R⊕YAL
INTRIGUE

OTHER BOOKS AND AUDIOBOOKS
BY TRACI HUNTER ABRAMSON

UNDERCURRENTS SERIES

Undercurrents

Ripple Effect

The Deep End

SAINT SQUAD SERIES

Freefall

Lockdown

Crossfire

Backlash

Smoke Screen

Code Word

Lock and Key

Drop Zone

Spotlight

Tripwire

Redemption

Covert Ops

Disconnect

Reconnect

LUKE STEELE SERIES

Hometown Vendetta

ROYAL SERIES

Royal Target

Royal Secrets

Royal Brides

Royal Heir

Royal Duty

GUARDIAN SERIES

Failsafe

Safe House

Sanctuary

On the Run

In Harm's Way

Not Dead Yet

Unseen

DREAM'S EDGE SERIES

Dancing to Freedom *

An Unlikely Pair

Broken Dreams *

Dreams of Gold

The Best Mistake *

Worlds Collide

FALCON POINT SERIES

Heirs of Falcon Point

The Danger with Diamonds

From an Unknown Sender

When Fashion Turns Deadly

PEN AND DAGGER SERIES

Novel Threat (April 2025)

STAND-ALONES

Obsession

Proximity

Twisted Fate *

Entangled *

Sinister Secrets *

Deep Cover

Mistaken Reality

Kept Secrets

Chances Are

Chance for Home

A Change of Fortune

The Fiction Kitchen Trio Cookbook

Jim and Katherine

Shadows of Trust *

* Novella

R◉YAL INTRIGUE

a novel

TRACI HUNTER ABRAMSON

All statements of fact, opinion, or analysis expressed are those of the author and do not reflect the official positions or views of the US Government. Nothing in the contents should be construed as asserting or implying US Government authentication of information or endorsement of the author's views.

Cover image: *Majestic golden crown with blue gemstones, royal symbol of authority and glory, digital illustration-* AI Generated, by furyon ©stock.adobe.com

Cover design by Julie Olson
Cover design copyright © 2025 by Covenant Communications, Inc.

Published by Covenant Communications, Inc.
American Fork, Utah

Library of Congress Cataloging-in-Publication Data

Name: Traci Hunter Abramson
Title: Royal Intrigue / Traci Hunter Abramson
Description: American Fork, UT : Covenant Communications, Inc. [2025]
Identifiers: 2024939262| 978-1-52442-806-8
LC record available at https://lccn.loc.gov/2024939262

Printed in the United States of America
First Printing: June 2025

31 30 29 28 27 26 25   10 9 8 7 6 5 4 3 2 1

for Ashley Gebert
May you live your happily ever after.

ACKNOWLEDGMENTS

THANK YOU TO MY FAMILY for your continued support in doing what I love. Thanks to Lara Abramson and Susan Carl for your help with the early drafts as well as my many critique partners: Daniel Quilter, Eliza Sanders, Ashley Gebert, Steve Stratton, Millie Hast, Brian Goddard, and Ann Feinstein.

My continued appreciation goes to the Covenant team and the individuals who do so much behind the scenes to bring my books into the world. Thanks as well to the CIA Publication Classification Review Board for all your efforts on my behalf.

And finally, thank you to the readers who have made this career such a joy and given me a reason to keep writing even when things get tough. I appreciate you more than you know.

CHAPTER

1

PRINCESS ANNABELLE OF SERENO STOOD on the upper deck of her family's yacht and breathed in the scent of salt water and freedom. In the distance, the coastline of Alameda came into view. Rocky cliffs, long stretches of sandy beaches, and sailboats dotting the blue-green water of the Mediterranean was evidence of why this ally nation had long been her favorite vacation spot.

And she needed a vacation now. For the past two years, she had juggled her royal duties while using every spare moment to create a business she could call her own, a business her family would be proud of, a business *she* could be proud of. Of course, a full six months of that time had been consumed by creating a business plan and coming up with a name. Who knew naming a cosmetics company could be so complicated? In the end, she had kept it simple: Sereno Cove Cosmetics. The name reflected her origins as well as her favorite spot on their island nation.

Now, with the marketing efforts already underway and her first products hitting the shelves in August, she was ready for a much-needed holiday. This trip was only the second time since her sister's coronation that she was traveling for pleasure rather than duty. With both of her sisters pregnant, she suspected the juggling act between business and royal engagements would increase significantly by Christmas.

Annabelle rested her hand on the railing as they neared the coastline, her gaze instinctively drawn to the white lighthouse that separated a particularly rocky area from the small harbors that lay beyond it.

A set of footsteps sounded, and Annabelle turned as her personal guard approached.

"Your Highness, you should come inside. We've already passed into Alameda's territorial waters."

Annabelle raised both eyebrows. "Rocco, I think you're letting your over-protective streak take over again." She gestured toward the open space in front of her. "Alameda has been an ally my entire life."

"Yes, but it's best not to announce your arrival through someone's social media page." Rocco nodded at the nearest boat. "Cameras are everywhere, and you are third in line for the throne."

"Not for long." A smile bloomed on her face and was mirrored on Rocco's.

"Two new babies in the royal family in one year." Wonder resonated in his voice. "That will be cause for celebration."

"I still can't believe Cassie and Victoria are pregnant at the same time." Her family was growing. If only her parents had lived to see the grandchildren who would soon arrive. "Two babies to spoil rotten. I can't wait."

"Just make sure that we're sent somewhere warm if the king and queen banish you for spoiling their son," Rocco suggested.

Annabelle laughed. "I'll do my best, but shipping me off somewhere won't be easy." She glanced toward the approaching coastline once more. "I plan to be close by while my niece and nephew are growing up."

"Then you've chosen the perfect time for this trip." Rocco took a step back. "Come on. You can watch the coastline through the windows in the lounge."

"Fine." Annabelle led the way into the large living space. A serving bar was situated in the center of the aft side of the room, and several couches and small tables had been arranged throughout the rest of the space to allow occupants to enjoy the view through the windows.

Annabelle sat in a plush chair on the starboard side. Instantly, a steward approached.

"May I get you anything, Your Highness?" Vincenzo asked.

"A water with lime would be wonderful."

Vincenzo nodded and returned to the bar.

"I need to check with the captain to make sure everything is in place for our arrival." Rocco took a step toward the stairs. "I'll be back in a bit."

"Take your time." Annabelle leaned back in her chair and picked up the fashion magazine she had left on the table beside her. If she had her way, her new line would be featured in this magazine by next year.

Her mobile rang, and she pulled it from the pocket of her slacks. When she spotted Tayla's name on the screen, her mood brightened.

The two of them had grown up together, and their close family ties had given them a bond that was nearly as tightly knit as the ones she shared with her older sisters. Annabelle and Tayla had even attended university together in Switzerland.

"Tayla, is your navy telling you we've crossed into your waters?" Annabelle asked, humor in her voice.

"Actually, yes, but that isn't why I'm calling."

"Is everything okay?"

"I had a little glitch in my plans," Tayla said. "Isaac planned a dinner with his mother for tonight, and we had to cancel on her the last two times we tried to get together. We can't cancel a third time. I'm so sorry."

Isaac, as in Tayla's fiancé.

"I'll be here for three weeks. We'll have plenty of time to visit," Annabelle said. And eating alone in her room at the palace wouldn't be the end of the world.

"We will. I promise," Tayla said. "There's just one more thing."

"What's that?"

"Since my parents are coming with us to talk about wedding plans, my brother will be the one meeting you when you arrive."

She instantly stiffened. "Thanks for the warning."

Prince Leonardo was only three years older than Tayla and Annabelle, but he had considered himself too mature to spend time in their presence since their teenage years.

"Who knows. Maybe you'll get lucky, and he'll bring Chrishelle with him. Then you'll have someone else to talk to."

Annabelle had seen photos of Prince Leonardo and his American girl-friend repeatedly over the past few months, but Annabelle had expected him to dump this one just like the others who came before her. "It sounds like you like her."

"I do like her," Tayla said. "I'm not sure she and Leo are a good match though."

Annabelle paused when Vincenzo approached with her water. She mouthed a thank-you before returning to her conversation. "Chrishelle has lasted longer than most." She took a sip of water. "Of course, knowing Leo, the relationship will end before the summer is over."

"I don't know about that. My father gave him our grandmother's engagement ring."

"Leo's planning to propose?"

"The only reason I can think of for my father to pass that to him would be if a wedding is in his future."

"Wow." An odd weight dropped in her stomach. "It's hard to imagine Leo married."

"I know. Of course, it's hard to imagine me getting married either, but the wedding is only nine months away."

"It will be here before you know it."

"I know. We do need to go shopping before my engagement party. I have nothing to wear."

"You say that before every big event." Annabelle laughed.

"And it's always true," Tayla said. "Oh, did you remember to bring the samples to use for the gift bags?"

"Enough for a hundred." Annabelle had offered a moisturizer and some basic makeup products to both spread the word about her new cosmetics company and help Tayla provide a unique gift for her guests. "Just make sure you don't expand the guest list more than that."

"Would I do that?"

Annabelle laughed again. "Yes. You would."

- - -

From his seat in the back of the limo, Leo skimmed through the latest report on the gold-mining operation in the southern part of Alameda. The enhanced safety measures had taken longer than expected to implement, in part due to the discovery of a body that had been buried nearby. But finally, the mine was operational again and one of the major sources of his nation's wealth was flowing freely. Only one more mine left to complete, and this project would finally be behind him.

The vehicle turned, slowing as it approached the security gate that protected the private harbor from intruders. Leo looked up as the remote section of the Mediterranean came into view. The water sparkled beneath the afternoon sunlight, a swath of trees providing shade for the small parking lot and shielding the harbor from view of anyone who might sail by. Several workers stood on the long wooden dock that had been built to accommodate larger vessels, such as the sleek yacht spanning the length of the structure that had already been secured to the metal cleats.

The crew lowered the gangplank and secured it in place. Princess Annabelle had arrived.

How Leo had gotten stuck with greeting duty was beyond him. Normally, he wouldn't have minded rearranging his Tuesday meetings, but something about his sister's best friend grated on his nerves. He couldn't quite put his finger on why.

Maybe it was her overly cheerful disposition. She made being royal seem like a permanent holiday, even though he knew she was actively involved in running several of her family's charities. And then there was the way she always looked so perfect, never a hair out of place and constantly dressed as though she was about to be photographed for the cover of *Vogue*.

If there was a bad photo of her on the internet, Leo certainly hadn't seen it. He, on the other hand, seemed to have a knack for being spotted in the worst possible situations. And it had all started with a photo of him and Annabelle when he was a mere eighteen years old. An innocent dance had turned to speculation. The press had quickly pointed out that he was an adult, and she was not.

Since then, every handshake or conversation with a woman inevitably turned into him either beginning a new relationship or cheating on whomever was supposed to be his girlfriend of the moment. In truth, he hadn't dated nearly as much as the tabloids claimed. It wasn't until his last year of his doctoral program at Harvard that he'd settled into a serious relationship.

He could hardly believe he and Chrishelle had been together nearly two years now. Of course, more than half of that had been long-distance, with him back home in Alameda and her finishing her degree in Boston.

Leo's driver pulled into a spot beside the dock, and his security detail parked across the road a short distance away to secure the entrance. Beyond the dock, a patrol boat had already taken position to ensure no civilians could interrupt the privacy of the harbor that was exclusive to the royals and their trusted employees.

"Would you like to remain in the car until the princess disembarks, Your Highness?" his driver asked.

"No, thank you. I could use a break from these reports."

By the time Leo closed his laptop, his driver already stood beside him, his door open.

Leo stepped out. "Thank you, Norvin."

Norvin gave his customary nod before motioning to the suitcases that were already stacked beside the parking lot. "Would you like me to load Princess Annabelle's luggage?"

Leo hadn't expected the crew to have already unloaded it, much less transport it the thirty meters between where the yacht was docked and the parking area. Apparently, they were more efficient than he expected. "That would be appreciated. Thank you."

Leo circled past the three large suitcases, his security detail falling into place behind him. Their presence was a constant reminder of the life he had been born into. His parents had allowed him the freedom to choose his field of study—environmental science—but his military service had been decided for him. And though the two years between university and his doctorate degree had been emotionally and physically demanding, working alongside those dedicated to protecting Alameda gave him a much-needed understanding of how the military worked—and how to protect himself.

He reached the base of the gangplank at the same moment Annabelle stepped into his view. Her dark hair hung loose today, the ends of it lifting in the breeze, and her eyes were bright with wonder as though she hadn't ever stepped foot on Alamedan soil before.

He waited, his gaze remaining on her.

When she spotted him, her carefree expression faded, and her jaw tightened. Apparently, she wasn't any happier about him being on greeting duty than he was.

A man stepped beside her and adopted a protective stance. It only took a moment for Leo to identify him as Rocco, Annabelle's longtime personal guard.

Annabelle and Rocco walked down the gangplank.

Though technically Leo should have met her halfway, he couldn't bring himself to treat Annabelle as an equal in status. No, she was his little sister's best friend, and neither Annabelle nor Tayla would ever understand the pressures of preparing to someday wear the crown or lead their country.

"Prince Leonardo." In typical Annabelle fashion, the princess dropped into a perfectly executed curtsy. "It's lovely to see you again."

"You as well." Leo turned his attention to the man standing beside Annabelle.

"You remember Rocco," Annabelle said.

"Of course." Leo extended his hand. "Accommodations have been made for both of you. Please let our chief of security know if there is anything you need during your stay."

Rocco bowed his head. "Thank you, Your Highness."

"Shall we?" Leo gestured toward the waiting limo.

Annabelle fell into step with him, her guard taking position on her other side.

"Thank you for coming to pick us up," Annabelle said. "Tayla called to tell me she had to do some wedding planning with her fiancé and his family."

"Yes. They've had some scheduling challenges." He didn't look forward to dealing with his own wedding details when that time came. A heaviness settled inside him like it always did when he thought of getting married. He fought against it. It was just nerves. Nerves and a fear of commitment. According to his mother and the tabloids, he had suffered from the latter since reaching puberty.

They reached the limo, and the driver opened the back door.

"Should we wait for our luggage?" Annabelle asked.

"I already loaded it," Norvin said.

"That's not possible." Annabelle pointed back at the yacht.

Leo glanced behind him to where the crew was hauling suitcases down the gangplank and stacking them on the dock. "If those are your cases, where did the ones come from that were already stacked over here?"

Rocco stepped forward. "May I see them?"

Leo gave a nod of approval to Norvin.

The driver unlocked the trunk and pulled it open.

Rocco approached the open trunk and studied the suitcases. He turned back to look at them. "Maybe you should all clear the area."

"You don't think—" Annabelle didn't finish her sentence, but Leo could easily sense her and her guard's concern.

"This area is secure," Leo assured them. "This dock is only used by the royal family."

"Be that as it may, it would be best for you to all stand back." Rocco pulled the largest case out. He studied it again before unzipping it and slowly opening it.

Annabelle took a step back.

Leo stepped forward.

As Rocco lifted the top, Leo focused on the contents, expecting to see a variety of designer clothes, handbags, and shoes. Instead, he caught a flash of red, like the numbers he would expect to see on a digital alarm clock. Except the numbers didn't display a time, but rather a countdown. The number twenty-eight turned to twenty-seven.

For a split second, Leo froze. Surely, that couldn't be—

Rocco whirled toward them. "Run!"

Annabelle sprinted the opposite direction. "Leo, come on!"

The gravity of the situation finally caught up with him, and he raced after her. "Everyone, take cover!" Leo shouted at the crew on the dock.

"How much time?" Annabelle asked, her breathing already heavy from exertion.

"Twenty seconds." Rocco huffed out.

Twenty seconds before a bomb detonated. And they had nothing to protect them. If they didn't find cover now, these frantic breaths might very well be their last.

Leo spotted a few crew members on the dock moving toward them with puzzled expressions on their faces. He waved both arms to stop them. "Get back!"

Footsteps pounded as Leo and Annabelle raced forward, Norvin already several meters ahead of them, Rocco beside them.

"Over here." Leo grabbed Annabelle's arm and redirected her away from the yacht, heading instead for the open space of the dock in front of it.

Seconds ticked off in his head. They were out of time.

They were a step away from the edge of the wooden planking when the ground shook with a thunderous explosion.

With his hand still firmly on Annabelle's arm, Leo leaped into the air, the two of them splashing into the water together, Rocco and Norvin following right behind them.

CHAPTER

2

ANNABELLE SPUTTERED TO THE SURFACE, despite the weight of her wet clothes dragging her down. One of her brand-new shoes had already come off, and she used her bare foot to free herself of the other one. She wasn't going to think about the three hours she had spent browsing through stores and dodging the paparazzi when she had bought that particular pair.

She treaded water and scanned the surface, relieved to see three other heads bobbing in the water. Leo, his driver, and Rocco had survived too. Smoke plumed into the air from the remnants of the limo, flames licking at the nearby trees.

Someone had just tried to kill them. Had Rocco not opened the suitcase when he did—

Annabelle's throat closed up as she fought against the awareness of just how close she had come to dying, how close they had all come to having their lives tragically end.

Leo stroked through the water toward her, his white shirt nearly transparent now that it was soaking wet. The stunned expression of a minute ago was gone, but his breathing was still rapid. He reached her side and swiveled toward his driver and Rocco. "Is everyone okay?"

Both men nodded.

"I think so," Annabelle said. Her head was still ringing from the impact of the blast, but as far as she could tell, she hadn't sustained any other injuries. "What about you?"

"I'm fine."

Annabelle shifted her attention to the source of the explosion again. Her breath shuddered. "Why would someone try to kill us?"

"More importantly, who was the target?" Leo turned a sharp eye on Annabelle.

Her chest tightened, and she shivered in the cool water. "You think that was meant for me?"

"I wasn't supposed to be here today," Leo reminded her. "Tayla planned to pick you up."

"Who else knew Princess Annabelle's schedule?" Rocco asked. His question reinforced Leo's belief that Annabelle had been the target of the explosion.

She shivered again.

Shouts carried to her from above, and she looked up. Several workers stood on the dock above them. A few pointed. Others shouted down to them and to each other. Only a moment passed before a ladder was lowered to the water's surface.

All of them swam to the bottom of the ladder.

Leo grabbed the edge of it and held it steady. "Annabelle, you go first."

"No, I'll go first," Rocco said. "I want to make sure there aren't any other issues waiting for us up there."

Rocco gripped the ladder and placed his foot on the lowest rung. Water flowed off him as he went, but despite the weight of his soggy clothes, he made his way steadily to the top.

As soon as he was within reach, two workers helped lift Rocco onto the solid surface of the dock.

"Do you want to go next, Your Highness?" the driver asked. "Or shall I go help him?"

"Maybe we should wait—" Annabelle began.

Leo cut her off and spoke to his driver. "Norvin, go ahead." Leo held the bottom of the ladder until his driver climbed to the top. Then he turned to Annabelle. "You go next."

"Not yet." Annabelle's teeth chattered, and she clenched them together. She moved her arms back and forth through the water in the hopes the movement would help warm her up. "Rocco won't want us up there until he's sure it's safe."

Leo drew his eyebrows together. "You're freezing. We need to get you out of the water."

"It's not that bad," Annabelle said, even as another shiver rippled through her. "And being cold isn't nearly as dangerous as getting up there and finding out there's another bomb."

"You're seriously going to wait here until he comes back for us?"

"Yes." Her teeth chattered together again. "You can go up if you want, but I advise against it."

"I'm not going to leave you here alone." He seemed to contemplate for a moment. Then he reached his arm toward her. "Come here."

Before she processed his intention, Leo hooked his arm around her waist, pulling her closer.

"What are you doing?"

"It's called the huddle method. It will keep us both warm while we wait."

She remembered the term from her water safety classes, but she never anticipated she would put it into practice by holding on to Tayla's brother.

"Hang on to me," Leo said, drawing her close so they were torso to torso.

With little choice, she slipped her arms around his waist. Leo threaded his other arm through the opening of the rope ladder at the water's surface and then wrapped that arm around her as well.

The warmth of his body seeped into her, but it still wasn't enough to stop her shivering.

"You really are freezing." Leo rubbed his hands over her back as though trying to get her blood circulating again, but the result sent a different kind of shiver through her. She lifted her eyes to meet his, and for a brief moment, her gaze lingered on his lips. How many women had Leo held close like this? She shook that thought away. He was only holding her to protect her from hypothermia.

Rocco's voice carried down to them. "Come on up. It's all clear."

"Go ahead." Leo kept one arm around her and turned his body so the ladder would be in easy reach. She released him and gripped the first rung. With her other hand, she smoothed her hair out of her face.

She didn't want to think about what she looked like right now, and she certainly didn't want to find out the hard way that her waterproof mascara didn't work in sea water. Even worse would be the image of her and Leo together while both soaking wet. This incident and their resulting appearance would need to remain their little secret, or Leo would once again suffer from the paparazzi's interference. With his pending engagement, that was the last thing he or his girlfriend needed.

"Go ahead," Leo urged. "I'll be right behind you."

"I'm going." Annabelle climbed up the first two steps. "But you had better not have any photographers up there."

- - -

Photographers. The woman had practically died from an explosion, she faced hypothermia, and she was worried about how she looked for the tabloids?

Leo was still trying to process what had happened today at the dock, but that comment from Annabelle had stuck with him. Maybe she really was as shallow as he'd always thought.

It was just as well. For a brief moment, while he had been holding her in his arms, he'd forgotten she was his little sister's best friend and that he had a girlfriend his parents hoped he would marry. Instead, all he'd been able to think about was her composure in the face of danger, her concern for him when he had wanted to follow her guard up the ladder. And yes, perhaps he had been distracted by the way her body fit so perfectly against his.

Leo finished changing his clothes and sat on the sofa in his living room to put on his shoes. He was tying the laces on the first one when a knock sounded at his door.

"Come in."

His girlfriend rushed in, her blue eyes shining with concern. "I just heard what happened. Are you okay?"

Leo tied his other shoe and stood. "I'm fine."

"I was so worried." Chrishelle tucked a lock of her blonde hair behind her ear before she closed the distance between them and leaned in for a kiss.

The kiss ended almost before it began, and Chrishelle stepped back so she could see him more clearly. "What exactly happened? The guard told me there was a fire."

Leo needed to talk to someone, and one thing he always appreciated about Chrishelle was her ability to protect a confidence. "There was a fire," Leo said. The rest of the words took a bit more effort to form. "But the fire was caused by a bomb."

"What?" Chrishelle grabbed his arm and stepped directly in front of him. "Is everyone okay?"

"Yes, but we're trying to keep the facts contained until my father decides how he wants to handle the situation," Leo said. "We can't afford to let details leak out, especially before we know what we're really dealing with."

"Leonardo, someone tried to kill you. Word is going to get out."

"I don't think I'm the one someone was trying to kill," Leo corrected.

"If not you, then who?"

Whom. He silently corrected her grammar, instantly irritated at himself for doing so.

Chrishelle's question replayed through his mind. Even though he suspected Annabelle had been the target, the logic behind such an attack didn't make any sense. She was third in line to the throne, and within the year, she would be fifth.

"Leonardo?" Chrishelle said his name, bringing him back to the present.

Leo shook his head, struck by the oddity that Chrishelle still called him by his full name rather than the nickname commonly adopted by his close friends and family. "Like I said, we don't know who the bomb was meant for, and it's best if we don't fuel any speculation the press might have."

"But you have your suspicions."

"One or two." Leo took her hand and gave it a reassuring squeeze. "I doubt I was the target. I wasn't even supposed to be there today."

That thought stretched out. He wasn't supposed to be at the dock. Tayla was.

A streak of panic pierced him. "I need to check in with security." Leo pressed a kiss to Chrishelle's cheek. "I'll talk to you later."

He left his private quarters and headed toward the security chief's office in the administrative wing of the palace. Saul, his personal guard, followed behind him.

"Saul, is Esteban in his office?"

"Yes, Your Highness. I believe he's meeting with Rocco."

"Thank you." Leo continued down the hall until he reached his intended destination.

Saul took his position in the hall.

Leo knocked twice on the closed door before he opened it. When he entered, his security chief stood, as did Rocco, who had been seated across from him.

"Sorry to interrupt," Leo said, even though the words were far from sincere. "I'd like an update on today's incident."

"Of course, Your Highness." Esteban motioned to the seat beside Rocco.

Leo closed the door. "What do you know so far?"

To his surprise, Rocco answered. "The bomb had a C4 base, single detonator, no remote access."

"How do you know all that?"

"I saw it, remember?" When Leo continued to stare at him, Rocco added, "Instruction about explosive devices is part of our training in Sereno."

"I see." Leo suspected that training was a direct result of an attempted bombing a few years ago, before Princess Victoria got married. "Do you have any idea how the bomb got there?"

Rocco nodded. "As a matter of fact, we do."

CHAPTER

3

ANNABELLE APPROACHED THE SECURITY OFFICE, her hair hanging loosely over her shoulders and only a light dusting of makeup on her face. A hot shower had done wonders for her, and now that her shivering had stopped and she once again wore dry clothes, she was ready for answers.

Her body trembled with the adrenaline that had yet to dissipate. So maybe the shivering hadn't *completely* stopped, but at least it was no longer caused by wearing wet clothes.

She knocked on the closed door, waiting until a man's voice called out, "Come in," before opening it.

Rocco, Leo, and the man sitting behind the desk all rose to their feet, but it was Leo who spoke. "What are you doing here? You should be resting."

She appreciated his concern, but resting wasn't going to help her mental state. "I'm fine."

Rocco motioned to the man on the far side of the desk. "Your Highness, this is Esteban, the chief of security here at the palace."

Annabelle stepped forward and extended her hand. "It's good to meet you. I wish it were under better circumstances."

"As do I, Your Highness." He shook her hand and bowed his head slightly before releasing her.

Annabelle turned her attention to Rocco. "What do you know so far?"

"We were just discussing the bomb and potential targets."

Potential targets. A lump formed in her throat. "Am I one of them?"

"I don't think so." Rocco motioned for her to take his seat beside Leo, and he retrieved another chair from a spot behind them.

As soon as Annabelle sat down, the men followed suit. "If you don't think I was the target, then who?" She turned to the man on her right. "Leo?"

Leo's jaw tightened, a silent confirmation that she had guessed correctly.

"The suitcases were delivered after Prince Leonardo parked, but before it was clear who was inside the car," Esteban said. "That means Prince Leonardo is one possibility. Princess Tayla is another."

"Tayla?" Annabelle whipped her head around to look at Rocco. "Why would anyone want to hurt Tayla?"

"I don't know." Rocco looked past her and asked Leo, "Can you think of any reason why someone would want to hurt you or your sister? Any civic protests, family members who have ambitions for moving up in rank, terrorist threats?"

"Nothing specific comes to mind." Leo furrowed his brow. "We had some protests last year about the safety protocols in several of our gold mines, but we've been upgrading those for months. The last one will be finished in August, and that mine is inactive until the construction is complete."

"Terrorist threats?" Rocco asked.

"Nothing beyond the usual." Leo held up a hand. "And no, I don't think any of my cousins are trying to kill me or my sister in a quest to someday become king or queen. They're all quite grateful that they're free to pursue their own interests rather than step more fully into the family business."

"Then we're missing something," Rocco said.

"I agree." Esteban picked up a remote off his desk and pointed it at the flat-screen TV on the wall. "Whoever we're dealing with understands our protocols well enough to know where to leave the suitcase carrying the bomb."

He pressed Play, bringing the image to life of someone entering the parking lot and stacking three suitcases. Suitcases that looked exactly like hers.

Annabelle leaned forward. Judging from the person's height and build, it appeared the person stacking the cases was a man, though his face wasn't visible. But her focus was on the luggage. "Can you zoom in on the cases?"

"Yes." Esteban reversed the video feed and adjusted the image. He hit Play again.

When the label from the luggage appeared on the screen, Annabelle straightened. "Freeze it right there."

"What is it?" Rocco asked.

She stared at the frozen image for a moment longer before she turned her attention to Rocco. "Whoever planted that bomb doesn't just know Alameda's security protocols; he also knows ours."

"What are you talking about?" Leo asked.

She faced Leo. "That luggage is identical to mine, right down to the number of cases I usually bring and the brand."

Leo's eyes widened. "Who would have that information?"

"Someone who has worked for both royal families," Rocco said.

"I can't think of anyone working for the royal guard who once worked in Sereno," Esteban said. "Princess Annabelle, how long have you owned that luggage?"

"Three years. Papa gave me a set just like it before I left for college, and Cassie replaced it when one of the zippers broke."

"So you've really had the same luggage for six years," Esteban said.

"Yes."

"Then it could be someone who knows you and works for us," Leo surmised.

"He's right," Rocco said. "Unless you're going on a weekend trip, you always travel with three cases. At least, you did until this trip."

"Why is this trip different?" Leo asked.

"Because of my business and your sister." At the confused look on Leo's face, Annabelle continued. "I brought samples of my new cosmetic line with me for Tayla to use as party favors for her engagement party." And to use to show to some local stores to expand her distribution. That wasn't likely to happen now.

"So, except for people who saw you leave Sereno, anyone who knows you well would assume you would have three."

"Yes." But out of those close to her, who would plant a bomb? And why? She struggled against the sense of betrayal that rose inside her as another thought formed. "Most of my friends are also friends with Tayla. Maybe that's where we need to start."

"I'll also go over the work schedules to see who wasn't on duty," Esteban said.

"We'll want to verify their presence on security footage while we're at it." Rocco stood. "In the meantime, with your permission, I'd like to speak with Prince Alan about bringing in one of our bomb-detection dogs so we can do a sweep of the guest quarters and the palace residence."

Leo stood as well. "I think that would be wise."

"Is there anything I can do to help?" Annabelle asked.

"Perhaps you and I can start making a list of who else would know your travel habits," Leo suggested. "We can work in my office. We'll have fewer interruptions there." Leo offered a hand to Annabelle and drew her to her feet.

Annabelle nodded. "Lead the way."

- - -

Annabelle's hand was every bit as soft as he remembered, and Leo hated himself for noticing. He'd been avoiding her for nearly a decade for this exact reason. He didn't want to have any interest in her. She was his little sister's best friend, for heaven's sake.

As soon as they reached the hall, he released her and motioned toward his private office. "It's this way."

She walked with him, the heels of her shoes clicking on the tile floor. She clasped her hands together in front of her. "I still can't believe a bomb went off on the docks."

Nor could he. The whole day still felt like a nightmare he had yet to wake up from. "The fact that no one was seriously injured is a miracle." Leo didn't want to think about what would have happened had Annabelle's guard not insisted on checking the luggage. "Your guard was quite the hero today."

"So were you."

"All I did was run for the water."

"And warn everyone to do the same," Annabelle said. "Judging from the burn marks on the bow of our yacht, had those workers not been warned, some of them might not have made it."

He had noticed the scorched hull too, another reminder of how close they'd come to not surviving the day. "I suppose someone should have a maintenance crew take a look at the yacht," Leo said. "The captain won't want to put out to sea again until it's been thoroughly inspected."

"I'm sure you're right, but I have no doubt the captain is already taking care of it."

They turned the corner into the administrative hallway where his offices were located, along with the offices belonging to his sister.

"This is my office here." He stopped beside the open door.

"I know. I remember." Her lips twitched into a half smile.

The memory of his last birthday pressed to the front of his mind, complete with helium balloons filling his entire office. "I should have known."

Annabelle blinked innocently. "Known what?"

"That you were part of my birthday surprise last year."

Her eyes lit with humor. "You only turn twenty-nine once."

Some of the stress eased from his body, and he shook his head. "I don't know how you and Tayla managed to sneak all those balloons past the guards without anyone noticing."

"That was easy." She walked through the door and glanced over her shoulder. "We didn't."

"You didn't sneak them past the guards?" Leo followed her inside to where his personal assistant sat at his desk. Marcus was nearly old enough to be his father and at times took on a parental role even when it was far from necessary.

"Nope." Annabelle turned to greet his assistant. "Marcus, it's good to see you again."

Marcus stood, the concern on his face instant. "Are you both okay? I heard what happened."

"We're fine," Leo assured him. "Princess Annabelle and I have some business we need to attend to. Will you please reschedule my meetings for this afternoon?"

"Esteban already asked me to cancel all visitors for today and tomorrow." Marcus picked up a pad of paper off his desk. "Several news outlets have called for comments, but I've forwarded those to the press office. And your parents called. They'll be remaining with your sister at the summer retreat until tomorrow."

"Thank you."

"Oh, one more thing." Marcus opened his desk drawer. "You'll be wanting this." He handed Leo a new cell phone. "I understand all your phones were damaged from the water."

"Thank you." Leo glanced at Annabelle. "Would you also please arrange for replacement phones for Princess Annabelle and her guard?"

"Of course, Your Highness. I'll take care of that right away."

"Thank you, Marcus," Annabelle said. She crossed the threshold into Leo's private office. "And Leo, thank you for thinking of that."

"It's not a problem." Leo closed the door and motioned for her to take a seat in one of the chairs opposite his desk. "We'll have far more luck creating this list if you have access to your contacts."

"True."

Leo waited until she settled into her seat before he claimed his own and turned on a laptop.

"I think we should start with the friends who came to Tayla's last birthday celebration," Annabelle said. "I wasn't able to come for the entire week like everyone else, so I'm pretty sure I was the last to arrive and first to leave."

"Which means they all would have seen you coming and going."

"They could have, anyway," Annabelle said.

"I'll email our social director and ask for the guest lists for the last six years for all the events you attended."

"That's a lot of events."

She didn't have to tell him that. Even though he didn't want to, Leo always noticed when Annabelle was present. "Yes, I know."

CHAPTER

4

ANNABELLE HELD THE BORROWED PHONE against her ear and paced her sitting room. The suite she had been granted was the same one she always stayed in when visiting Alameda.

"Are you sure you don't want me to send the plane for you?" Cassie asked. She was known as Queen Cassandra to the rest of the world.

"I don't think Rocco will want us to leave until we have more answers," Annabelle said. "And I'm sure between him and the royal guard here at the palace, I'll be more than safe."

"You'd better stay safe," Cassie said, more like a protective parent than an older sister.

"I'm sure Rocco has already talked to Levi and Alan about how best to ensure my safety," Annabelle said. Her brothers-in-law were both well-versed in security measures. Cassie's husband, Levi, was a former intelligence operative who specialized in security, and Victoria's husband, Alan, was an explosives expert. Sometimes it was hard to believe both of her sisters not only ended up marrying Americans, but also married men who had worked for the CIA.

"Rocco briefed Alan earlier, and Levi is working with the chief of security there on a few enhancements," Cassie said.

"Dare I ask what sort of enhancements?" With Annabelle's luck, she'd be confined to her suite for the foreseeable future.

"Alan is sending Federico and Zeus to stay at the palace while you're there."

Federico was one of the guards trained in bomb detection, along with his K-9 companion. "Actually, after what happened today, that's a good idea." Annabelle paced to the balcony window and looked out at the water. "When will they arrive?"

"Later tonight."

"It will be good to have them here."

A knock sounded at her door.

"Someone's here. I should get going."

"Okay. Stay safe and be careful."

"I will," Annabelle said. "Give Victoria a hug for me."

Annabelle said her goodbyes and opened her door. As expected, Rocco stood on the other side.

"Are you ready for dinner?"

"As ready as I'll ever be." She stepped into the hall.

They made their way through the long hallway, down the stairs, and toward the private dining room. When she had envisioned what tonight would look like, it certainly hadn't included dining with Leo and his girlfriend, at least not without Tayla by her side.

"I spoke with King Josep a few minutes ago," Rocco said. "We're working on some security enhancements to be implemented during your stay, but we're concerned with you remaining in Alameda given the current threat level."

"I was afraid you were going to say that."

The last thing Annabelle wanted was to return home before she even saw Tayla, but she could understand her guard's concern. "How bad is the damage to the yacht?"

"It's relatively minor, but because the damage is so close to the water line, the captain doesn't want to set sail until after the repairs are complete."

"How long will that take?" Annabelle asked.

"Best guess, three weeks. Maybe four."

"What a nightmare." Annabelle let out a sigh. "I'm sorry we landed in the middle of this."

"Me too. My job is to prevent situations like this one."

"Yes, but regardless of the training my brothers-in-law put you through, defusing bombs is not something most people are prepared to do."

Regret flashed in his eyes. "I didn't defuse the one today."

"You also didn't have access to prevent this one from being planted."

"The breakdown in Alameda's security protocols is a concern," Rocco said. "Even though Federico and Zeus are arriving tonight, it would be best for us to transport you home at the earliest opportunity."

They approached the dining room, and Annabelle noted the two guards standing by in the hall. "I'm sure I'll be fine during dinner. Why don't you get something to eat? I'm sure one of Leo's guards can escort me back to my room."

"But—"

"You need to eat too," Annabelle said. "And I'm sure you'll want to confer with Federico when he gets here, which means you won't have time to eat later."

"Fine. I'll speak with Esteban to ensure his staff attends to your needs."

"Thank you." Annabelle stepped through the doorway into the dining room where Leo and a blonde woman sat at the oval table.

At her entrance, they both stood.

Leo bowed slightly. "I hope your accommodations are to your satisfaction."

"Yes, thank you." Annabelle crossed to the chair beside Leo, where a butler stood, her chair already pulled out.

"Princess Annabelle, may I present Chrishelle Montgomery from America."

"It's lovely to meet you." Annabelle nodded her head and stepped in front of her seat.

"You as well. Leonardo and Tayla have told me so much about you."

Leonardo. The use of his full name caught her attention, but Annabelle supposed she was using it as a formality, unaware that Annabelle had been a family friend since she was barely old enough to walk.

"Please, sit down." Leo waited until the women took their seats before lowering into his own.

Instantly their salads were placed before them.

"Have you spoken to Tayla yet?" Annabelle asked Leo.

"No, but I spoke with my father. They anticipate returning to the palace within the next day or two."

"I'm sorry your schedules have been turned upside down like this," Annabelle said.

Leo winged an eyebrow up. "I could say the same about yours."

"The only thing I had on my schedule was to spend time helping your sister with wedding plans." And to promote her new cosmetics line, but she kept that thought to herself. Leo would undoubtedly consider her business trivial at best. Keeping her focus on her friend, she continued. "Once I have a new phone, I can still help Tayla, even if we need to video chat."

"Your new phones should arrive first thing in the morning," Leo said. "But feel free to use the phone in your suite to call anyone you'd like."

"Thanks." She would if she knew everyone's numbers by heart.

"I don't know how all of you are so calm right now," Chrishelle said. "I would be a nervous wreck if I had come so close to being killed by a bomb."

Annabelle tensed as memories came rushing back. The ringing in her ears, the heat at their backs as they jumped off the dock, the freezing cold water.

Was it too much to ask that they pretend life was normal for a little while before facing the terrifying reality that they had almost died today?

As though sensing her inner turmoil, Leo sat up a little straighter. "Sometimes it helps to take a little time to pretend life is still normal."

Annabelle gave him a grateful look.

"I hope some good food will help too." Leo kept his gaze on Annabelle. "I told our chef you would want crema catalana for dessert."

Annabelle blinked. "You remembered."

"Of course," Leo said the words as though he were expected to know such things about her, even though he spent most of his time avoiding both her and Tayla whenever Annabelle was around.

"I don't think I've had that before."

Leo shifted his attention to Chrishelle and put his hand on hers. "You're in for a treat. It's the Spanish version of crème brûlée."

Annabelle smiled. "It's been one of my favorites since Leo and I were children."

Chrishelle's smile faded. "I'm sure it will be a nice diversion."

Annabelle sensed Chrishelle's change in mood, but she wasn't sure what had caused it. Ready to change the subject, she turned to Leo. "Tayla said you finished your doctorate program in America. Do I have to address you as Dr. Leo now?"

Her comment earned her a typical Leo eye roll. "I believe for you I should be addressed as Your Highness Doctor Leonardo."

"Sorry." Annabelle shook her head. "That's too much of a mouthful."

Two members of the kitchen staff entered carrying dinner plates. One set a plate in front of Annabelle while the other served Leo and Chrishelle.

Leo picked up his fork, indicating that everyone could now start eating. "Bon appétit."

Annabelle took her first bite of clam and pasta. "Oh, this is wonderful."

Leo took a bite of his own and nodded. "I agree. Duran has outdone himself."

Annabelle took a second bite. Good food, surprisingly good company, and they were all alive to enjoy it.

CHAPTER

5

HE COULDN'T SLEEP. EVERY TIME Leo closed his eyes, the explosion rocked through his memory, altering and changing into a nightmare in which he and Annabelle didn't survive. Rather than continue reliving the alternative outcomes, Leo chose to keep his eyes open. And if he was going to keep his eyes open, there was no reason to remain in bed.

Dressed only in a pair of sweatpants, Leo pulled a T-shirt over his head and crossed to his balcony.

He tugged the hem of his shirt all the way down before he stepped through the French doors. Heaven forbid some long-range camera get a shot of him shirtless. A sleepless night would instantly turn into tabloid fodder.

Or perhaps news of the bombing today had already leaked and taken over the headlines. He hadn't dared look.

He lifted his gaze skyward, the stars twinkling in the otherwise dark sky. Only a sliver of the moon was visible, and the expanse of the Mediterranean stretched out before him.

On the far side of the gardens, a palace guard patrolled the area. Another stood beside the terrace entrance. Leo had no doubt the number of security personnel had doubled after today's threat.

He still couldn't quite put the memory into the reality category in his brain. Rather, it was as if he and Annabelle had been acting out some ridiculous action movie. Only the bomb hadn't been make believe, nor was the danger that remained. Someone had tried to kill them. Or had tried to kill Tayla. But who? And why?

He had been truthful when speaking to Rocco earlier. No one in line for the throne was a likely suspect. Two uncles, one aunt, eight cousins, all of whom were willing to help with royal duties but were more than happy to leave the heavy lifting to his immediate family. The protests over the working conditions in the gold mines had come to a halt months ago, and the economy was solid enough, especially since he had started dating Chrishelle. Who knew that dating an American would have such an effect on tourism? Perhaps that was why his father had been so eager to pass his grandmother's engagement ring along to him.

Leo moved back into his room and turned on the lamp on his bedside table. After sitting on the edge of his bed, he opened the second drawer and pulled out his gun safe.

His insistence on keeping a gun at his bedside had become a source of argument between him and his mother when he first returned home after his military service. She argued he didn't need a weapon, not with so many members of the royal guard assigned to protect him and their home. Leo, however, had grown accustomed to protecting himself and preferred to know he could do so if the occasion arose.

Never had he expected that protecting himself would involve jumping off a pier rather than drawing a gun.

He pressed his thumb against the locking mechanism, and the lock popped open. Slowly, he lifted the lid to reveal a black velvet box tucked beside his pistol.

With a sigh, Leo pulled the ring box out of the safe and flipped open the lid. The center stone, a square cut emerald, flashed in the lamplight, the diamonds surrounding it sparkling.

Leo tried to imagine putting the ring on Chrishelle's finger. Tried and couldn't. He dropped onto the side of his bed. Why were his parents in such a hurry for him to marry? He was only twenty-nine, for heaven's sake. He doubted Annabelle had these kinds of pressures from her family. Of course, she wasn't the heir to the throne. Plus, she had two pregnant sisters. And she was younger than him by three years. Her family undoubtedly recognized that she had plenty of time to find a husband.

Then again, with Tayla getting married next year, what was the rush for him?

Still restless, Leo snapped the ring box closed and secured it and his gun back in his side table. A walk in the gardens and some fresh air. That's what he needed to clear his head.

Leaving the light on, he stepped into his shoes and left his private quarters.

As expected, a guard trailed behind him. When they reached the terrace, he spotted another guard at the edge, but he wasn't one Leo recognized. He took a step closer and took in the yellow, red, and green ribbon affixed to the man's lapel. Not a member of the Alameda royal guard, but rather a member of Sereno's security force. And if a guard from Sereno was present, so was Annabelle.

Leo's gaze swept over the area in front of him until he spotted Annabelle. She sat on a bench beside a climbing rose bush, the white flowers illuminated in the faint wash of light coming from the palace.

Leo spoke to her guard. "How long has she been out here?"

"Twenty minutes."

Leo nodded and crossed to her.

She startled when he approached, and her gaze whipped up to meet his.

"Sorry. I didn't mean to scare you."

Annabelle rubbed her thumb under her left eye as though wiping something away. "It's not your fault." She wiped at the other eye and glanced at the terrace where both of their guards had taken defensive positions. "What are you doing still up?"

"Probably the same thing as you; I couldn't sleep." He motioned to the spot beside her. "May I?"

She nodded and slid over to make room for him.

He sat down but didn't speak. An oddly comfortable silence enveloped them, both lost in their own thoughts.

After several minutes, Annabelle broke the silence. "I keep reminding myself how lucky we were today, but every time I close my eyes, I feel the blast of the bomb going off. And I imagine we're too far from the water to avoid the flames."

"I know what you mean." And he did. Annabelle had put his nightmare into words perfectly.

A tear spilled onto Annabelle's cheek. It wasn't until Leo spotted it that he realized she'd been crying and that her face was devoid of makeup.

"Hey, everything is going to be okay." Leo slid his arm around her shoulders.

He wasn't sure what to think when she nestled closer.

Holding Annabelle close wasn't something he had experienced in recent memory, and now he had taken the opportunity twice in one day. He settled his hand firmly on her shoulder, and his heartbeat thickened. A ripple of attraction flowed through him, and he fought against it. Yes, Annabelle was a captivating and attractive woman, but she was also his sister's best friend. Not to mention, he already had a girlfriend.

Annabelle's voice broke into his thoughts. "How long do you think it will take before the nightmares go away?"

"I don't know. Your family has more experience with this sort of thing than mine does."

"That's sad but true." Annabelle rested her head on his shoulder. "I talked to Cassie a little while ago."

"Did she have any advice for you?" Leo asked. Both of her older sisters had been the intended victims of violent attacks in the past, but from his understanding, Annabelle had largely managed to avoid those incidents.

"She said the same thing she always does. It helps to talk about it with someone who understands." A little sigh escaped her. "Talking to her helped a little."

Footsteps approached, and Leo looked up with the intention of sending the intruder away. Then he spotted Chrishelle.

"Am I interrupting?"

Annabelle looked up and hastily pulled away from him. "No, of course not."

Leo kept his hand on Annabelle's shoulder, undeniably disappointed that his conversation with Annabelle had been interrupted. "What are you doing up at this hour?"

"I heard voices through my window."

And she likely saw Leo with Annabelle.

"I should go in." Annabelle pushed to her feet.

Leo rose as well.

"Good night, Annabelle." Chrishelle stepped past her and slid her arm around Leo's waist.

Annabelle took a step back. "Good night." Tears still glistening in her eyes, she turned and crossed to the terrace. A moment later, she and her guard disappeared inside.

"Leo, what were you thinking?" Chrishelle dropped the arm that had gripped him possessively a moment ago. "What would happen if someone got a photo of the two of you together?"

Leo studied Chrishelle's currently irate features. "Are you worried about it looking like I was cheating on you or are you worried that I would follow through with such behavior?"

"Both."

The single word cut through him. "I thought you knew me well enough to know I don't cheat."

"So you've told me." Chrishelle folded her arms. "I've also seen nearly a decade's worth of photos in the press accusing you of exactly that."

The barb landed as she intended. Leo had fought against false rumors since his teenage years. He had hoped she'd learned that those past stories were just that: stories. His jaw tightened, and he took a moment to ensure his voice was even before he spoke. "Jealousy doesn't become you."

"I walked out here and found you with another woman snuggled up next to you." Chrishelle waved a hand toward the bench he had vacated a moment ago. "I think a bit of jealousy is a normal reaction in this situation."

"She's my sister's best friend."

"Are you sure that's all she is?"

"Yes." Even though he had briefly entertained thoughts of more at one point when they were teenagers, he knew better than to pursue them. Royal protocols could be demanding enough. Dating and ultimately breaking up with the woman who attended nearly every family event was not a prospect he wanted to face, even if her presence was a constant distraction.

Leo placed both of his hands on Chrishelle's arms and leaned forward, his gaze intent on hers. "And like I said before, I don't cheat."

CHAPTER

6

ANNABELLE NEEDED TO APOLOGIZE. SHE knew better than to spend time alone with a man she wasn't dating, particularly someone like Leo who had been accused of cheating far more times than she could count. As if anyone who knew him would believe him capable of such behavior.

Still, she had taken comfort in Leo's arms, and that clearly hadn't sat well with his girlfriend.

The phone beside Annabelle's bed rang, and she crossed the room to answer it. "Hello?"

"Are you okay?" her sister Victoria asked without bothering with a greeting.

"Yes, and I'm sure you already got that update from Cassie."

"And Alan and Levi, but that's not the same as hearing it from you."

"I'm fine." If she said the words often enough, she might start to believe them.

"Now that you've given me the expected answer, tell me how you're really doing," Victoria insisted. "I know what it's like to see your life flash before your eyes. So does Cassie."

Annabelle dropped onto the side of the bed. "I don't know how I feel." She sighed. "I don't know how I'm supposed to feel."

"There isn't a right or wrong answer to that. Everyone is different," Victoria said with understanding. "Did you get any sleep last night?"

"Not much, but I guess that must be somewhat normal because Leo showed up while I was outside getting some fresh air."

"I know the two of you don't always get along, but it might be good to talk to him about how you're feeling. I'm sure it will do you both some good."

"It's not that we don't get along, per se," Annabelle said. "He just doesn't typically want to be around me."

"More likely, he doesn't want to hang out with his younger sister."

"Maybe."

A knock sounded at her door.

"I'd better get going, but thanks for calling."

"I'm here any time you need to talk."

"Thanks." Annabelle ended the call and crossed into the sitting room. She pulled the door open, not surprised to see Rocco standing on the other side.

"Did you get any sleep?" Rocco asked, repeating her sister's question of a moment ago.

"Not much. You?"

He shook his head. "Believe it or not, that's the first time I've had a bomb explode on me." He tilted his head slightly. "Unless you count the times when we blew things up on purpose for training."

"Somehow I don't think a planned explosion has the same effect as an unplanned one."

"You've got that right." Rocco motioned down the hall. "Would you like me to escort you downstairs for breakfast?"

"I guess so." She would need to face Chrishelle eventually, and the sooner she put this apology behind her, the better.

She stepped into the hall beside Rocco and caught sight of Federico standing a short distance away with Zeus at his side. "Good morning."

Federico bowed his head before speaking. "Good morning, Your Highness."

Annabelle fell into step with Rocco. "Anything new on the investigation?"

"We're still gathering information," Rocco said, his answer frustratingly vague.

Annabelle stopped walking. "I know I'm far from an expert at this sort of thing, but I want to help. Whoever planned this clearly knows both me and the royal family of Alameda."

"I know." Rocco stopped beside her, waiting until she started moving again before continuing forward once more. "I already spoke with Esteban this morning. We'd like you and Prince Leonardo to keep working on the invitation lists from the social events for the past six years."

"When is Tayla supposed to get back to the palace?" Annabelle asked, continuing down the hall.

"King Josep and Queen Eva have already arrived," Rocco said. "I believe Princess Tayla and her fiancé will be back later this afternoon."

"Why didn't they all come back together?" The words barely crossed her lips before she answered her own question. "Security protocols, right?"

"Yes. With an active threat, no one wants to have any of the family traveling together right now."

"That's understandable."

They reached the family dining room, where a couple waited inside, but it wasn't the one Annabelle expected.

"Your Majesties." Annabelle curtsied to her best friend's parents. "I'm glad to see you made it home safely."

"Thank you, Annabelle." Queen Eva stepped forward and brushed her cheek with a kiss.

"So good to see you again." King Josep kissed her cheek as well. "We're so relieved you're safe."

"Thank you." Annabelle gestured to Rocco. "Your Majesty, I believe you remember Rocco of the Sereno Royal Guard."

"Yes, and I understand I owe you a debt of gratitude." The king shook Rocco's hand.

"It's an honor to meet you, Your Majesty."

"Thank you for protecting my son." Queen Eva reached up and kissed Rocco's cheek. "I can't imagine what would have happened had you not been there yesterday."

"I didn't do anything beyond recognizing the problem," Rocco said. "Your son was equally responsible in making sure everyone escaped injury."

"Regardless, you must join us for breakfast this morning."

"I'd be honored, Your Majesty." Rocco bowed briefly.

Grateful that the conversation had veered away from those terrifying moments of yesterday, Annabelle asked, "How's Tayla? I haven't talked to her since before the bombing."

"We wish to speak to you about that." King Josep motioned for everyone to sit. As soon as they were all settled, he continued. "Tayla is unaware of what happened yesterday."

"How is that possible?" Annabelle asked. "Surely it's hit the news cycle by now."

"Yes, but the media believes the incident was nothing more than a fuel barrel igniting accidentally," King Josep said.

Annabelle looked to Rocco for confirmation.

Rocco nodded. "We hope that by keeping the details of the bomb private, we can prevent the media from interfering with the investigation."

"Are you worried about the media or about Tayla?"

"Both," Queen Eva said. "Tayla has been under a great deal of stress trying to plan her wedding, and if it gets out that she is a potential target, I don't know how she'll handle it."

Annabelle read between the lines. The queen was worried the news would affect Tayla's anxiety. "Wouldn't it be better if she knows of the danger?"

"The likelihood that Tayla was the target is slim at best," King Josep said. "We'll inform her of the situation once we have more details on who the bomb was intended for and why."

And they undoubtedly didn't want to risk her having another nervous breakdown. Annabelle had been front and center when the stress caused by a persistent stalker had required Tayla to undergo extensive therapy.

"You're assuming we'll be able to find those answers," Annabelle said.

"We hope we will," King Josep said. "Thankfully, Tayla's wedding planning efforts will keep her close to home over the next few weeks."

"What about me?" Though Annabelle suspected her departure was already being planned, she forced out the needed question. "Would it be better for you if I go back to Sereno?"

"We know this is a lot to ask." Queen Eva hesitated and glanced at her husband. "But we hope you will continue with your original plans."

She was still processing the queen's request when King Josep spoke. "Leo believes that with your help, the two of you can assist our security forces in narrowing the suspect list."

Which was where she came in. "And if I stay, Tayla won't suspect that anything is wrong."

"Precisely." The king nodded.

Annabelle turned to Rocco. "What do you think?"

"The security here at the palace is solid, and King Josep has agreed to let Federico do regular security sweeps for explosives," Rocco said. "I can speak with King Levi about King Josep's request."

Their conversation was interrupted when Leo entered with Chrishelle.

King Josep and Rocco stood at their entrance.

"Mother, Father." Leo kissed each of his parents' cheeks. "Welcome home."

"Thank you." King Josep motioned for Chrishelle and Leo to join them.

Everyone sat, and Chrishelle reached for the basket of croissants in front of her.

Annabelle froze, not sure Leo's girlfriend recognized her faux pas. Serving oneself before the king started eating was a serious breach of etiquette.

Leo leaned over and whispered something in Chrishelle's ear, and she lowered her hands into her lap.

The king waited a moment as though testing to see if Chrishelle would actually start eating before him. Then, seemingly satisfied that Leo had corrected the problem, he nodded at a nearby server, who stepped forward and placed a plate in front of him.

As everyone was being served, King Josep said, "Leo, I trust you can clear your schedule to work with Annabelle again today on that information we spoke about."

"Yes, Father," Leo said. "I've already told Marcus to postpone my meetings for the rest of the week."

"Good. Keep me updated."

Queen Eva cut into her poached egg. "Chrishelle, what do you have planned for today?"

"I hadn't thought that far yet." Chrishelle looked at Leo. "I had hoped Leonardo and I would be able to spend some time shopping in town."

"I'm afraid it would be best to limit your outings for the time being," King Josep said. "Perhaps you can spend some time by the pool."

"Our library is also well stocked with books in several languages."

Leo didn't give Chrishelle the chance to answer. "I'm sure Chrishelle can find something to occupy her time while Annabelle and I are working."

"Yes," Chrishelle said. "I'm sure I can."

CHAPTER

7

His parents were home, and his sister would be arriving within hours. Leo was ready to have his whole family safely at the palace. If he and Annabelle could just help find the person behind the bombing yesterday, they could get back to the business of getting his sister married.

He led the way out of the dining room, leaving his parents chatting with Annabelle. With the way Chrishelle had gone silent during the meal, he suspected he needed to have a private conversation with her before turning her loose on the palace grounds.

"What are your plans for today?" Leo asked once he was sure they were well out of earshot of his parents.

"I had planned to spend the day with you." Chrishelle waved a hand through the air. "And I have to be honest; I'm not thrilled with you spending all day with Princess Annabelle."

"Annabelle and I simply have work we need to do that will be more efficient if we do it together."

"Maybe I could help too."

The names and contact information of Tayla and Annabelle's friends would fall into the confidential category, and Leo couldn't bring himself to include Chrishelle in his circle of need to know. "I'm sorry, but some of the details we'll be working with are classified."

"Of course it is." She huffed out a breath. "Seriously, what am I supposed to do while you're working?"

"You knew I'd planned to work today even before the incident yesterday."

"Yes, but I thought you would at least be able to spend some time with me."

"We will spend time together." Although he wasn't sure when. "Maybe we can meet for lunch."

"I guess that's better than nothing." Chrishelle waved at the windows overlooking the gardens. "I'll be by the pool if you need me."

"Try to enjoy your day." Leo leaned down and kissed her cheek. "I'll see you later."

With a little twinge of guilt, he left her behind and made his way to his office. He'd barely turned on his laptop when Annabelle appeared in the open doorway, a cell phone in her hand.

"You got your new phone."

"Yes. Esteban gave it to me after I promised not to tell your sister what happened yesterday." She sat in one of the chairs beside the worktable in the far corner of his office. "I'm still not thrilled about keeping this a secret from her."

"I know, but I can understand why my parents don't want her to know. At least not yet."

"So can I." She set her phone on the table. "If Gonzalo Caballero wasn't still in jail, he would be my first suspect." Her eyes narrowed. "He is still in jail, right?"

"As far as I know, but I'll ask to make sure." Leo texted the question to Esteban and retrieved his laptop from his desk. He crossed to where Annabelle sat and took the spot beside her.

She faced him. "How upset was Chrishelle with you last night?"

"She's fine."

Annabelle gave him the same look as when he'd told her he'd had nothing to do with the frog in her bed when she was nine and he was twelve. "She didn't look fine."

"It was just a little jealousy."

"I need to apologize."

"There's no need." At least, there shouldn't be a need for it. If Chrishelle trusted him, she would have seen the situation for what it was: two friends supporting each other after a traumatic day.

Annabelle stared at him for a moment before she lifted her phone. "Where do you want to start?"

"Let's finish organizing the names from the guest lists."

Annabelle sighed. "I still can't fathom the idea of one of our friends trying to hurt you or Tayla."

"Neither can I."

- - -

"I think that's the last of them." Annabelle set aside the printed guest list that she'd been using to double-check the data in Leo's spreadsheet.

"That's good timing. My sister should be back anytime now."

"I guess it would be awkward if we had to explain why I was spending time with you instead of her." Annabelle checked the time on her watch. "It's already after one? I'm so sorry. You must be starving."

"I'm the one who should be apologizing." Leo clicked on his keyboard. "I haven't been the best of hosts."

"We had work to do." Annabelle leaned back in her seat. "Finding answers is a lot more important than eating lunch at a reasonable time."

"Let me email this list to Esteban, and then we'll raid the refrigerator."

"Deal." Annabelle stood, crossed to his desk, and picked up his office phone.

"What are you doing?" Leo asked.

"Warning Duran that we're on our way down."

Leo cocked his head to one side. "I think I can be trusted to make my own sandwich."

"Maybe, but if I tell your chef we're coming, I bet he'll let us have some of the leftover crema catalana." She made her call, pleased that Duran did indeed have extra dessert from last night. Smiling, she hung up and turned to face him. "Success."

"You and your desserts." Leo chuckled. "It's amazing you can eat the way you do and still look like that."

As far as Annabelle could remember, Leo had never commented on her looks before, other than to complain about her and Tayla taking too long to get ready for any number of events over the years. "Look like what?"

"Like you just stepped out from in front of a camera." Leo clicked on his mouse. "It's no wonder the paparazzi love you."

It was an offhanded compliment, but she'd take it. It wasn't often Leo spoke to her in complete sentences, and the last two days together had been a rather welcome change. "The paparazzi love anyone who will give them headlines," Annabelle corrected, "which is why you are such a target. You're just a little too popular with the press and the public."

"The media only wants my photo when they can claim I'm cheating on my girlfriend or that I have a new romance in my life."

Her sympathies stirred. "It's not fair, is it?"

"No, it's not." Leo stood and moved his laptop back onto his desk. "But you know as well as I do that part of being royal is dealing with the press and their speculation."

"I know, but anyone who knows you at all would never think you were capable of cheating on your girlfriend."

Leo turned and stared at her for a long moment. "Thank you."

"For what?"

"For knowing me well enough to not believe the drivel in the press."

Annabelle simply shrugged one shoulder. "Now, if they said something about putting frogs in a princess's bed, that would be something else entirely."

Leo held both hands up. "In my defense, I thought Tayla was sleeping in that bed." He took her by the elbow and steered her toward the door. "And I was only twelve."

"I think you were thirteen by then, but either way, I think we've likely passed the statute of limitations on that particular story."

"Does that mean my secret is safe with you?"

She tilted her head upward and lifted both eyebrows. "Do you even have to ask?"

His expression turned thoughtful. "No. Come to think of it, I don't."

Marcus stood when Leo and Annabelle emerged into the outer office. "Your Highnesses." He bowed his head.

"Any calls?"

"Several, but most of them can wait." Marcus lifted a notepad from his desk. "Chrishelle stopped by around noon to see if you were ready for lunch, but since you were still working, she decided to eat by the pool."

"Thanks for the message." Leo guided Annabelle to the door. "I'll be back in an hour or so."

"Yes, sire."

"Do you want us to bring anything back for you, Marcus?" Annabelle asked.

"No, thank you, Your Highness." Marcus set his notepad down. "One of the other staff members covered my desk earlier so I could take my lunch."

"We'll be back soon." Leo continued into the hall. "Did Duran mention what he fixed for lunch?"

"I didn't ask, and he didn't offer." And with the way her stomach was grumbling, she didn't care. Any meal would be welcome.

Leo glanced down at her. "I forgot. You rather like surprises."

"I do. At least I did." Yesterday's surprise was one that she could have easily lived without.

Leo stopped walking and put his hand on her arm. "Don't let yesterday's excitement change who you are."

"How did you know that's what I was thinking about?" Annabelle asked.

"Because you get a little line on your brow when you're worried."

"Really?" No one had ever mentioned that before.

Footsteps approached, and Tayla's voice carried from an adjoining hall.

"Where else could she be?" Tayla emerged into the main hall and spotted Annabelle. "There you are!"

Tayla rushed forward and hugged Annabelle. "I'm so sorry I wasn't here to greet you."

"It was just as well. You wouldn't have been happy if your hair ended up smelling like smoke."

Leo shot her a warning look, no doubt to remind her that Tayla hadn't been told about the explosion.

"I can't believe there was a fire at the docks while you were there," Tayla said.

"The good news is the fire is out, and everyone is fine." Annabelle motioned to Leo. "We were about to get some lunch. Do you want to join us?"

"No, thanks. Isaac and I are taste testing food for the rehearsal dinner in a little while. I don't want to fill up too soon."

"We can help with that too if you need us," Leo offered.

"Thanks, but you two are the worst at this sort of thing. You both like everything anyone puts in front of you."

Annabelle slanted a look at Leo. "She may have a point. Where is Isaac?"

"He had some phone calls to make, but we'll all get to visit tonight."

"Good. I look forward to seeing him again."

"Come on, Annabelle. Let's get something to eat. I'm starving." Leo started forward again and called over his shoulder, "We'll see you later."

Annabelle fell into step with him. As soon as Tayla headed back the way she had come, she lowered her voice and said, "I say we put in our votes for the rehearsal dinner while we're in the kitchen with Duran."

Leo nodded. "I like the way you think."

CHAPTER
8

LEO STRODE DOWN THE WIDE hall leading to his father's office. The number of guards had doubled since yesterday, and Federico's dog sniffed at the base of a plush chair. Leo offered a nod of greeting as he passed, continuing toward his destination. The summons to meet with his father had come shortly after he finished lunch with Annabelle.

His sister's safe return brought with it a sense of relief, but he didn't care for keeping Tayla in the dark about the bombing yesterday. He hated keeping secrets from her, and despite her past challenges with anxiety, Tayla was far stronger than many gave her credit for, including their parents.

Leo entered his father's outer office and was promptly admitted into his inner chamber. Rocco and Esteban stood at his entrance.

"Anything new?" Leo asked.

His father waited until the door was closed and everyone was seated before responding. "Esteban has accounted for all his staff during the time of the bombing. Whoever planted the bomb, it wasn't a member of the royal guard."

"What about the guards who were off duty?" Leo asked.

The king gave a subtle nod toward Esteban, a silent command to answer.

"More than half the off-duty guards were having lunch together," Esteban said, "and the others have at least one person who can account for their whereabouts."

"What about other staff members?" Leo asked. "Drivers, household staff, gardeners. Someone could have overheard a conversation between Annabelle and Tayla and known Tayla was going to meet Annabelle at the docks."

"We're still looking into that," Esteban said.

Someone living among them could be responsible. That really was a terrifying thought. "Annabelle and I have compiled the list of her and Tayla's friends who might have both seen her luggage and also visited us here at the palace."

"Have you narrowed down which of them knew Annabelle was arriving yesterday?" Rocco asked.

"Not yet," Leo said. "We really need to compile a list of everyone both Annabelle and Tayla have spoken to since they made their plans."

"They've been planning this trip for months," Rocco said. "And it's possible someone overheard them talking when Tayla visited Sereno in April."

"Rocco is right," Esteban said. "We'll run a search of everyone on the list to see who is currently in Alameda."

"You work on confirming who's here," Rocco said. "I'll work backwards and focus on proving who wasn't here."

"You're assuming one of Tayla and Annabelle's friends not only planned this but also executed it." Leo shook his head. "I find it much more likely it was a hired hand who placed the bomb."

"That's true," his father said. "The majority of their friends come from wealthy families. They aren't likely to have the knowledge of how to build a bomb, much less chance being caught planting it."

"But they would have the means to pay someone else to do it," Rocco finished for him.

Leo nodded.

"Sounds like you and Annabelle may need to do some more analysis," his father said.

"I agree." Rocco leaned forward in his seat. "If you can highlight those who Annabelle spoke to about her plans as well as those who were at Tayla's birthday party, that will help us focus our search."

"What about the people who Tayla spoke with?" Leo asked. "If we don't tell her what happened, we won't be able to ask her directly."

Esteban spoke now. "I've already pulled her cell phone records. One of my staff is analyzing her recent activity, both calls and texts."

"I can work with Annabelle, but I'm not sure how I'll get her away from Tayla."

"I suggest you both pretend to turn in early tonight," his father said. "You can then work after Annabelle has excused herself for the evening."

Which would be fine if it wasn't for how he and Annabelle alone together might be perceived, particularly at a late hour. "I don't know that your idea is the best plan. Chrishelle is already upset about how much time I've been spending alone with Annabelle."

"If she is going to be your future queen, she'll need to learn that sometimes duty comes before all else."

Leo clenched his jaw. For a man who had spent his life teaching Leo about the importance of discretion, his father didn't seem to be overly concerned with Leo's reputation right now. And to mention a possible engagement in front of Rocco, a man who was in the employ of another government, was inexcusable.

Though he made it a point not to comment about his private life in front of people outside his inner circle, today he couldn't risk his father's assumption being shared with anyone.

Leo drew a slow breath and forced calm into his voice. "A royal engagement is not imminent, and it would be wise not to assume otherwise."

His father lowered his chin in the way he did when he didn't approve of what he heard. "Regardless, the security of you and your sister remains my priority. You and Annabelle need to identify the problem. Soon."

Resigned to finding an excuse to steal Tayla's best friend from her, Leo nodded. "Yes, sire."

- - -

Annabelle strolled with Tayla through the exhibit hall, absorbing the beauty of centuries past. The artwork displayed here was truly magnificent, from the paintings on the walls to the sculptures scattered about the room.

An early Renoir caught her eye. "Oh. This is new." Annabelle stepped closer.

"Yes. Leo procured it a few months ago, not long after Isaac proposed."

"I still can't believe you're getting married."

"Nor can I."

Fabric rustled behind them, and Annabelle turned. Chrishelle stood in the wide archway leading into the exhibit hall.

"I'm sorry. I didn't mean to disturb you." Chrishelle's gaze swept the room. "I was looking for Leonardo."

"I believe he's meeting with my father," Tayla said.

Even though Leo insisted Chrishelle didn't need an apology, Annabelle needed to clear the air. "Chrishelle, do you have a moment?"

Chrishelle's eyebrows lifted, and for a second, she didn't respond. Then she nodded.

Annabelle placed her hand on Tayla's arm briefly. "Will you excuse us for a minute?"

"Of course."

Annabelle led the way out of the exhibit hall and headed for the nearest exit. As she approached the doors leading to the gardens, she gave a subtle nod toward the guard beside it.

He bowed his head and opened the door.

"Thank you," Annabelle said as she exited.

Chrishelle followed. "Why are we going outside?"

Annabelle waited until the door closed behind them before speaking. "Because palace walls have ears." She noted the guards stationed nearby, one on the side of the terrace, another beside an entrance thirty meters away.

Annabelle continued to the gardens. As soon as she was satisfied they had their privacy, she stopped and faced Chrishelle. "I wanted to apologize for last night."

A flicker of accusation sparked in Chrishelle's expression. Apparently, an apology truly was in order.

"Leo and I are old friends, nothing more." She tilted her head slightly toward the palace. "He would never cheat on you, and I would certainly never try to steal someone else's boyfriend."

The tension in Chrishelle's body eased slightly.

Annabelle continued. "What you saw last night was simply two people struggling to overcome a difficult memory."

"Thank you for explaining." Chrishelle laced her fingers together. "Leonardo and I have been apart for so long; it's been difficult trying to find our footing again."

"How long have you been in Alameda?"

"Only five days."

"Give it time," Annabelle said. "I'm sure everything will get back to normal before long."

"I hope so."

"It will. Trust me." Annabelle looked out over the gardens, the memory of Leo's first summer home from university washing over her. "As much as Leo loves adventure, he also needs to know what to expect from one day to the next. I'm sure after so many months apart, he's still trying to figure out what his expectations should be while also trying to be sensitive to yours."

"You know so much about him."

"He's been a dear friend for most of my life." The moment the words were out of her mouth, she recognized the truth in them. While Leo had been admittedly standoffish during her late teens and early twenties, he had been part of her life for as long as she could remember.

"Thanks for talking to me about all this." Chrishelle tucked a lock of hair behind her ear. "I'm sure you can understand why I'd be jealous of the two of you together."

"I know how it may have appeared, and I hope you now know that Leo is someone you will never have to worry about." Annabelle clasped her hands together. "He's always been a perfect gentleman, and I don't expect that will ever change."

- - -

Leo had his marching orders, and he wasn't happy about it. He dressed for dinner, mulling over possibilities in his head of how he could meet with Annabelle without his sister knowing and without upsetting his girlfriend. He wasn't sure which would be the bigger challenge.

He knotted and straightened his tie and shrugged into his dinner jacket before walking out of his bedroom, through his private quarters, and out the door.

Saul fell into step behind him as he headed for the dining hall.

When Leo reached the hallway leading to the guest quarters, he hesitated, unsure whether Chrishelle would have already gone down to dinner or if she would be waiting for him. Best to check rather than upset her again.

He was three doors from Chrishelle's room when Annabelle emerged from her room. Her room. Odd that he couldn't remember anyone else staying in that particular suite besides her in recent memory. Was she really at his home so often that she had created her own space without him ever noticing it?

Her vibrant yellow dress swished around her calves when she stepped toward him. Her voice low, she asked, "Does Esteban have any new leads?"

"No." Leo glanced at Chrishelle's closed door before he continued. "My father wants us to work together tonight on narrowing down their suspect list."

"How are we supposed to do that without Tayla knowing why we're meeting together?"

"He suggested we both pretend to turn in early, but I have to be honest; I'm not thrilled with sneaking off with you alone when my girlfriend is already jealous of you."

"Then I suggest we only sneak around behind your sister's back," Annabelle said. "Tell Chrishelle the truth."

"She won't be happy about this."

"I don't blame her," Annabelle said with entirely too much understanding. "She came to visit you here, and within a few days, you not only have to juggle your regular duties, but all of your free time is spent investigating a bombing instead of with her."

He supposed when considering Chrishelle's side of things, he could understand her frustration, but her lack of trust from last night still stung.

"And if it makes you feel any better, I did speak with her today and apologized for my part in upsetting her last night."

"You didn't have to do that."

"I know, but I think it helped."

Chrishelle's door opened, and she emerged from her room. She spotted Leo and Annabelle, but this time, there wasn't any hint of accusation in her stare.

She approached Leo. "I was about to come find you."

"I came to escort you to dinner."

Chrishelle glanced at Annabelle. "Both of us?"

"No. Annabelle came out as I was coming to your room." Leo glanced from Chrishelle to Annabelle. When Annabelle tilted her head toward Chrishelle and gave him a just-tell-her look, he turned his attention back to his girlfriend. "My father has asked Annabelle and me to work together again tonight without my sister's knowledge."

Chrishelle sighed. "I'll be so glad when all of this is behind us."

"Me too." Then speaking to Annabelle again, he said, "Perhaps we can meet in my office around eight. I can say I need to do some work, and you can say you're turning in early." He glanced at Chrishelle. "And I'll ask Marcus to stay late so Annabelle and I won't be alone."

"I appreciate that," Chrishelle said. "I prefer to avoid more speculation that you're cheating on me."

No one had to lecture Leo on the importance of avoiding even the mere appearance of impropriety.

"What do you think, Annabelle? Are you willing to continue our search tonight?"

"Yes, of course."

"In that case, shall we go to dinner?" Leo offered one arm to Chrishelle and the other to Annabelle.

"We shall," Annabelle said. She took his arm, while Chrishelle put her hand inside the crook of his other elbow. Together the three of them made their way to the main staircase.

When they reached the top, Annabelle released his arm, opting to use the curved railing to steady herself as she descended the stairs.

Leo and Chrishelle followed, and Chrishelle squeezed his arm. "I'm sorry I jumped to conclusions last night."

Surprised by her apology, he stared for a brief moment. "I appreciate that. And I'm sorry I've been so busy since you've been here."

"Maybe we can do something together this weekend," Chrishelle suggested.

It should have been a simple request, one he would have happily granted if the royal guard wasn't already working overtime to ensure the family's safety. The sailing trip he had planned for them for Saturday would likely have to wait, as would their excursion into town for dinner at his favorite spot.

Chrishelle looked up at him, clearly waiting for an answer.

"I'll see what I can do."

"I guess that's the best I can ask for at the moment," Chrishelle said.

"I'm afraid so."

CHAPTER

9

ANNABELLE SAT ACROSS THE TABLE from Tayla and Isaac, the dinner conversation on the happy topic of their upcoming wedding. Three couples and her. Not exactly the ideal dinner seating arrangement, especially since King Josep had designated her the spot to his left, forcing Leo and Chrishelle to sit farther down the table.

And although talking about which flowers would be in bloom in March for the wedding would normally appeal to Annabelle's artistic side, such details felt trivial in comparison to the work she and Leo would attempt tonight.

At least her chat with Chrishelle seemed to have put Leo's girlfriend at ease with their situation.

"Cherry blossoms will be in bloom at that time of year, and they are a beautiful shade of pink," Queen Eva said.

"What do you think, Annabelle?" Tayla asked.

Annabelle took a sip of her lemonade. "Pink has been your favorite color since we were five."

Tayla turned to her fiancé. "Isaac?"

"I've told you before, when it comes to the decorations, I don't have an opinion as long as it's what you want."

Smart answer.

"I'll have the wedding planner prepare some ideas for us with cherry blossoms as your central theme," Queen Eva said.

From his spot beside Annabelle, Leo asked, "Isaac, have you wrapped up your latest case?" He was clearly ready for the topic to move away from flowers and wedding colors.

"I expect I'll make my closing arguments on Friday."

Though not particularly interested in legal proceedings here in Alameda, Annabelle asked, "What case have you been working on?"

Isaac looked at her like she had just crawled out from under a rock. Then, as though remembering that Annabelle hadn't been in Alameda for months, he said, "I've been prosecuting the man accused of embezzling over seven million euros from Alameda's largest shipping company."

"Wow. That's a lot of money." Since preparing for the launch of her new company, Annabelle had gained a new appreciation for the value of a euro and just how quickly money could disappear if not managed well. Nerves fluttered inside her. She needed this venture to go well, and spending so much of her time working with Leo instead of keeping up with her correspondence wasn't working in her favor.

"It's the largest embezzlement case in recent history," Isaac said, breaking into Annabelle's thoughts.

"That's impressive." She took a bite of her swordfish, wishing this meal would end so she could escape this dinner conversation.

"How is it going so far?" King Josep asked.

"Very promising."

"I'm sure you'll make the prosecutor's office proud," King Josep said.

"It'll be nice when this case is behind him so we can get more of the wedding details in place," Tayla said. "We're supposed to meet with a caterer tonight and three more next week."

Four meetings that could give the would-be assassin access to Tayla. "Are the caterers coming here?" Annabelle asked.

"The one tonight for the rehearsal dinner will be here, and so will the cake tasting, but the catering appointments are in town."

Annabelle glanced at the king and queen. Neither commented, but she could only imagine their thoughts mirrored her own.

Keeping her response neutral, Annabelle said, "I'm sure you'll be glad to get those details behind you."

"Yes. But then there are the photographers, the videographer, the florist, my gown."

"One thing at a time," Annabelle said. "You don't have to take care of everything right now. And I'm here to help."

"And I appreciate it," Tayla said. "We should start with some shopping in town tomorrow. Chrishelle, you're welcome to join us."

Chrishelle's face instantly brightened. "That sounds wonderful."

Annabelle didn't have to see Leo's face to sense his panic. Grasping at anything that would keep them on the palace grounds, Annabelle said, "Chrishelle and I had already planned to go horseback riding tomorrow." Not giving

Chrishelle the chance to respond, Annabelle continued. "She hasn't been given the grand tour yet."

"But—"

"Be sure to take her to the overlook," Queen Eva said, cutting off Tayla's intended protest. "That's always been one of my favorite places."

"And Chrishelle is quite the accomplished rider," Leo said. "I'm sorry I haven't been able to take her out yet."

Chrishelle leaned forward, her awareness evident. "I do love to ride."

The tension that had built up inside Annabelle eased, grateful Leo's girl-friend was astute enough to play along. "Yet another reason to take advantage of the gorgeous weather we're having."

Resigned, Tayla shrugged. "I guess we're going riding tomorrow then."

"I promise, it will be fun." Annabelle flicked a glance at Tayla. *And safe.*

- - -

With two highlighters in hand, Leo plucked the printout off the printer tray and settled on the sofa in the far corner of his office. He typically used this little seating nook when needing a break or perusing reports after-hours. Reviewing the list of Tayla and Annabelle's friends would certainly be an after-hours event.

Annabelle announced her arrival with a knock on his open door.

Leo stood and patted the cushion beside him. "Please. Sit down."

Annabelle gestured to the door. "Do you want this open or closed?"

"I'm sure Chrishelle would prefer it open, but with the sensitivity of who we're discussing, you'd better close it."

She did so and crossed to the sofa. "Surely you trust Marcus."

"I do, but I don't want to put him in the position of having to announce every time someone walks into the outer office."

"That I understand." She sat on the end of the sofa. "We both know that palace staff have excellent hearing."

"As evidenced by the time we were grounded after my parents learned about my planned fireworks display in the gardens."

Annabelle's face lit up. "It would have been spectacular, assuming we hadn't blown ourselves up first."

Leo's lips twitched into a smile. "Perhaps ten was a bit young for me to attempt that on my own."

"Especially with two seven-year-olds as your assistants."

Leo handed Annabelle half the printout and sat beside her. "I thought it would be easier to work off a hard copy and highlight everyone you've had contact with in the past two months."

"This really would be easier if Tayla was helping us."

"I agree, but between you talking to her all the time and Esteban's access to her phone records, we should be able to accomplish this without her."

Annabelle held up her highlighter. "Do you have another color? I might as well distinguish who I know was aware I was coming on this trip."

"There should be one in my desk." Leo started to rise, but she waved for him to remain where he was.

"I can get it." She circled the coffee table and crossed to his desk. "Which drawer?"

"The center one."

She opened it and stared for a moment before she lifted something from the drawer, but it wasn't a highlighter. Leo only had to take a quick glance to remember the photo he had tucked there, out of Chrishelle's sight.

"I haven't seen this photo in forever." Annabelle held it for a moment before turning it toward him. The photo of him with his family and Annabelle had been taken when he graduated secondary school. "Why is it in a drawer?"

"I was trying to head off Chrishelle's jealous streak," Leo admitted. "For me, that's a happy family photo. For her, it would be your picture on my desk instead of hers."

Annabelle replaced the photo and retrieved a blue highlighter. "You know there's a cure for that."

"What?"

"Put her photo on your desk too."

"I don't think I'm ready for that."

Annabelle sat back down and picked up her portion of the printout. "I thought you were about to propose."

Heat rose in his face. "Where did you hear that?"

"Don't get mad." She held up a hand, complete with blue highlighter, to placate him. "Tayla mentioned your father gave you your grandmother's engagement ring. We both assumed—"

"Please don't assume."

"I'm sorry." Annabelle set the highlighter down and put her hand on his arm. "I shouldn't have."

The sincerity of her apology soothed the worst of his anger. "It's my sister who should know better."

"We both should have." She squeezed his arm before releasing him. "I think Tayla didn't want to ask you about it because she was afraid you'd get mad."

He couldn't blame his sister for that. He would have been furious had she broached the subject with him, not because he didn't trust her, but because the topic always made him feel cornered. Trapped.

"You can tell my sister that I am not making plans for an engagement."

"Do you think Chrishelle is the person you'll marry?" Annabelle asked. "You've been with her far longer than anyone else."

"We were also apart for half of that time." He leaned back on the sofa. "It was actually quite nice. I had the label of a girlfriend, so I wasn't constantly being pressured by my parents and friends to date, but I also had the freedom to do basically whatever I wanted."

"I'm sure daily phone calls take far less time than in-person dating," Annabelle said.

Leo didn't correct her assumption and admit that his calls with Chrishelle fell into the once-or-twice-a-week range. "Yes. A lot less time." He uncapped his highlighter. "We should get started. I'll match up the names on Tayla's phone records, and you can highlight everyone you talked to or who was at Tayla's birthday party."

"So you're taking the easy job."

A lightness rose inside him. "Absolutely."

CHAPTER

10

ANNABELLE STIFLED A YAWN AND pulled on her riding boots. She'd struggled to stay awake through her eight o'clock video conference with her board of directors for Sereno Cove Cosmetics. It was her own fault. She'd chosen to stay up until nearly midnight reviewing their list of friends and acquaintances. Ultimately, she and Leo had ended up with thirty-one people who could have both seen her luggage and known about her planned visit to Alameda. Of those, she was certain four of them fit both categories. Because of that certainty, those four friends had risen to the top of their suspect list.

A knock sounded at her door, and Annabelle answered.

Rocco stood on the other side.

"Come in." Annabelle stepped aside.

As soon as he entered, Rocco closed the door. "Any luck last night?"

Even though Annabelle hated putting her close friends on a suspect list, she said, "We have thirty-one possibilities, but only four who I'm sure knew I was coming here and when."

"Who?"

"April Cronin, Remy Dufour, Selina Meier, and Russell Manning." Just listing her friends' names as potential suspects churned her stomach. "All of them graduated with us, but I can't imagine what would motivate any of them to try to hurt Tayla or Leo."

"I met April Cronin and Russell Manning when they visited Sereno last summer," Rocco said. "Who are the other two?"

"Remy Dufour lived next door to us our senior year. He's French and was studying art history."

"What does his family do?"

"They own a vineyard in the Bordeaux region."

"And Selina Meier?"

"She was a freshman when we were sophomores, but she went to school year-round so she could graduate early." Anticipating his next question, she continued. "She's Swiss, and her dad is a chocolatier. I believe she's working at a bank in Linz."

"It could be any of them," Rocco said.

"Or none of them."

Rocco inclined his head slightly to acknowledge that truth. "I'll work with Esteban to track their recent movements and activity."

"What's your impression of Esteban?" Annabelle asked.

"I trust him."

Nothing Rocco could have said would have given her more comfort. "I'm afraid I'll be out riding the better part of the morning. If you and Esteban could solve this whole puzzle before I get back, that would be great."

Rocco cocked an eyebrow. "I'll do my very best."

Annabelle smiled. "You always do."

- - -

Leo buttoned his shirt, already dreading the day he would spend in the office. He'd emailed his and Annabelle's list of potential suspects to Esteban last night, thus concluding his part in the investigation. Unfortunately, today would be filled with meetings as he attempted to catch up on the work he should have been completing over the past two days: teleconferences with dignitaries from Spain and Italy, reviewing the latest progress report from the gold-mine safety enhancements, and another call with the nation's tourism council. Too bad he wouldn't be able to break free and join Annabelle, Tayla, and Chrishelle on their ride today.

In no mood to deal with Chrishelle's inevitable request that he do just that, he headed for the kitchen with the intent of grabbing a quick bite on his way to his office. When he walked inside, Annabelle sat on a stool beside the prep counter, a glass of milk in front of her and a chocolate croissant in her hand.

Leo let the door swing closed behind him. Duran never let people eat in his kitchen. Annabelle caught sight of him, and her expression brightened. "Good morning."

"What are you doing in here?"

She held up her breakfast. "I stopped by to see what Duran was making and had to stay to taste test."

"He let you?"

Duran approached with a baking sheet in his hand, the scent of croissants and melted chocolate wafting toward him.

Leo stepped forward. "Is one of those for me?"

"I've never known you to stop at just one." Duran set the tray beside Annabelle's breakfast. He retrieved a spatula and transferred two onto a plate.

Leo slid onto the empty stool beside Annabelle. "You need to visit more often. Duran never lets me eat in here."

"Today's an exception, and only because the princess is here to keep you out of my baking supplies."

"Sneak a few chocolate chips when you're ten, and you're branded for life."

"It was three pounds, and you were sick for days," Duran said.

"That was Tayla." At least, she'd been the one who'd gotten sick. He'd managed his portion of chocolate chips without any negative side effects.

"He's right." Annabelle picked up her glass. "That's why Tayla still won't eat chocolate."

"Don't let him fool you into thinking he wasn't involved." Duran poured Leo a glass of milk and set it before him. "His Highness might not have suffered sufficiently afterward, but he was every bit as guilty."

Leo avoided commenting by taking a bite of his breakfast. Warm chocolate inside the delicate croissant. He took a second bite and debated how to negotiate for an extra serving.

Duran crossed his burly arms over his chest. "Well?"

"This may be even better than your beignets." Leo held up the remnants of his pastry. "You should fix these for the wedding breakfast."

"Your sister doesn't eat chocolate, remember?" Duran asked.

"That doesn't mean the rest of us should suffer." He took a sip of milk and stood. "I should get to my office."

Annabelle put her hand on his arm. "It won't hurt for you to finish your breakfast before you go to work."

A timer went off, and Duran crossed to the bank of ovens on the far side of the kitchen.

Leo picked up his plate. "I do need to go. I have a lot to do today."

"Okay." Annabelle gave him a you-don't-know-what-your-missing look.

Instantly suspicious, he asked, "What am I missing?"

"The scent of raspberry scones." She nodded toward Duran. "The ones Duran is pulling out of the oven."

Leo set his plate back down. "Maybe I can spare a few minutes longer."

Annabelle's eyes lit with humor. "I thought so."

- - -

Annabelle reined in her horse, or rather Leo's horse, at the top of the bluff overlooking the Mediterranean. The stallion was one Leo had claimed as his own several years ago, and she could never pass up the opportunity to ride him. Calypso pranced beneath her, and she put a hand on his neck to settle him.

Pure joy rushed through her as he tossed his head as though reminding her that few would ever have the opportunity to ride such a magnificent animal. She truly felt like a princess, the sort who spent all her days pursuing a life of luxury, one who had no responsibilities to carry or worries to bear beyond where to ride next. But this brief departure into the fairy-tale world was an illusion. It would never be real.

Even though her brothers-in-law now helped with the official functions, Annabelle still tried to balance carrying her share of the burden with the increasing demands of her new company. She'd already responded to a dozen emails this morning before heading to the stables after breakfast, and she had no doubt there would be many more when she returned to the palace.

Pushing aside the reality that awaited her when she returned, she took in her beautiful surroundings. The vast waters spread out before her, sailboats dotting the water, the path down the hill tempting her to continue to the beach below so she could walk along the shoreline.

A light breeze tugged at her ponytail, and a bead of sweat dripped down her spine and dampened the lightweight button-up she had donned with her riding pants this morning. Tayla and Chrishelle stopped on either side of her.

"This view is amazing," Chrishelle said.

Tayla stared out at the water, a distant look in her eyes. "It's always been one of our favorite places."

Annabelle knew that look on her friend's face, the one that nearly hid a storm brewing beneath the surface. Perhaps Tayla's parents had been wise to keep the bombing attempt from her.

"Is everything okay?" Chrishelle asked.

"I was just thinking it's too bad Isaac doesn't like to ride." Tayla leaned forward so she could see past Annabelle to Chrishelle. "Leo's lucky you like horses."

"This was my passion growing up." Chrishelle patted her mount's neck. "I got a pony for my fifth birthday, and I never looked back."

"I'm glad we could do this today." Tayla wiped a bead of sweat from her forehead. "Although with this heat, maybe we should have opted for sailing instead."

Annabelle stared out at the water again, but the sense of peace this view normally invoked didn't come. Someone had tried to kill Tayla or Leo, someone who knew them, who knew her, and here she was leisurely riding with her best friend and Leo's girlfriend.

Tayla's watch chimed with an incoming message. She read it, and her eyes brightened.

"Isaac?" Annabelle asked.

"Yes. It looks like the defendant agreed to a plea bargain, so he'll be back early today."

"Is he staying at the palace?" Annabelle asked.

"Yes, for the next few weeks anyway," Tayla said. "We're hoping to get the majority of our wedding plans in motion before you leave."

"No pressure," Annabelle said even as pressure built inside her. Meetings with caterers, florists, bakeries, musicians. All while the royal guard attempted to find a would-be assassin—an assassin Tayla didn't know existed.

"Do you mind if we head back?" Tayla asked. "I want to get cleaned up before Isaac gets home."

"That's fine." In truth, Annabelle would love the chance to check in with Esteban for updates, although she doubted he would tell her much unless she enlisted Leo's help. He would undoubtedly want the information as well.

Chrishelle checked the time on her watch. "Maybe we'll get back in time for me to eat lunch with Leonardo."

Annabelle's image of enlisting Leo's help vanished. She turned her mount toward the stables. "I'm sorry he's been so busy since you've been here."

Chrishelle followed her lead. "I have to admit, this isn't what I expected of royal life."

"How so?" Tayla asked.

"Leo is so incredibly busy." Chrishelle ran her hand along her horse's neck. "I thought he would have more time for moments like these."

Annabelle's sympathies stirred. Leo lived a royal life, but Chrishelle wanted the fairy tale.

CHAPTER

11

LEO FLIPPED THROUGH THE BACKGROUND report for Selina Meier, music from his favorite Italian band pulsing through the portable speaker on the far end of the library table. A six-inch stack of dossiers lay at his right elbow, an empty plate at his left.

Someone knocked lightly on the library door before pushing it open. Annabelle stepped inside a moment later.

She'd changed out of her riding clothes, now dressed in a blue dress with little white buttons up the front.

She closed the door and continued to the table. "Have you found anything?"

"Nothing beyond what Esteban already told me."

"Which is?" Annabelle sat at the table across from him.

"April Cronin and Russell Manning have both been in the UK since last Thursday."

"So they couldn't have been involved unless they hired someone."

The song playing on the speaker ended, and the first notes of the next tune rang out.

Leo leaned back in his chair. "Esteban has already requested the financial information for everyone we have on our list. With any luck, we'll be able to find transaction records that will prove who was involved."

"How is he going to get their financials?" Annabelle asked. "It's not like any of them are Alamedan citizens."

"Prince Alan seemed to think he could expedite the process."

"You can drop the 'prince' from his name," Annabelle said. "He only wears the title when absolutely necessary."

"Regardless, Alan has put in a request with someone, and Esteban is hoping their financial records will magically appear."

Annabelle motioned toward the files. "What about Remy Dufour and Selina Meier?"

"I'm reading through Selina's information right now." Leo lifted the file in his hand.

Annabelle stretched out a perfectly manicured hand. "Hand me Remy's."

Leo complied. "How was your ride this morning?"

"Challenging."

"How so?"

"Keeping secrets from your sister is a new experience for me." She flipped open the file. "I don't like it."

"I'm not thrilled with it either." He flipped to the next page in the file.

"On the plus side, Chrishelle is an excellent rider."

Riding was one of the few things he and Chrishelle both enjoyed. "Lucky for us, it's one of her passions."

"So true. It wouldn't have been good if she'd said she was afraid of horses; riding was the only activity I could think of that Esteban and Rocco would approve of." Annabelle fell silent, her attention on the dossier in front of her.

Leo read through Selina Meier's information one more time. "I don't see anything suspicious here. Selina posted several photos on her social media of her at a restaurant opening in Vienna on the day of the bombing. I checked to make sure the event really happened on the same day, and everything lines up."

"Based on the video feed, we're pretty sure the person who planted the bomb was a man anyway."

"That's true." Leo rolled his shoulders to battle the stiffness that had settled there. "But I don't see anything that would cause Selina Meier to turn terrorist either."

"Same here." Annabelle closed her file. "Did Esteban say anything about Gonzalo Caballero? Is it possible he could be out of prison?"

"According to Esteban, he's still there, but maybe it's worth paying him a visit." Leo wouldn't mind giving himself that peace of mind to be sure his sister's stalker wasn't involved in the bombing.

Annabelle shook her head. "There's no way your security chief is going to let you anywhere near a prison."

"True, but I'm sure he can arrange for me to receive the video of him being interviewed."

"Maybe, but what good will questioning him do?" Annabelle asked. "If he's in prison, he certainly didn't have the ability to arrange for the bomb."

"Yes, but Gonzalo followed Tayla around for months. If there was anyone else paying special attention to her, it's possible he noticed."

"I suppose it's possible, but that was over two years ago." Annabelle reached out her hand. "Pass me another file."

Leo handed over a file folder containing another of her friends' background information. Annabelle opened it. He took one for himself and read through it. They worked in silence for two more files.

"I'm striking out," Annabelle said. "Nothing in any of these background checks suggests any of my friends are involved." She set another folder aside and asked, "Do you have meetings this afternoon?"

"Yes." He checked the time. "I should get back to my office."

"I'll keep searching through these files until Tayla looks for me," Annabelle said. "Since she planned to spend some time with Isaac, I suspect I won't see her until dinner."

"Let me know if you find anything." He stood, and the oddity that she had located him in the library in the first place surfaced. "How did you find me here anyway?"

"I followed the music."

- - -

Annabelle read through every file, but not a single detail about her friends suggested any of them would have reason to harm Tayla or Leo. Her friends. Perhaps they had been looking in the wrong direction. What if the culprit was one of Leo's friends who happened to notice Annabelle's luggage?

With that thought in mind, Annabelle gathered the files off the library table and headed down the hall toward Leo's office. She only made it as far as the terrace doors before Tayla stepped inside, the scent of the ocean and roses spilling into the hallway. Isaac followed, his white dress shirt contrasting against his tanned skin. He had discarded his tie, and the top two buttons were unfastened.

"Annabelle. I was hoping we would find you." Tayla crossed to her. "Are you ready to work on wedding plans?"

"Can't we just elope?" Isaac asked hopefully.

"No, we can't." Tayla barely spared him a glance.

Annabelle held back the smile trying to break free. "Nice try, Isaac."

"I thought so."

"What do you say, Annabelle? Are you ready to pick my colors so we can put Isaac out of his misery?"

"More than ready." Though Annabelle was also more than ready to speak with Leo or, even better, learn that the bomber had been identified and captured. She held up the stack of files in her hands. "Let me put my work in my room first."

"We'll meet you in the grand salon." Tayla and Isaac continued down the hall.

Annabelle waited until they turned the corner toward the salon before she hurried to Leo's office. Her intended conversation with Leo died when she stepped into his outer office. Chrishelle and Leo stood by the doorway to his private office, deep in conversation. Marcus sat at his desk, a phone to his ear.

"I'm sorry to interrupt." Annabelle held up the files. "Leo, I wanted to return these to you."

"Any luck?"

"I have an idea, but we can talk about that later."

"It's okay." With a surprising sense of calm, Chrishelle took a step toward the door. "I was just leaving."

Marcus held up his phone. "Your Highness, King Alexander is on line three."

"I'm sorry." Leo focused on Annabelle. "I have to take this."

"That's okay. We'll talk later." Annabelle shifted the files into his arms.

As soon as Leo disappeared into his office, Annabelle asked Chrishelle, "What are you doing now?"

"No plans."

Sensing Chrishelle's obvious discomfort at being left to her own devices yet again, Annabelle led the way into the hall. "Would you like to join me and Tayla? We're doing some wedding planning."

"I don't want to intrude."

"Since Isaac would prefer to elope, we may need reinforcements." Annabelle started down the hall. "Today's objective is to pick her wedding colors."

Chrishelle's expression brightened, but she still asked, "Are you sure Tayla won't mind?"

"I'm sure."

They turned down the hall toward the grand salon. Annabelle walked into the beautiful space, taking a moment to appreciate the elegant crystal chandelier hanging in the center of the room.

Isaac and Tayla sat on a loveseat in the seating area closest to the marble fireplace, the vase of freshly cut flowers on the square table beside them scenting the room.

Isaac stood upon their entrance.

Annabelle crossed to them. "I hope you don't mind, but I enlisted some help."

"We may need an extra opinion." Tayla flicked a glance at her fiancé.

Annabelle chose a spot on one side of a loveseat. Chrishelle sat across from her.

As soon as Isaac reclaimed his spot beside Tayla, he said, "My darling fiancée seems to think pink is the ideal color for the wedding."

"I gather that isn't your first choice," Annabelle said.

"No." He lifted up a color palate that highlighted a dozen shades ranging from blush to bubblegum. "I prefer not to accessorize in any of these colors."

"What's your favorite color?" Annabelle asked Isaac.

"Green."

"What about sage and pink?" Chrishelle asked.

"That could work." Tayla tapped her forefinger against the color swatch in her hand. "This pale pink would work beautifully with sage."

"Add a base color to tie them together, and you're all set," Chrishelle agreed.

"What about this one?" Annabelle held up a card. "Champagne would be stunning with the sage and pink, and it would give Isaac more options for the groomsmen."

"I like it."

Over the next few minutes, they narrowed down their options until Tayla made her final choices.

"Now that we've decided on the colors, we have to pick our announcements," Tayla said.

"When do we have the next taste testing?" Isaac asked.

"We have three next week."

Three tastings, three opportunities for a would-be assassin to strike. Annabelle dreaded the chaos the next week might bring.

CHAPTER

12

LEO SETTLED AT HIS DESK, the video feed for the interrogation room at the federal penitentiary already open on his computer. The metal table in the center of the room was bolted to the floor, as were the bench seats that stretched along either side.

Any minute, a guard would escort Gonzalo Caballero into the room. Whether this conversation with his sister's stalker would give them any insight into the bombing was doubtful, but he was willing to try just about anything to find answers.

The door opened, and Esteban walked in. He faced the camera. "Your Highness, please text me if you can hear me."

Leo texted him. *Audio is fine.*

As soon as Esteban read his message, he nodded. "The guard should be bringing Gonzalo any minute."

Leo glanced at the latest construction report on the corner of his desk. He could review it while he waited, but he doubted he would be able to concentrate. They were running out of time. Tayla's first catering appointment was next week, and keeping her home when she expected to go into town wouldn't be easy. If he abided by his parents' wishes to protect her from the truth, they needed answers, and they needed them now.

Seconds ticked by, his patience fraying with each passing minute.

The door finally opened again, and a guard entered alone.

"Sir, I'm sorry, but Gonzalo isn't here."

Leo straightened.

"What do you mean he isn't here?" Esteban asked. "I called to make this appointment yesterday."

"According to the system, he should be here, but the prisoner in his assigned cell isn't Gonzalo."

"Then where is he?" Esteban demanded.

"We don't know."

Leo pushed to a stand as the implications of the guard's words sank in; if Gonzalo wasn't in prison, he could have been the person who planted the bomb. And he was free to try again.

Panic clawed up his throat, and Leo rushed to his office door. He yanked it open and spoke to Marcus. "Call security and have them do a perimeter sweep of the grounds. And double the guards on Princess Tayla."

"Yes, Your Highness." Marcus reached for his phone, a look of confusion on his face.

Though Leo was tempted to retrieve his weapon from his room, he didn't want to miss out on any information the prison could share. He rushed back into his office and moved back behind his desk.

On his screen, the guard motioned toward the exit. "The warden is pulling up Gonzalo's records."

"I want to see the surveillance feed of when he arrived too." Esteban headed out the door, lifting his mobile to his ear as he did so.

Leo snatched up his phone as soon as it rang.

"Did you hear that?" Esteban asked.

"Yes. Is it possible Gonzalo escaped, and we were never informed?"

"Highly unlikely."

Leo paced across the room. "How else can you explain why the prison doesn't know where he is?"

"I don't think he escaped," Esteban said. "But it's possible he was never here."

"Call me as soon as you know anything."

"I will, Your Highness."

Leo dropped his phone onto the couch. It bounced once before falling motionless onto the center cushion. Perhaps his parents had been wise in keeping the news of the bomb from Tayla. He paced the room again, circling back to where he'd started.

A rapid knock sounded at his door, and he drew his eyebrows together. Either Marcus had stepped away from his desk, or the person on the other side of the door was his father. Before he could call out, the door burst open, and Marcus and Saul rushed in.

"We have an intruder on the grounds." Saul hurried to the window.

Leo shot to his feet. "Is it Gonzalo?"

"We don't know, Your Highness." Saul checked out the window before closing the blinds. "We need to move you to a safer location."

If it was Gonzalo on the grounds, he wasn't the one in danger. "Where's Tayla?"

"I'm not sure."

Leo rushed to the door and put his hand on Marcus's shoulder. "Marcus, make sure the guards get Tayla to the panic room."

"Yes, sire."

Leo moved past him, Saul quickly taking the spot behind him. When Leo turned toward his room, Saul called to him. "Sire, it's this way."

"I'm not going to the panic room," Leo called out over his shoulder. "I'm getting my gun."

- - -

Annabelle hung up the phone and raked her fingers through her hair. The marketing plan was set, and she'd delegated her upcoming responsibilities to her trusted employees. Nerves tangled inside her, an ache starting in her center and spreading outward. What if this business wasn't successful? What if she failed her family? What if people like Leo thought she was just wasting her time on frivolous pursuits?

Not that Leo's opinion should matter.

Footsteps pounded outside her door, followed by muffled voices. Then someone knocked on her door with an unexpected urgency.

"Your Highness!" Rocco shouted through the door.

Annabelle rushed across the room and pulled the door open. "What's wrong?"

"We need to get you to the panic room," Rocco took her by the arm and tugged her into the hallway. "A guard spotted an intruder on the grounds."

An intruder who could be the bomber. Her heart seized, memories of the explosion rushing to the forefront of her mind.

She hurried down the hall with Rocco, one of the Alamedan guards leading the way. Within moments, Rocco ushered her into the palace's panic room, located in the royal family's residential wing.

Tayla and her parents were already inside, Tayla huddled on the couch with the king on one side and the queen on the other, but Leo was nowhere to be found.

"Where's Leo?" Annabelle asked.

Tayla didn't even look up, as though her brain couldn't process her presence, let alone her question.

Chrishelle entered a moment later. "What's going on?"

"Just a precaution." King Josep gripped Tayla's hand. "I'm sure the guards will have the situation under control shortly."

Annabelle hoped so for everyone's sake, but she needed to know where Leo was. "Your Majesty, where's Leo?"

King Josep lifted his gaze to meet hers. "I'm not sure."

- - -

Leo gripped his pistol as he ducked behind the hedge on the east side of the gardens. Saul remained at his side, his own weapon in hand.

Another guard signaled to them to indicate the direction of the problem.

A bush rustled. A man's voice carried to him in a foreign tongue Leo couldn't immediately identify.

Leo's heartbeat quickened, and he held up his hand. Methodically, he lowered one finger at a time. When Leo fisted his hand, the guards moved in tandem, rushing toward the problem, with Leo right behind them.

"Hold it right there!" one guard demanded.

"Hands up!" Saul yelled.

A woman screamed, and a man yelped in surprise.

Leo moved to Saul's side to get a better look at the intruders. The couple was dressed in black, and the woman had a camera around her neck. The man held his hands up, a phone gripped in one of them.

Leo lowered his weapon and used his mobile phone's flashlight feature to shine a light on the intruders. They weren't locals. And they weren't Gonzalo.

- - -

Annabelle heard the screams. And she didn't miss the way Tayla's eyes had filled with terror.

Queen Eva pulled Tayla closer and looked over her head to King Josep. "We should call the doctor. Tayla may need something to calm her nerves."

King Josep nodded and pulled out his phone. He didn't get the chance to dial before it rang.

"Status?" He paused. "Are you sure?"

Annabelle strained to hear both sides of the conversation, unable to make out any of the words coming through the king's phone.

After a moment, King Josep ended the call and lowered his phone into his lap. "It was a false alarm. A couple of tourists made it onto the grounds and were trying to take photos of themselves in the gardens."

Queen Eva rubbed Tayla's back. "Did you hear that, Tayla? It's nothing to worry about. The guards have everything under control."

Tayla lifted her head, her eyes beginning to clear.

"Everything is going to be fine." King Josep took Tayla's hand in his.

"Are you sure?" Tayla asked.

"We're sure." King Josep nodded.

"I'm fine," Tayla whispered to herself, her breathing rapid, her body shaking. "I'm fine." She looked up at her parents. "We're fine."

"Yes, we're fine, but before you get back to whatever you have planned for this afternoon, I suggest you have a meeting with the doctor. I'm sure he has something you can take to help settle your nerves."

Tayla took another gasping breath and nodded. Annabelle turned to the door, her original question still humming through her—Where was Leo?

- - -

Leo still couldn't believe that a couple of tourists had tripped the alarms at almost the exact same time that he'd learned Gonzalo wasn't in prison. What were the chances?

His pulse had yet to settle, and he'd been more than happy to turn the interlopers over to the police. Unsure of the status of the rest of the family's whereabouts, he returned to his office where Marcus had already resumed his duties.

"Do you know where my father is?"

"The family has already left the panic room," Marcus said. "I'm not sure where they are now, though."

The words were barely out of Marcus's mouth when Leo's father walked in. "What's the latest?"

"A couple of tourists thought they would document their trip here by taking selfies in front of the palace." Leo walked into his office and waited for his father to join him inside before he closed the door. "They're now in police custody."

"Good. And the other matter? Did you speak with the prisoner today?"

"I'm afraid not."

His father glanced at his watch. "I thought the interview was scheduled for two hours ago."

"It should have begun two hours ago, but it's been postponed, perhaps indefinitely." Leo fisted his hands and shoved them in his pockets. "The warden can't find Gonzalo Caballero."

His father's face paled. "How is that possible?"

"That's what I asked. I'm waiting for an update now." Leo pulled his hands from his pockets and gestured helplessly. "If Gonzalo isn't in prison, we can't let Tayla leave the palace grounds."

"I know, and it won't be easy to keep her home with all the appointments she has scheduled. Although with today's scare, she may be more inclined to remain on the palace grounds."

"How is she doing?" Leo asked.

"She's rattled, but she's meeting with the doctor now," his father said. "She seems determined to continue with her afternoon plans."

Leo sat on the sofa. "Maybe we should enlist Isaac's help."

"That's not a bad idea. He should be able to change the location of the appointments to here at the palace instead of in town."

Leo's phone rang, and his father grabbed it before he was able.

His father answered and put it on speaker. "Have they found him?"

"No, Your Majesty," Esteban said as though he had expected the king to answer his call. "Gonzalo Caballero isn't here. He never was."

Esteban went on to explain how the surveillance feed of the van that should have transported Gonzalo to the prison two years ago had arrived with five prisoners when there should have been six. Yet, the prison records had logged all six names into the system despite the missing prisoner.

"Gonzalo must have had someone helping him to keep him off that prison van and to falsify the records," Leo said.

"I've asked the warden to pull the names of everyone who would have had access to them," Esteban said.

"Tell the warden to turn those names over to the investigators and send them to us as well. I want you back here," Leo's father said.

"Yes, sire."

Leo's father ended the call and stood. "I need to tell your mother about this."

"And I should tell Annabelle, assuming I can get her away from Tayla."

His father's eyebrows lifted slightly before he said, "I think that would be wise."

- - -

Annabelle passed the tablet back to Chrishelle, still trying to come to grips with the excitement of earlier. Only three hours had passed since they'd left the panic room, yet Tayla had insisted on moving forward with the wedding planning.

Chrishelle zoomed in on the image of the screen. "Oh, that table setting would be stunning."

Tayla took a steadying breath as though trying to push away the last dregs of her earlier panic attack. "I agree. Let's use this one."

Another decision made. And if Tayla kept planning her wedding from the safety of the salon, she wouldn't need to spend time outside the palace walls.

Isaac had joined them an hour ago and disappeared within minutes of his arrival, supposedly to check in with his office. Annabelle couldn't blame him for not rushing back. He never had cared much for the fussy details that came with grand events. Rather, he preferred to enjoy the people.

"I can't believe how much we've already accomplished," Tayla said. "Colors, flowers, announcements, the table settings."

Chrishelle held up the notepad that she had been using to take notes. "We're simply planning a party of grand proportions."

"And you're clearly a master at party planning," Tayla said. "Those skills will come in handy if you end up in this family." Tayla said the words, and her cheeks colored. "I'm sorry. I don't mean to presume what will happen with you and Leo in the future."

"It's okay," Chrishelle said. "Up until coming here, I had that same vision."

Annabelle caught the wisp of uncertainty in her voice.

"Don't let Leo's work schedule scare you off," Tayla said. "Being royal is a job, but it can be incredibly rewarding."

"It's not just his work." Chrishelle set the notepad on her lap. "He's different when he's here."

Choosing her words carefully, Annabelle said, "The fire at the dock rattled him a bit."

"He was different even before that."

"You've lived apart for a long time," Tayla said gently. "I'm sure it will take time to find that comfort with each other again."

"Maybe."

Leo walked in, and his gaze met Annabelle's before he spoke to his sister. "Have you cleaned out the flower market yet with your plans?"

"Very funny." Tayla held up the tablet. "We won't need the flowers until the wedding day."

"So you're only *planning* to wipe out the flower market," Leo corrected.

Tayla shrugged one shoulder. "Maybe."

"I hate to interrupt all of this important business, but do you mind if I borrow Annabelle for a moment?"

Tayla's eyebrows lifted. "Annabelle?"

Leo looked at Chrishelle belatedly before he said, "She has a call from Sereno."

"I'd better take it then." Annabelle stood.

Leo put his hand on Chrishelle's shoulder. "I'll see you at dinner?"

"Of course."

Leo headed for the hall.

Annabelle followed.

"I gather it's Alan on the phone?" Annabelle couldn't think of anyone else who would try to reach her through Leo instead of calling her directly.

Leo glanced over his shoulder and shook his head. "I lied. No one called." He put his hand on her back to guide her forward. "I need to speak with you privately."

Annabelle lowered her voice to a whisper. "What's happened?"

Leo continued down the hall until they reached the music room. He led her inside and turned to face her. The concern on his face sent a chill through her.

"Leo, you're scaring me. What happened?"

"Gonzalo Caballero escaped."

"What? When?"

"As far as we can tell, he escaped during his original transfer from the courthouse to the prison."

"Two years ago?"

"According to the surveillance video, that's when it happened." Leo shook his head. "I still can't believe Gonzalo has been listed as a resident of the prison for all this time, but he's been on the loose since the day of his conviction."

"If he's been free this whole time, why is he coming after Tayla now?" Annabelle asked. "And how did he know she was supposed to be at the dock on Tuesday when I arrived?"

"Excellent questions, both of them."

"But you don't have any answers."

"No, I don't."

"What are we going to do about Tayla?" Annabelle asked. "Right now, she feels safe. Or she's trying to anyway. After today's scare, it's likely she'll go into town just to prove to everyone that she can."

"I don't know what to do." Leo dropped onto the piano bench. The fact that he did so while she was still standing testified to the depth of his distress.

"What are our options?" Annabelle sat beside him. "If we tell her he's out, she might very well have a nervous breakdown, but if we don't, she'll keep going out as though there isn't anything wrong."

"My father and I discussed speaking with Isaac."

"That's a good idea. We should talk to him now while Tayla is with Chrishelle." Annabelle put her hand on his knee. "Isaac should be in the library."

"Might as well get this over with." He stood and held out his hand to help her up.

She placed her hand in his, an odd tingle working up her arm. Where did that come from? The moment she rose to her feet, she released his hand. It wouldn't do for her to think of Leo as anything other than her best friend's brother. He had a girlfriend, and it wasn't her.

Eager to redirect her thoughts, she followed Leo from the room. "It's amazing how fast my perspective has changed with all of this. Earlier today, I was wondering if we might need to look at your friends rather than mine and Tayla's."

"That would have been the next logical progression in the investigation," Leo said.

"How do you think Isaac will take the news?"

"I don't know. He was on the prosecution team when Gonzalo was convicted. I can't imagine he will be thrilled."

"That's an aspect I hadn't even thought about." Yet the news media had capitalized on the connection between Tayla and Isaac throughout the trial, especially since they started dating only a few weeks after Gonzalo was convicted.

Annabelle stopped outside the library door. "Are you ready for this?"

"No." Leo drew a deep breath and squared his shoulders. "But it has to be done."

CHAPTER
13

Lights shone brightly in the library from both the chandelier overhead and the sconces lining the walls. Leo led Annabelle inside where Isaac sat at the rectangular worktable in the center of the room, his laptop open before him.

"Isaac, we need to talk," Leo said.

Isaac closed his laptop and looked up. "As long as it isn't about invitations and wedding colors."

"Those topics would be preferable to this." Leo closed the heavy wooden door to ensure privacy. He motioned for Annabelle to sit at the table, and he claimed the seat beside her, both of them facing Isaac. "We believe someone may be trying to kill Tayla."

"What?" He put both palms on the table and stood. "Why would you think that?"

"The fire at the dock wasn't just a fire." Leo forced the words out. "It was a bomb."

"A bomb?" Isaac whispered the words and lowered back into his seat. He looked from Leo to Annabelle and back again. "Tayla and I were supposed to be there on Tuesday."

"I know." Leo was all too aware of what could have happened had his sister picked up Annabelle instead of him.

"We were fortunate that my guard recognized the problem," Annabelle said. "If it hadn't been for Rocco, Leo and I wouldn't still be here."

"I can't believe this." Isaac shook his head. "I should go check on Tayla."

"You can check on her in a minute, but first, there's more you need to know." Leo rubbed two fingers back and forth on the table. "We learned today that Gonzalo Caballero isn't in prison."

"Of course he's in prison," Isaac said with absolute certainty. "I'm the one who put him there."

Technically, Isaac had been only a small part of the team, but Leo didn't bother to correct him. Isaac had a tendency to aggrandize his memories.

"Esteban went down there today to interview him. Not only was he not there, the warden confirmed that he never arrived."

Isaac leaned forward. "Do you know who's behind this?"

"The warden is pulling the list of the employees who were involved in the transfer. Between him and the police, they'll interview everyone. We'll get to the bottom of this, but in the meantime, we need your assistance."

"My assistance with what? I don't know how Gonzalo escaped."

"I didn't think you did, but my father doesn't want Tayla to know about the threat against her," Leo said.

"We need your help to keep Tayla here at the palace where she's safe," Annabelle added.

Isaac blew out a breath. "That won't be easy."

"No, but you could use your work as an excuse to hold your wedding appointments here instead of in town."

"I'll see what I can do, but convincing Tayla will be a challenge."

"I'll back you up," Annabelle said. "Hopefully, between the two of us, she'll be okay with everything coming here."

"Maybe you can call the vendors and reschedule the first catering appointment to be here at the palace," Isaac suggested. "Then we can act like that was so convenient, we want to do it with all the others."

"If you give me the schedule and contact information, I'll do what I can," Annabelle said.

"I'll email it to you." Isaac pushed back from the table and picked up his laptop. "In the meantime, I want to check on Tayla before dinner."

"Of course, you know that this information we've shared with you is confidential," Leo said.

"Of course." Isaac nodded to both of them and left the room.

Leo remained where he was. "What do you think?" he asked Annabelle. "Do you think we can pull this off without Tayla knowing about Gonzalo?"

"I'm not sure." She sighed. "I'm not even sure we should. She's stronger now. I think she can handle the truth."

Annabelle could be right. But if she wasn't . . . he couldn't imagine going through months of his sister barely conversing with anyone, of her fear overwhelming her to the point of her shutting down completely. Last time was torture to watch. "Right now, it's my father's call."

"Then I'd best get used to being your sister and future brother-in-law's personal secretary."

"While running your own business."

A flicker of surprise crossed her face. "Thankfully, I have a fantastic executive board that is doing a great job running the day-to-day activities. And Tayla's safety is more important than launching my business." Annabelle held up her phone. "If I don't get the email from Isaac in the next hour, I'll ask Tayla who her first appointment is with. I should be able to make a call in the morning to move it here."

"You know we'll need the names of everyone coming, for security."

Annabelle tilted her head to one side, her dark hair spilling over her shoulder. "Trust me. After all my family has been through in the past five years, I am very well-versed with security protocols."

"I'm sure you are."

- - -

Annabelle hung up the phone and collapsed into the chair beside the balcony doors. Isaac had emailed her Tayla's list of upcoming appointments, and she'd been on the phone ever since.

The taste testing scheduled for Monday would now occur on Tuesday to give security time to do the necessary background checks on the staff. In truth, some of the current precautions would ease the burden on security's preparations for the wedding itself. Of course, the best preparation would be to find Gonzalo Caballero and put him behind bars where he belonged.

Someone knocked at her door, and Annabelle laid her head back against the chair cushion. Couldn't she have five minutes to relax? Just five minutes?

With a sigh, she pushed out of her chair, took a moment to lift her chin and adopt her princess I'm-at-your-disposal persona, and answered the door.

Federico stood in the hall with Zeus by his side. He held up the file folder in his hand. "I have something you need to see."

She stepped aside and let him in, leaving the door open. "What is it?"

"Prince Alan sent this information for you. He suspected you might need it."

Annabelle opened the file. The photo of a man appearing to be in his thirties took up the top of the page, and his name and personal information were listed at the bottom.

"Who is Julian Benitez?" She flipped to the next page, which contained another bio, as did the next three pages—two women and three men. "And the rest of these people?"

Federico leaned out into the hall and looked both ways before lowering his voice. "These are the five people who had both the knowledge of the prison transport Gonzalo was supposed to be on as well as the ability to either forge the arrival documents or replace them."

"Have you already given this information to Esteban?"

"No." He lowered his voice further. "Prince Alan was concerned that the royal family here in Alameda might not approve of where he obtained the information."

"He tapped into his American connections again, didn't he?"

"I'm not at liberty to say." Federico had the decency to look apologetic. "Prince Alan suggested you familiarize yourself with these names. When Esteban or Prince Leonardo shares this information with you, you can determine if anyone is missing off their suspect list."

"Why would someone be missing?" Annabelle asked.

"One of the men and the two women on the list are still working in their original positions. They each have the ability to alter the information that is sent to the royal family."

"And if one of their names is left off, it's possible it's because he or she is the guilty party."

"Correct."

"Do you know if Esteban has received the suspect list from his people yet?"

"No, but I believe he expects it by this evening."

"It's already after four. Maybe I'll touch base with him and see if he has any news." She flipped through the bios again, memorizing the names. "I don't suppose you have any updates on where Gonzalo Caballero might be hiding, do you?"

"Nothing yet, but from what Prince Alan and King Levi have indicated, they believe he is still here in Alameda."

Annabelle lowered the file folder to her side. "That's what I'm afraid of."

CHAPTER
14

LEO STROLLED THROUGH THE GARDENS with Chrishelle by his side. After spending so much of his time working and in meetings about the bombing investigation, he wanted to spend some time with his girlfriend for a change. She deserved no less.

A light breeze rippled the fabric of his shirt, giving relief from the overly warm day.

"How busy will you be this weekend?" Chrishelle asked, breaking the comfortable silence.

"We have a formal dinner tomorrow evening with the Spanish ambassador as well as a charity appearance on Saturday morning."

"Is that wise?" Chrishelle asked. "I thought you didn't want to leave the palace grounds until after the person behind the bombing is caught."

He had debated whether to cancel the upcoming events, but doing so would practically shout "security threat" to the media. The ambassador's visit had been scheduled for months, as had the benefit on Saturday morning.

"Security will take care of Friday's event, and based on our latest reports, I'm not the person at risk."

Chrishelle stopped walking. "You really think someone is trying to kill Tayla?"

Though the thought was still inconceivable to him, he nodded. "We have a good idea who we're looking for."

"Then this could all be over soon."

"I certainly hope so."

"Do you think we could go horseback riding on Saturday?" Chrishelle asked. "Maybe after the charity thing?"

He doubted he'd have time, but Leo didn't want to admit it. "We'll have to check the weather. This time of year, afternoons are often too hot for the horses. Or we have thunderstorms roll in." He caught the flash of disappointment on her face. Not wanting to make any promises he couldn't keep, he asked, "Have you given any more thought to whether you want to take the job in New York or branch out on your own?"

"I've thought a lot about it, but I'm not sure I want to live in New York," Chrishelle said. "I'm a California girl at heart." She lifted her hand to encompass the view of the Mediterranean. "I need to be close to the water."

"New York City is on the Atlantic coast."

"Sometimes it's hard to remember that since every time I go there, all I see are skyscrapers."

"It is a different world." Leo stepped up to the retaining wall that separated the flower gardens from the dunes that led to the beach below. So much of his childhood had been spent at the water's edge, his feet always sandy when he reached the palace, his skin tanned by the daily exposure to the sun.

He wanted that for his children someday, to have that joy and freedom.

"Do you think there's a place for another event-planning business here in Alameda?" Chrishelle asked.

He realigned his thoughts and studied her. "I don't know." And he didn't.

This wasn't the first time she had hinted at living in close proximity, of possibly taking their relationship to the next level. Yet no matter how many times he tried to envision a future with her that included marriage and children, he couldn't quite wrap his mind around the image.

Chrishelle was beautiful and polite, but as of late, Leo found himself holding back, only giving Chrishelle whatever information was needed to keep her content. He doubted she would ever be one to challenge him, to encourage him to do more, to be more. And she certainly wasn't the sort who would ever borrow his horse without asking.

Chrishelle spoke, breaking into his thoughts. "I've enjoyed helping Tayla with her wedding plans."

"Thank you for that. It's been a stressful time, and I appreciate you helping Annabelle provide a distraction for her."

"Distracting a future bride." Chrishelle let out a sigh. "Not exactly a promising job title."

"But you have the choice of what you want your future job title to be," Leo said. "That's a luxury I've never enjoyed."

"I understand that, but like it or not, many of my future decisions will be determined by where we stand when I leave here." Chrishelle took his hand in hers. "Where do we stand, Leonardo?"

The vulnerability in her eyes tugged at him, and Leo couldn't help but lean down to press his lips to hers. The kiss was simple and familiar, but as much as he wanted to experience a connection that would last a lifetime, he couldn't deny that it wasn't there.

When he pulled back, Chrishelle stared up at him. After a moment of silence, she asked, "Well, Leo? Where do we stand?"

Honesty. She deserved that much. "If you're asking if we're going to be together forever, I'm sorry, but I just don't know."

"I'm not asking about forever. I'm asking about now."

Her words sounded sincere enough, but something in the lift of her eyebrows gave him the sense that she did need to know if their relationship would ever lead to marriage.

"Let's worry about my sister's wedding plans for now, before we consider where we go next."

"If nothing else, I'm getting an education in royal protocols by working with Tayla and Annabelle."

"I'm glad you're able to spend time with them."

"Yes." She looked out to the water again before returning her gaze to him. "Me too."

- - -

Annabelle left Esteban's office, a little unsettled by the way her brothers-in-law could manage to snatch information seemingly out of thin air when the security forces of Alameda had yet to receive intel that had originated within their country's borders. And the idea of keeping valuable information from Esteban and Alameda's royal family in order to protect her sources—or rather, Alan's and Levi's sources—left her uneasy.

She reached a peaked window overlooking the Mediterranean. A single sailboat was silhouetted on the horizon, the sun low in the sky. Ground lights illuminated the winding paths through the gardens, two lamp posts shining from the main entrance beside a wide archway covered with ivy. The entire scene was so lovely, right down to the scent of roses and poppies wafting in the air.

She caught sight of Leo and Chrishelle walking beside the gardenias, Leo's arm wrapped around Chrishelle's waist.

Annabelle leaned against the windowsill. She should step back and give Leo and Chrishelle some privacy, but she couldn't help being drawn into the moment and the sheer romanticism of it. This was what fairy tales were made of: the handsome prince and the beautiful woman from a different world who had captured his heart.

Maybe someday she would have that for herself, a man in her life who would make her the center of his world. Although, sadly, Leo hadn't been able to give that to Chrishelle over the past few days. He'd likely spent more time with Annabelle than his girlfriend.

The upcoming weekend would be an interesting dynamic, with both Leo and Tayla paired off while she was most decidedly single.

King Josep and Isaac approached from the king's office, and Annabelle straightened.

"Your Majesty." She dipped into a curtsy.

"What are you doing up here?" King Josep asked.

"I was checking with Esteban to see if he had any updates."

"That's where we were headed," King Josep said.

"Does he have his list of suspects yet?" Isaac asked.

"No. He thinks he'll have them tomorrow morning," Annabelle said. "He hopes the police will be able to conduct all of their interviews with the suspects by tomorrow evening."

"It would be nice to have this business behind us before the dinner tomorrow night with the Spanish ambassador."

"Most certainly." The sooner this was all behind them, the better.

Isaac glanced at his watch. "Your Majesty, if you'll excuse me, I'd best prepare for my meetings tomorrow."

The king nodded his assent.

Isaac continued down the hall to the stairwell.

"Has my wife spoken to you about tomorrow evening's guest list?" King Josep asked.

"No." Suspicion bloomed. The queen didn't care to have an uneven number of guests at her table, and since the ambassador was married, and the entire royal family had a plus-one, Annabelle was most certainly the odd person out. "Who has she paired me with this time?"

"Prince Timeo of Crovacia," King Josep said. "I believe you are already acquainted."

More than she cared to admit. She had dated the prince briefly during her freshman year at university, but his insatiable love of polo and sports cars had bored her before two weeks had passed.

"Will he be staying here at the palace?"

"Yes, for a few days. And don't worry. Prince Timeo may be my wife's way of keeping the number of guests even, but she assured me that she isn't trying to do any matchmaking," King Josep said.

"That's a relief."

King Josep clasped his hands in front of him. "I needn't tell you that the sensitivity of the situation with Tayla mustn't be discussed in Prince Timeo's presence."

"That goes without saying." A few days waiting for information that could only be shared in front of a select few people while also avoiding getting trapped by Prince Timeo's running diatribe of the best sports cars would make for an interesting challenge. Perhaps she could retreat to the kitchen and convince Duran to let her help with some meals. She rather liked to bake, especially if she could sample the results of her efforts.

The king lifted his arm, gesturing toward the far stairwell that led to the dining hall. Annabelle fell into step with him.

"I haven't spoken today with Federico," Annabelle said. "I assume he hasn't found any issues."

"No." King Josep gripped the railing to the circular staircase and started his descent. "It was kind of your brother-in-law to arrange for him to stay here during this difficult time."

"It was kind of you to agree to his offer," Annabelle said. "Levi and Alan tend to be rather protective of me."

"As older brothers should be."

"Yes, I suppose so." Annabelle smiled. Alan and Levi might not be related by blood, but they were very much her family. Turning her thoughts back to the impending dinner tomorrow, she asked, "What are the chances that the queen would be willing to let me help with the seating chart for tomorrow's dinner?"

"I can put in a good word for you." King Josep reached the bottom step, and he turned to wait for her to reach his side. Lowering his voice, he added, "As long as I don't have to sit next to him either."

Annabelle fought back a smile. "I'll make sure of it."

CHAPTER
15

LEO FINISHED DRESSING FOR THE day, his thoughts pressing in on him. He opened the safe in his side table drawer and retrieved his grandmother's engagement ring, leaving his pistol where it lay. He flipped the top of the velvet case open to reveal the emerald, sparkling from inside.

Part of him wished his father hadn't given him the ring yet, that marriage wasn't expected at an early age here in Alameda. He was only twenty-nine. He had plenty of time to find the right woman, to settle down and provide an heir. Yet the ring signified his parents' belief that he had already found the right woman.

His conversation with Chrishelle last night played through his mind. She needed a commitment from him, and he'd been unable to give it. What was wrong with him? She was gorgeous and kind, and his family loved her. Even Annabelle seemed to approve of his girlfriend, not that her opinion should matter.

A knock sounded on his door, and Leo set the ring on the table, exchanging it for his wristwatch. He only made it as far as his sitting room before the door to his suite creaked open and his father called out his name.

"I'm in here."

His father entered his sitting room, his mobile phone in his hand. "Have you checked your email this morning?"

"Not yet." Leo slid his watch onto his wrist. "Why do you ask?"

"Esteban sent both of us the police's initial suspect list. They'll be interviewing all of them today."

"How many are on it?"

"Four."

Leo returned to his room to retrieve his phone so he could check his messages.

"What's this?" His father motioned to the ring.

"I had a long talk with Chrishelle last night, and I find myself debating what my future should look like."

"I'm sorry, son. I didn't mean to pressure you," his father said. "You and Chrishelle seemed so well matched."

Leo picked up the ring and closed the box. "You say that as though you no longer believe that to be the case."

"I don't think it is."

Even though his father's comment mirrored his own thoughts, Leo's need for clarity rose to the surface. "What changed your mind about Chrishelle?"

"It's not Chrishelle who has altered my opinion, but you."

"How so?"

"Chrishelle is a lovely girl, but she isn't the woman you're in love with."

Leo returned the ring to the safe and locked it. "I've never been in love with any woman."

"Are you sure about that?"

Surprised by the tone of his father's voice, Leo furrowed his brow. "If not Chrishelle, who is it you think I'm in love with?"

"I found it very telling that when we learned about Gonzalo Caballero, your first instinct was to tell Annabelle."

"Of course I needed to tell Annabelle." Leo gestured in the general direction of the guest quarters. "She's every bit as invested in ensuring Tayla's safety as we are."

"It's often said that the person whose calls you always answer is the one you're in a relationship with." His father tilted his head slightly. "The same is true for whom you want to first share important news."

Leo and his sister's best friend. His father must be more stressed than he thought. "You're seeing something that isn't there."

"Perhaps, but Annabelle is a lovely young woman."

He couldn't deny that, nor did he care to debate Annabelle's virtues with his father. "How soon do you expect the report from the police?"

"I asked for an update by this evening, but that doesn't mean we'll have answers that quickly."

"I should let Annabelle know." The moment the words escaped him, he held up his hand. "And no, I'm not seeking her out because of some personal interest. I simply know she's waiting on the information too."

His father's lips twitched, and he stepped aside. "Don't let me keep you."

Leo led the way out of his bedroom and into the living room.

"Oh, one more thing," his father said. "I hope you don't mind that you'll be sitting between Annabelle and Chrishelle at dinner."

"Why would I mind?"

"Because Prince Timeo will be on the other side of Chrishelle." He shrugged a shoulder. "Annabelle needed a buffer between herself and the prince."

"I should probably warn Chrishelle what she's in for this evening."

"Maybe it would be best to let her experience an evening with Prince Timeo without coloring her opinion."

Chrishelle and Timeo both enjoyed being around horses, at least. "You could be right."

"I'll inform you as soon as we receive the update from the police."

"Thank you."

Leo left his room in search of Annabelle. He checked the kitchen first. One glance at the tray of croissants on the counter told him Annabelle had already been and gone.

From where he stood by the stove, Duran spotted him and held up his spatula. "You just missed her."

"How did you know I was looking for Annabelle?"

"Lucky guess." Duran transferred an almond scone onto a napkin and offered it to Leo. "I think she was heading to the breakfast room to meet your sister."

Leo held up the scone. "Thanks."

By the time he reached the dining room, he had reduced the scone to a few crumbs. As expected, Annabelle and Tayla sat at the table along with his mother.

"Where's Chrishelle?"

"She decided to go riding before it gets too hot today," Tayla said. "She thought you had meetings this morning."

"I do." Though he'd expected to see her this morning before he got bogged down with phone calls. It only took him a moment to realize Chrishelle wasn't the only person missing from the breakfast table. "What about Isaac?"

"He had some work he needed to take care of at the office," Tayla said. "He should be back this afternoon."

His mother motioned to the seat beside her. "Leo, sit down and eat with us."

"Sorry, I don't have time right now." He turned to Annabelle. "Do you have a minute?"

She nodded and stood. "Tayla, I'll meet you in the salon in a little while." Annabelle followed him into the hall. "Do you have news?"

"We have a suspect list."

"How many people are on it?"

"Four."

Annabelle stopped walking.

"Is something wrong?"

"I think so." Rather than elaborate, she asked, "Can you email the names to me?"

"I don't see any reason why not, but why do you want them?"

"I need to check something." She turned toward the main staircase. "Send the names now, and I'll meet you in your office in ten minutes."

Before he could ask where she was going, Annabelle hurried down the hall. Leo pulled his mobile from his pocket and forwarded the email Esteban had sent him. He then turned back toward the kitchen. Might as well grab another scone on his way.

Twelve minutes later, Annabelle entered his private office with a piece of paper in hand. "You need to have the police check on this person too."

"Why?" Leo circled his desk. "Who is he?"

Annabelle closed the door. "I'm not sure exactly where the information came from, but my country's intelligence service provided me with a list of five suspects. This name wasn't included in yours."

Leo stiffened. "How would someone in Sereno know more about this case than our police do?"

"Because we were concerned that someone still working within your justice system might have access to alter the records."

Leo stepped forward, his gaze intent on hers. "You've been feeding classified information to people in Sereno?"

Annabelle took a step back. "I was using my country's resources to help protect you and your family."

"You had no right."

"I have every right." Annabelle held up her hand, waving the paper in the air. "In case you've forgotten, I was nearly killed by that bomb too."

A fact of which he was all too aware. He fought against his simmering anger.

Annabelle held out the paper. "Whether you agree with my methods or not, it can't hurt to check this man out."

He *didn't* agree with her methods, but Leo couldn't afford to ignore a suspect. "Fine. I'll pass this name along."

"Thank you." Her anger seemed to fade. "I'm not trying to undermine any of your efforts. You should know that."

He did know that, even if she had an uncanny ability to send his emotions churning.

She put her hand on his arm. "We're one step closer to finding the truth."

And she was trying to help. Leo covered her hand with his. "Let's hope it's the last step we have to take."

"I'm already praying for that."

CHAPTER
16

ANNABELLE COULDN'T WIN. SHE COULD hardly tell Leo that both of her brothers-in-law worked for US intelligence, but she could understand Leo's need to protect the private details surrounding his family's current security issues. Now everyone was annoyed with her.

Logically, she knew she shouldn't have shared the confidential information with Leo before checking with Levi or Alan first—a fact Levi reminded her of when she had called to confess—but she hadn't been able to resist. The missing name very well might lead to the person responsible for freeing Tayla's stalker. And if they found that person, they might finally be able to find Gonzalo Caballero.

She tried to push thoughts of Gonzalo and the investigation from her mind as she neared the salon. Duran stormed toward her, his chef's hat slightly askew, his irritation clear.

Since she'd only snitched one croissant this morning, she was quite certain she wasn't the source of his anger. "What's wrong?"

"Did you know about the caterer using my kitchen on Tuesday?" he demanded. "How am I supposed to prepare lunch and dinner if I have people in my space?"

Annabelle put her hand on Duran's arm and tugged so he would follow her away from the salon entrance. "That's my fault."

"Why would you do this to me?"

"It's because we had some security concerns." Annabelle would never be able to work in intelligence. She couldn't keep a secret. Except from Tayla for a good reason, and even that was killing her. "Please don't give Tayla a reason to push to go into town."

"What's wrong?"

"I don't know exactly." That was mostly true.

Isaac approached, dressed in casual slacks and a polo shirt instead of his typical business attire. "Is something wrong?"

"We were discussing the need to meet with the caterers here at the palace instead of in town."

"Yes, that would be ideal," Isaac said.

Duran looked from Isaac to Annabelle. "I can't have people working in my space unless I'm able to supervise."

"That sounds like a reasonable compromise," Annabelle said. "And from what I understand, the caterers should be bringing most of the food already prepared."

Duran held up a finger and wagged it at Annabelle. "You're lucky I like you."

"I have that same thought every morning at breakfast."

He shook his head, but the corners of his lips twitched into the beginnings of a smile. "I need to get back to the kitchen. I have a banquet to prepare."

"We're all looking forward to it," Annabelle said.

As soon as Duran turned back to the kitchen, Isaac asked, "Where's Tayla?"

"In the salon. I'm heading there now." Annabelle started down the hall. "Where have you been?"

"I had some work I needed to take care of at the office."

"Are you ready to dive back into wedding planning?"

"What's on the agenda today?"

"I have absolutely no idea." She entered the salon, where Tayla sat with her mother and Chrishelle. "Look who I found."

"Isaac." Tayla's expression brightened. "I didn't know you were back."

"I just arrived." He leaned down and kissed her cheek before sitting beside her. He waved a hand at the iPad on her lap. "What are you working on?"

She turned the iPad upside down. "We were looking at wedding dresses, but now that you're here, we can get back to planning our reception."

"How would you feel about a horse-drawn carriage to bring you from the church to the palace?" Chrishelle said.

"Is that what you want?" Isaac asked Tayla.

"It does sound romantic."

"Then add that to our plans."

"Do you want a full parade?" Annabelle asked.

Queen Eva nodded her approval. "That would allow our subjects to feel they are part of the event while also giving us a reason for the royal family to split up throughout the procession."

"Security protocols," Annabelle said under her breath.

The queen focused on her and nodded again. "Precisely."

- - -

Throughout the day, his father's words kept circling through his mind. Leo couldn't fathom how anyone would think he was romantically interested in Annabelle, but as he pondered his relationship with Chrishelle, he had come to agree with one point his father had made: He wasn't in love with Chrishelle, and he didn't see that ever changing. It was unfair of him to let her believe otherwise.

With the business side of his workday complete, Leo left his office in search of his soon-to-be ex-girlfriend. He passed by the banquet hall where tonight's dinner would be held. Already, the dishes were in place atop the linen-covered table in the center of the room, cut flowers in glass vases scenting the air.

Pablo, the chief butler, looked up from where he stood polishing silverware beside a cart before placing each piece on the table. He bowed his head. "Your Highness. May I help you with something?"

"Have you seen Chrishelle?"

"I believe she's in the grand salon with Princess Tayla."

"Thank you." Leo continued down the hall until he reached the salon.

The moment Chrishelle spotted him, she lowered the iPad in her hand. "I'm afraid Princess Annabelle isn't here."

The oddity that Chrishelle would speak to the location of his sister's friend struck him as yet another sign of the disconnect between the two of them. "I wasn't looking for Annabelle; I was looking for you."

"Oh."

"Can you spare a few minutes?"

Chrishelle nodded, her expression revealing her surprise more than anything else. She handed her iPad to Tayla. "I'll see you later."

"Thanks for all your help," Tayla said.

Leo led Chrishelle outside onto the terrace, stopping when he reached a cluster of chairs facing the Mediterranean. He gestured toward one of them, waiting for Chrishelle to sit before he claimed his seat.

Even though Leo had more experience with breakups than he cared to admit, he drew a deep breath and gathered his courage. "I think we need to talk."

"I agree." Chrishelle's gaze met his. "I need to decide what to do with my future. I need to know if you have any interest in being part of it."

He didn't want to hurt her, but he couldn't keep pretending. "I'm sorry. I care for you, but—"

"But you're not in love with me." Chrishelle pressed her lips together. "I suppose I was foolish to think I would be different that the other women you dated."

"You are different. I just think we've come to that point that we need to admit that there isn't a future for us as a couple."

Chrishelle stared at him for a long moment before she put his hand on his arm. "I think these last few days have demonstrated that we're not as well matched as I thought we were."

Relieved beyond words that Chrishelle's thoughts so closely mirrored his own, he covered her hand with his. "I'm sorry."

"Don't be." Despite the touch of sadness in her voice, she offered him a weak smile. "I've enjoyed our time together, and visiting your country has been a wonderful experience."

"Even though I ignored you for most of it."

"You've been busy, and I understand that." She pulled her hand from his and gestured toward the palace doors. "And your sister and Princess Annabelle have been good company."

"I'm glad." He glanced toward the gardens where he'd spent time with Annabelle after the bombing. "And even though we're no longer a couple, I hope you'll stay as our guest until your planned flight leaves."

"Are you sure that won't be awkward?"

He had expected that would be the case, but with Chrishelle agreeing that they were better off apart, he said, "We were friends before we started dating. I hope we can be friends now."

"I would love to continue helping your sister with her wedding plans."

"I'm sure she would appreciate that," Leo said. "And my mother will be thrilled that you'll be in attendance tonight. She doesn't care for an odd number at her dinner table."

"What about Princess Annabelle?" Chrishelle asked. "Does she have a date?"

"No, but Prince Timeo will be in attendance." Leo debated how much to tell Chrishelle and opted for ambiguity. "I believe you're seated next to him tonight."

"I have to admit, I'm a little nervous about dinner. I've never been to an official event like this before."

"It's just dinner."

"With a table full of people who have royal titles attached to their names."

He supposed that was true. "If you have any questions on protocol, just follow my lead."

She clasped her hands together. "If nothing else, this will be quite the experience."

"That it will."

CHAPTER

17

ANNABELLE SET A CHAIR IN front of the mirror in her dressing room, where her makeup and hair supplies were arranged on a long counter. "Who wants to go first?" she asked Tayla and Chrishelle.

"You don't have to do my hair," Chrishelle said. "Really."

"I love this sort of thing," Annabelle insisted. "I do my sisters' hair all the time."

"She does." Tayla sat in the chair. "You can do mine first."

Annabelle picked up a comb. "What are you wearing tonight?"

"My gold Valentino." Tayla went on to describe her planned accessories and how she wanted her hair styled.

Annabelle complied, pinning Tayla's dark hair into a complicated chignon. As soon as she finished, she stepped back and handed Tayla a mirror so she could see the back.

"This looks fabulous." Tayla stood and set the mirror down. "Thank you."

"You're welcome." Annabelle patted the back of the now-empty chair. "Your turn, Chrishelle. How would you like your hair styled?"

"How about something like this?" Chrishelle held up her phone to show her an image of a model with an intricate updo. "Is that too complicated?"

"Not at all." In fact, Annabelle rather liked the challenge. She plugged in her curling iron and waited for Chrishelle to settle into the seat before she started brushing out her hair.

"I can't wait to see the looks on Isaac's and Leo's faces when we walk in tonight," Annabelle said. "They aren't going to be able to take their eyes off the two of you."

"I don't think Leonardo will be paying much attention to how I'm wearing my hair," Chrishelle said, her voice somber. "We broke up today."

"What?" Annabelle set the brush aside and stepped forward so she could see Chrishelle's face rather than simply her reflection in the mirror. "When did this happen?"

"This afternoon." Chrishelle lifted a hand. "It's for the best. The two of us had drifted apart, and it's better we end it now rather than push a bad situation and make it worse."

"I'm sorry things didn't work out for you two," Tayla said. "I was rather hoping you would be around for a lot longer."

"Leonardo invited me to stay for the next couple weeks. I'd love to keep helping with your wedding plans. That is, if you don't mind."

"That would be wonderful," Tayla said.

Annabelle picked up the brush again. "Well, even if Leo isn't your boyfriend anymore, he's going to notice you when you walk in tonight."

"I think he's much more likely to notice you."

Annabelle narrowed her eyes. "Why?"

"The two of you seem very close."

She couldn't deny a unique connection between her and Leo since the bombing, but that was due to their shared experience and shared secret. "We have a lot of history together, but most of that involves him surprising me with slimy reptiles rather than friendship."

Tayla laughed. "Oh, the look on your face when you found the lizard in your shoe."

"I can't imagine Leonardo playing a practical joke like that."

Then maybe it was best Chrishelle and Leo didn't last. Annabelle couldn't imagine him not being the sort to look for fun whenever he could. A little twinge of regret twisted inside her. Both of them had spent so much time worrying about Tayla's safety that neither had been able to step back and enjoy any simple moments. They needed to change that.

Annabelle picked up the curling iron and sectioned off a lock of Chrishelle's hair. She curled several strands.

"I can't believe I'm sitting here in a palace while a princess is fixing my hair."

"You're in a palace letting a friend fix your hair," Annabelle corrected. After spending many hours working on wedding plans together, she did consider Chrishelle a friend.

Chrishelle's gaze met Annabelle's in the mirror. "Thank you for helping me feel so at home here."

"I'm not sure I did much," Annabelle said. "I'm a visitor here too."

"No," Chrishelle said. "You're very much part of this family."

"She's right," Tayla said. "You've been more family than friend for as long as I can remember."

"Well, as family-slash-friend, I vote we add some chocolate mousse to the wedding menu."

"You know I won't eat it."

"Yes, but everyone else will love it."

"You already told the caterer to bring samples, didn't you?" Tayla asked.

"Maybe." Annabelle piled Chrishelle's hair onto the top of her head and pinned it into place. She stepped back. "What do you think?"

Chrishelle blinked twice before she spoke. "I think we are all going to turn some heads tonight."

"We'd better get dressed."

"Isaac is meeting me at my suite." Tayla stepped toward the door. "I'll see you both down there."

Suspecting Chrishelle wouldn't feel comfortable attending by herself, Annabelle asked, "Did Leo plan to escort you tonight?"

"He didn't mention it."

"In that case, we can walk downstairs together."

Relief shone in Chrishelle's eyes. "Thank you. I'd appreciate that."

- - -

Leo retrieved his dinner jacket from where he'd draped it over the back of the sofa in his living room.

Someone knocked on his door.

"Come in," Leo called.

His parents entered, an uncharacteristic look of alarm on his mother's face.

His father closed the door behind them. "The police just found Julian Benitez in his apartment. He'd been shot to death."

Julian Benitez. The person Annabelle had named as a suspect. "Do you have any idea what his involvement may have been in Gonzalo's escape?" Leo asked.

"He was the officer who recorded the prisoners who arrived the day Gonzalo was supposed to be transported," his father said. "Based on the evidence, he created a fake document that showed the correct names on the manifest for when the prisoners arrived and then modified it after they were checked in."

"Which is how Gonzalo was believed to be there when he's been free this whole time."

His father nodded. "We believe so, but that's not all."

Leo set his dinner jacket back on the couch. "What else did they find?"

"A receipt for a set of luggage that matched Annabelle's."

"You think he's the one who planted the bomb." Leo tried to wrap his mind around that new development. Benitez did match the general description of the man they caught a glimpse of on the security feed. "Any clues as to who tipped him off about when Annabelle was arriving or what luggage she carries?"

"Nothing yet," his father said.

"This is all so unsettling." His mother tucked her hand into the crook of his father's arm.

The simple connection gave him a comfort he hadn't expected. Throughout his entire life, despite the many intrusions of the press and the various political challenges, his parents had always been a unit, a continual sign of solidarity. That was what he wanted someday, to find someone he could face any challenge with, someone who would be his partner in every way. It really was too bad he and Chrishelle weren't quite the right match.

Leo shrugged on his jacket. "Any clue as to Gonzalo's whereabouts now?"

"No news yet, but the police are still investigating." His father leaned against the back of the sofa, his only outward sign of weariness. "For tonight, we need to keep this news to ourselves."

"Annabelle will want to know." Leo caught the slight lift in his father's eyebrows. He opened his mouth to defend himself, but promptly closed it again. Annabelle deserved to know the status of the investigation, and it had nothing to do with any special interest in her, romantic or otherwise. "Our guests should be arriving." Leo opened the door to the main hallway. "Shall we?"

"Yes." His father escorted his mother into the hall, where two guards waited. "Isaac will be escorting Tayla to the banquet hall, and the royal guard has done an extra security sweep of the grounds."

"Including our borrowed resource from Sereno?" Leo asked.

"Yes." His father continued forward. "Federico and his dog did another search of the main level, and they are at the main gate now ensuring that all of the incoming vehicles are properly cleared."

"Good." Slightly mollified that his family had done everything possible to keep his sister safe, Leo descended the stairs behind his parents, one guard leading the way and the other falling in behind them.

They reached the reception room, and the chief butler announced their arrival. Leo followed his father inside, staying to his side and one step behind him as protocol dictated. The men in the room bowed, and the women curtsied.

Leo caught sight of his sister, Isaac, and Chrishelle speaking with the Spanish ambassador, while Annabelle spoke with Prince Timeo.

Annabelle glanced at him, giving a subtle tilt of her head. The sign was subtle, but he didn't miss her silent request to be rescued from Prince Timeo's company. With the way Annabelle looked, her hair pulled up to reveal her slender neck and her vibrant red gown enhancing her complexion, it was no wonder Prince Timeo had zeroed in on her so quickly.

He supposed the least he could do for his sister's friend was run some interference.

With his father already speaking to his foreign minister, Leo leaned close to his mother and whispered in her ear. "Would you mind engaging Prince Timeo in a bit of conversation?"

His mother spotted Annabelle before whispering back, "It's the least we can do for the dear girl."

Together, he and his mother continued across the room until they reached Annabelle and the prince of Crovacia.

"Prince Timeo." His mother extended her hand to him. "Thank you for joining us this evening."

"I could hardly refuse your invitation." Timeo took the queen's hand and bowed his head.

"I understand your mother has enjoyed quite a bit of success with her roses."

"Her gardens are her love."

Not the least bit interested in the various species of roses, or any other bloom for that matter, Leo moved toward the corner of the room. As expected, Annabelle took advantage of the distraction his mother provided and followed. She lifted her glass to her lips and took a sip of clear liquid before she whispered, "Thank you."

"You're welcome."

Annabelle angled her body so she was facing him. "I heard about you and Chrishelle. I'm sorry."

"You have nothing to be sorry about." Leo's gaze swept the room, noting that his mother had guided Prince Timeo across the room to where Chrishelle stood. "Chrishelle and I both knew that we weren't right for each other. This visit made it obvious."

"Still, it's never easy when a relationship comes to an end."

"I suppose that's true, but this is probably the most amenable breakup I've ever had."

"That's a testament to both you and Chrishelle," Annabelle said. "I really do like her."

"I like her too, but I'm not in love with her." Leo fell silent when a waiter approached with a tray of champagne. He shook his head to decline the offering and waited for the server to move on before continuing. "With the expectations growing that I would soon propose, I suspect this breakup will be a welcome reprieve for both me and Chrishelle."

"I suppose that's true." Annabelle lifted both eyebrows. "And this time the press doesn't have any fuel to say you've been seeing someone else."

"Leave it to you to find a bright side in any situation."

"That hasn't been easy as of late."

The latest news about the investigation burned on Leo's tongue, but he swallowed the words. This wasn't a topic to be discussed with an audience, and he was ready to know exactly where Annabelle had received her information. Someone was feeding her important intelligence, and he needed to know if any other details had been withheld.

- - -

Annabelle stood on the terrace with the ambassador's wife, the subtle notes of Chopin carrying from the salon where the rest of their dinner party still mingled.

"Two new members of the royal family," Gloria said. "Your citizens must be thrilled."

"Oh, they are," Annabelle said. "As am I."

"One aspect I've always admired about your family as well as the royal family here in Alameda is your absolute loyalty to one another."

"We've both been blessed in that area." Annabelle looked through the window where Tayla and Chrishelle chatted with Timeo. "Princess Tayla and I couldn't have asked for better siblings." Except for the toad and lizard incidents with Leo, but Annabelle kept those details to herself.

"Do you think we'll have a second royal wedding here in Alameda in our immediate future?"

Even though Annabelle was quite certain she knew the answer to that question, she wasn't about to share details about Leo's personal life. "That's not information I'm privy to."

The ambassador's wife wisely let that topic drop. "How much longer will you stay in Alameda?"

"Another fortnight."

The ambassador and Leo emerged through the French doors.

The ambassador reached his wife's side and put his hand on her waist. "My dear, we should be going."

"Of course." She nodded to Annabelle. "It was nice chatting with you." She then turned her attention to Leo and curtsied. "Your Highness."

Leo nodded his head. "Thank you both for coming."

The couple disappeared back inside.

"Have the other guests started to leave?"

"Prince Timeo is still in there, but Chrishelle has kept him occupied. I didn't realize she knew so much about horse bloodlines."

"Neither did I, but I'll have to thank her later." Annabelle stepped to the side so she was out of view of those still mingling inside. "How were things tonight, having Chrishelle at dinner when everyone still thinks you're dating?"

A little crease formed on his brow, a sure sign he was pondering her question. "Oddly, it was rather pleasant."

"I was wondering. After all, sitting between your ex-girlfriend and your little sister's pesky friend could be a trial on the nerves."

"I think you outgrew the pesky stage quite a while ago."

Annabelle took a step back and stared. "Prince Leonardo. Did you just pay me a compliment?"

"No. I was stating a fact." Humor laced his tone when he added, "Don't prove me wrong."

"I'll do my best."

He took another step away from the palace doors. "There is something I need to speak to you about."

His serious tone suggested the topic was Tayla and the threats against her. "You know something."

"Julian Benitez was found dead in his apartment today. Murdered."

She stepped back. Not only was Levi's information correct, but the death of their lead suspect suggested Gonzalo was making sure he wouldn't be found. "Do the police have any leads on Gonzalo's current location?"

"Not that I know of." Leo stepped farther into the shadows, this time taking her arm to ensure she followed. "Who told you we should look into him?"

Though Annabelle trusted Leo implicitly, she couldn't be certain he would protect her source. "I'm sorry. I can't say."

"You realize that whoever told you about him could have information about Gonzalo and where he is now."

"If he did, he would share it with me."

"He?" A hint of irritation flashed in his eyes. "That's all you'll tell me? This is my sister's safety we're talking about."

"I know." But that didn't mean she could admit that her brother-in-law was former CIA. "I'll make a call and ask if he has any new information, but I promise, neither of us would ever hold back anything that would help capture Gonzalo or keep your family safe."

His tone turned cold. "I wish I could believe that."

Annabelle took another step back, his words stinging more than she thought possible. She drew a deep breath to make sure her voice was steady before she spoke. "I've never lied to you. You should know that."

"How can I when you clearly know so much more than you're telling me?"

"It's called trust." Annabelle moved toward the door, casting a last glance over her shoulder. "Maybe you should try it."

Without waiting for a response, she continued through the French doors, leaving him in the dark.

CHAPTER

18

LEO STOOD ON THE EDGE of the west lawn, a bow gripped in his hand, an arrow pulled back beside his cheek as he focused on the target fifty meters away. He let his breath out slowly and released.

The arrow whizzed through the air, hitting the outer ring. This wasn't his day. Then again, yesterday hadn't been stellar either. First, he'd broken up with his girlfriend of two years, and then he'd alienated Annabelle.

Leo retrieved another arrow from his quiver, his indignation rising. He had every right to want to know the source of Annabelle's intel. After all, it was hardly fair for her to demand he trust her when she clearly didn't trust him.

He took aim again, drawing the arrow back. He released. Again, he missed the bullseye by a wide margin.

Tayla approached wearing her riding clothes. She took one look at the target and asked, "Girl trouble?"

"Chrishelle and I broke up."

"I know." She handed him an arrow. "Usually, you can't hit a target when you're *planning* to break up with someone, not after you're past it. What's wrong?"

Where to start? That Tayla's stalker was somewhere out there and no one could find him? That a man had been killed, a man who might have been able to lead them to the threat? That Annabelle knew more than she was willing to share?

With so little he could share with his sister, he said, "Annabelle and I had a fight."

"Annabelle?" She drew her eyebrows together. "Since when do you care what she thinks?"

"I don't." At least, he shouldn't. He nocked the arrow on his bowstring.

"Well, you'd better play nice at the benefit today, because Papa asked her to accompany you."

Leo pointed the arrow at the ground and whirled to face her more fully. "He did what?"

"You heard me," Tayla said. "He asked if I would take Chrishelle riding since it might be awkward for her to accompany you today, but he didn't want you to go alone."

"So he's sending Annabelle? Why can't Mama go with me?"

"I don't know. I didn't ask."

"Great." Leo sighed. Lifting the arrow toward the target again, he took aim and let the next arrow fly. This one caught the very edge of the target.

"Looks like you and Annabelle need to make up." Tayla took his bow from him. "Either that or you need to give up archery practice for a while."

"It was a minor disagreement."

"Then figure out how to get along during the benefit today." She set the bow beside his quiver. "Speaking of which, shouldn't you be getting ready?"

Leo checked his watch. Less than an hour until he needed to leave. "Probably. Are you sure you don't want to go with Annabelle, and I'll go riding with Chrishelle?" The moment he asked the question, he was reminded of how impossible both situations would be.

"You don't want to ride with Chrishelle, and I don't want you and Annabelle fighting," Tayla said. "You two should know how to get along by now."

They had been getting along until last night.

Chrishelle appeared on the path leading to the stables.

Tayla put her hand on Leo's arm. "Seriously, please try to sort things out with Annabelle. I hate it when you two are at odds."

Leo let out another sigh. "I'll do my best."

"Good." Tayla left him and joined Chrishelle, the two heading for the stables without a backward glance.

Leo gathered his arrows—no need to leave the evidence of his poor target practice—and headed for his private quarters. Forty-five minutes later, he entered the main hall dressed in one of his I'm-making-a-public-appearance suits. He'd barely reached the bottom when Annabelle appeared on the stairs wearing a pale pink dress that fell just below her knees. Her hair was down today, falling halfway down her back, and as always, her skin looked flawless. Not that he need notice such things.

Annabelle spotted him and lifted her chin slightly.

Trying to take his sister's advice, he waited at the bottom of the stairs. "Thank you for coming with me today."

"Your father asked this favor. I'm doing this for him."

"You're still mad."

"Anger isn't an emotion I'm fond of experiencing." She reached him and tilted her chin up again, her gaze meeting his this time. "What I am is hurt."

The bluntness of her statement didn't surprise him, but her words did. Mad he could deal with. Hurt, not so much. "I'm sorry, but surely you can understand my frustration."

"Yes, and you should understand my delicate situation," Annabelle countered. "I have someone who is risking his sources to help your family. You should appreciate the information instead of putting me in a position of making him not trust me and possibly not continue to share."

He hadn't thought of it that way. Indeed, had the situation been reversed and he'd been in the position to share classified material to help her family, he, too, would be bound by confidentiality protocols. Though it pained him to say it, he forced out an apology. "I'm sorry."

"Good," Annabelle said, the stiffness in her posture not easing in the slightest. "You should be."

- - -

A garden party. Annabelle hadn't thought much about the venue of this morning's event, but now, sitting in the back of the limousine, she couldn't help but take note of the logistical nightmare this must be for security.

She caught sight of Federico and Zeus, the black lab sniffing along the edge of a vehicle at the main entrance to the parking lot. A crowd of attendees had formed in what appeared to be a reception line.

Annabelle's chest tightened, and a wave of fear washed over her. She turned to Leo, who sat beside her. "Are we crazy for being here today?"

"Your guard and his dog did a complete sweep of the grounds before we arrived, and they're checking every vehicle to ensure no explosives could possibly be brought in."

That knowledge did nothing to settle the tension in her body. Annabelle closed her eyes, drew a deep breath, and slowly let it out.

When she opened her eyes, Leo was staring at her with an odd expression on his face, a sort of confusion like when he tried kiwi for the first time and discovered he liked it.

"What?" Annabelle asked.

"Nothing." He shook his head as though to clear his thoughts. He reached over and put his hand on hers. "This is a private event. All the guests have been thoroughly vetted, and the royal guard and local authorities have checked the area to make sure we won't have any surprises."

Of course, Leo was right. Rocco never would have allowed her here if her safety couldn't be guaranteed. She let that thought circle through her mind, trying to believe it. Finally, she said, "I'm ready when you are."

"Showtime." Leo gave a subtle nod to his driver, who climbed out of the car and circled to the rear passenger door.

Rocco appeared at his side, taking up a protective stance.

Norvin opened the door, and Leo stepped out. He nodded a greeting to the crowd before he turned back and offered his hand to Annabelle.

She took another deep breath before she grasped it and slid out of the car.

As soon as she was upright, Leo released her, and together they traversed the path from the limo to a table situated beneath a canopy.

A distinguished man with white hair and dressed in a crisp morning suit stepped forward. He bowed to Leo. "Your Highness, it is such an honor to have you here."

"Thank you." Leo turned to Annabelle. "Princess Annabelle of Sereno, may I present Sir Vicente. He oversees the charitable events for the royal family."

"It's so nice to meet you." Annabelle shook the older man's hand.

"I'm delighted to make your acquaintance, Your Highness." He bowed to her before releasing her hand. "I must admit, I didn't expect to have the pleasure of two royal families represented here today."

"The timing of my visit with Princess Tayla worked out perfectly to allow me the opportunity," Annabelle said. "I understand today's event is intended to benefit the children's art program."

"It is." Vicente's face lit up. "As you can imagine, the supplies for art classes in our primary schools can get rather expensive."

"The funds will also allow lower-income children access to summer art programs," Leo added. "Vicente volunteers his time teaching every summer."

"You're an artist, then." Annabelle smiled.

"Not a very good one, but I'm a few steps ahead of the children I teach."

"I'm sure you're being far too modest," Annabelle said.

Two men in their twenties approached, interrupting the conversation. Annabelle instantly recognized Leo's two younger cousins.

"About time you showed up," Sebastian, the older of the two, said.

Sir Vicente bowed and stepped back. "If you'll excuse me, Your Highnesses, I should check on the silent auction."

"Of course." Leo nodded.

As soon as Sir Vicente left, Rafael, the younger of Leo's cousins, shook Annabelle's hand. "How did you get roped into coming today?"

"I assure you, my sole purpose today is to torment Prince Leonardo at every opportunity."

"And sample every dessert that contains chocolate or strawberries," Leo added.

"That too." Annabelle grinned. "How have the two of you been?"

"Staying out of the headlines, unlike our cousin here."

Leo winced. "I'm afraid I'm about to make some more."

"Why this time?" Sebastian asked.

"Chrishelle and I broke up."

"Not ready to get married, huh?" Rafael asked.

Leo tensed, and Annabelle instinctively redirected the conversation. "What about the two of you?" she asked. "Do either of you have a special someone in your lives?"

"I'm too young to tie myself down," Rafael said. "And Sebastian is too busy pretending to be smart."

"Right." Annabelle lifted both eyebrows. "Last I checked, Oxford tended to admit only those who have a certain academic aptitude."

Sebastian scowled at his younger brother before he shot Annabelle an appreciative look. "Thank you."

Several more attendees approached, and before long, Leo's cousins excused themselves to visit the buffet table, though Annabelle suspected they were more interested in the group of young women standing nearby.

An hour passed of conversation with the various charity sponsors. A light breeze provided a small amount of relief against the overly warm day. Even Leo had discarded his morning jacket, which now lay draped over the back of his chair.

A server approached with a tray full of lemonade. Leo accepted a glass and passed one to her.

"Thank you." Annabelle sipped her drink, grateful for the cool liquid on her throat after chatting with so many people.

Several photographers stood nearby, their cameras constantly clicking.

Her gaze strayed to where Rocco stood, his eyes continually scanning. When he put his finger to his earpiece and started toward her, a new wave of apprehension rose inside her. Something wasn't right.

Leo must have sensed the change because he nodded to the couple before them. "If you'll excuse us." He put his hand on Annabelle's waist and leaned close. "We should go."

Annabelle turned, suddenly aware of the way she and Leo currently stood. His hand still on her waist, their faces bent close together.

As several photographers aimed their cameras in Annabelle and Leo's direction, Annabelle suspected a security threat wasn't the only challenge she and Leo were about to be subjected to.

CHAPTER
19

Leo didn't know what had changed, but the fact that both Saul and Rocco were heading their way indicated something wasn't right.

"What's the problem?" Leo asked as soon as the two guards reached them.

"The door to the roof of the resort was unlocked."

"Was anyone on the roof?" Annabelle asked.

"One of the guards thought he heard someone in the stairwell when they were conducting their search, but we aren't willing to take any chances that a sniper might be hiding out somewhere."

A possible sniper. Leo studied Annabelle. Her long, dark hair was nearly the same length as his sister's, and the two had a similar build. What had he been thinking bringing her here? Though her skin was several shades darker than his and Tayla's, from a distance a sniper could easily mistake Annabelle for Tayla.

He slid his hand more securely around Annabelle's waist and drew her closer. "We'll follow your lead."

"Norvin is pulling the car around now."

Annabelle looked up at him, and he didn't miss the fear shining in the depth of her dark brown eyes.

"It'll be okay." He leaned closer and whispered, "I won't let anything happen to you."

A photographer edged a little too close in his attempt to get a better shot of him and Annabelle together. No doubt, they would be linked together in the media by this time tomorrow.

Saul stepped between them and the photographers. "Stay back please."

The car pulled up, and within seconds, their guards were joined by two others. Flanking them, the security forces escorted Annabelle and Leo to the waiting limo.

As soon as they were safely inside, Rocco closed the door, Saul climbed into the front seat, and Norvin pulled away.

Beside him, Annabelle clasped her hands together in her lap and looked behind her. "Do you think there was really a sniper?"

He hoped not. In an attempt to reassure Annabelle, he said, "I'm sure the royal guard is simply being overly protective. It's better for us to leave early and let it look like it was planned than to risk a rushed exit that would make the tabloids."

"That exit felt pretty rushed to me."

"But to anyone attending, we were simply leaving with our security protocols in place."

Annabelle swiveled in her seat to look behind them. "We have plenty of security. It's too bad we're going to be in the news today. We should probably warn Chrishelle."

He hadn't thought of that aspect. Being linked to Annabelle wouldn't be such a big deal, but with his breakup still under wraps, he didn't look forward to the speculation about his relationship status or, even worse, the accusations of him cheating again.

"Maybe we should have someone leak your breakup to the media today," Annabelle suggested. "It would look better if people already suspect you and Chrishelle are no longer a couple, especially if the two of us are about to be linked in the press."

"I can't believe we left because of a potential sniper and you're worried about my image in the press." Leo lifted his hand as he made his point. "And because of my love life, no less."

"Wouldn't you rather think about that instead of the possibility that someone may have been hiding on a rooftop trying to kill your sister?"

"My sister who looks a lot like you."

"Tayla and I don't look anything alike."

"Not up close, but you do from a distance."

Her gaze met his. "I hadn't thought about that."

Sorry that he'd brought up the potential danger they had just escaped, he changed the subject. "You don't seem terribly concerned about being touted as my newest love interest."

Both elegant eyebrows lifted. "It's not the first time it's happened."

"Yes, but the last time, you were only fifteen, and I was already an adult."

"You were two days past your eighteenth birthday." She tilted her head. "I don't think you'd figured out the whole adult thing yet."

That much was true, but he was astute enough at the time to know that being linked to someone three years his junior would not go over well for his family or for hers.

When Leo didn't respond to her comment, she asked, "What are we going to tell Tayla if she asks why we came back early?"

"Maybe we shouldn't go back early." Leo leaned forward. "Norvin, can you please take us for a drive along the water? I think it would be best if we delay our return."

"Yes, Your Highness."

"That's one way of taking care of the problem." Annabelle smoothed her dress over her knees. "But I do want you to tell me when you receive the security report."

"I will, but we really need to find something else to talk about beyond security reports."

She shot him a regal look. "As long as our future conversations don't involve snakes, frogs, or lizards in relation to my sleeping chambers or my shoes, I'm happy to talk about anything you'd like."

Leo couldn't keep the corners of his lips from curving up. "I think your terms are agreeable."

"Good." Annabelle offered her hand as though sealing a business deal. "I'll sleep much better knowing we have a peace treaty in place."

- - -

Annabelle passed through the palace doors, grateful for her and Leo's safe return. They didn't make it past the front hall before Esteban was at their side.

"Any updates?" Leo asked.

"Nothing yet from the charity event, but I did receive the initial report from the murder scene."

"And?" Leo asked.

"Have the police found Gonzalo yet?" Annabelle asked.

"No luck finding Gonzalo, but the coroner puts the time of death between five and seven o'clock yesterday morning. They're searching through traffic and the security cameras at Julian Benitez's apartment complex in search of any sign of Gonzalo."

"Keep us updated." Leo put his hand on Annabelle's back. "Excuse us."

"Yes, Your Highness." Esteban bowed and headed back the way he came.

"Come on." Leo nudged her toward the opposite hallway. "We need to eat. Neither of us had a chance to enjoy the brunch at the garden party."

Annabelle didn't bother to argue. She was famished. "Duran won't be happy to have us interrupt his meal preparations."

"Some things can't be helped. And he likes you, remember?"

"Yes, but I don't typically interrupt him in the middle of the day." Unless she was snitching a taste of dessert. Come to think of it, she could use a little comfort food right about now.

She and Leo reached the kitchen, and Leo opened the door for her. She looked up and cocked an eyebrow. "You're making me go in first?"

"Like I said, Duran likes you."

With a shake of her head, Annabelle crossed the threshold. The scents of warm caramel and baking bread wafted toward her.

Duran looked up from the pot he was stirring. "If you're here to sample, you're too early."

"Prince Leonardo is hoping I can convince you to feed us lunch," Annabelle said. "We had to leave the charity event before we could eat."

Duran turned to his sous chef. "Prepare a plate for Prince Leonardo and Princess Annabelle."

The younger chef nodded and moved to the refrigerator.

"You'll have to make do with chicken salad and fruit. We've had to limit our options to make room for the caterers to store their ingredients."

"I'm sorry you have to go to the extra work," Annabelle said.

Duran took the pan off the heat and set it aside. "Is it truly necessary for the tastings to happen here at the palace?"

"I'm afraid so," Leo said. "Sometimes security outweighs convenience."

"I'm being invaded." Duran shook his head. Then he jerked a thumb at Annabelle. "It's bad enough that I need a full-time guard on duty to keep this one out of the sweets."

"I can't help it that you're the best pastry chef on this side of the Mediterranean," Annabelle said.

"There's no need for flattery. I already have crema catalana on the menu for dinner tonight."

"Twice in one week." Some of the tension that had built up in her shoulders eased. "You really do love me."

"It so happens that Prince Timeo is also fond of it."

"We'll let him think you're making it for him."

The sous chef carried plates to the table on the far side of the room and set them down.

"Thank you, Felix." Leo pulled out a chair for Annabelle.

"You're welcome, Your Highness." Felix bowed his head before returning to the preparation counter.

Annabelle took her seat and waited for Leo to take his place beside her before she picked up her sandwich. She ate a bite before she asked, "Do you know yet how much longer Prince Timeo intends to stay?"

"I'm not sure," Leo said.

"He'll be here through breakfast on Monday," Duran offered.

Annabelle swiveled on her stool to face him. "How did you know that?"

Duran held up both hands. "Because I'm the one who's feeding him."

"I'm surprised I didn't see him before we left today," Leo said.

"Maybe he was checking out the cars in your garage," Annabelle offered.

"He was in the stables," Duran said.

The surety of Duran's statement surprised her. "And you know that because . . ."

"Because he was included in the picnic lunch I prepared for your sister to take on her ride this afternoon."

"Are they back yet?"

"Not that I know of." Duran shot Annabelle a knowing look. "But guests don't often come into my kitchen."

"Only your favorites." Annabelle took another bite. "Thank you for lunch. You saved us from starvation."

"That's my job."

Leo held up the remaining half of his sandwich. "You do your job very well."

CHAPTER
20

LEO NEVER THOUGHT HE'D BE grateful for Prince Timeo's presence, particularly when Annabelle was also staying in his home, but he had to admit, the prince's shared interests with Chrishelle had greatly reduced the awkwardness between Leo and his ex-girlfriend.

The new seating arrangement at dinner had resulted in Annabelle being situated across from Leo, with Prince Timeo at his left and his mother at his right. And tonight, the conversation was all about the wedding.

"Annabelle, I don't think it's wise to have you do Tayla's hair and makeup," his mother said. "You simply won't have the time."

"Of course she will," Tayla said. "And having her do that for me will keep me calm."

Annabelle offered a diplomatic smile and aimed it at his mother. "I believe Tayla plans on me being a part-time therapist as well."

"But there are always so many details the maid of honor has to juggle on the day of the wedding," his mother said.

Knowing Annabelle wouldn't contradict his mother, Leo turned to Isaac. "Are you sure you don't want to elope?"

His mother didn't give Isaac a chance to respond. "Don't even joke about such a thing."

"Yes, Mother."

Across the table, Annabelle coughed, undoubtedly to hide the laughter she had been unable to suppress. His gaze met hers. Humor reflected in her eyes, confirming his suspicions.

"It appears an elopement is not an option," Isaac said.

"No, it's not," Tayla said firmly.

Ready for the wedding talk to be over, Leo asked, "Wouldn't it be wise to hire a wedding planner to juggle the details for you? This is a royal event after all."

"We have hired a wedding coordinator," his mother said, "but we don't want to involve her until after the core details are set."

"And why is that?" Leo asked, even though he already knew the answer.

"You know how much I enjoy planning parties," his mother said. She gestured toward Tayla. "And Tayla wants to make these decisions without someone she doesn't know trying to interfere."

"So you and Tayla want to orchestrate the events, something you have a great deal of experience with and undeniable talent," Leo said. He nodded toward Annabelle. "And Annabelle is offering to provide a service to which she is exceptionally gifted. And the wedding coordinator will handle the details you put in place, which will keep everyone happy."

His mother paused, studying him before turning her attention back to Tayla and Annabelle. "I suppose that's true."

In an effort to drive his point home, Leo added, "And it would be excellent publicity for Annabelle's cosmetics company if it's associated with Tayla's wedding, especially since we all know Tayla will be stunning."

His mother lifted an elegant hand. "Fine. Annabelle can do Tayla's hair and makeup."

Annabelle and Tayla both grinned.

At the head of the table, his father set his napkin beside his plate. "Now that we have that settled, I'm going to retire for the evening."

His mother stood. "I think I'll join you."

As staff members moved forward to remove his parents' dirty dishes, Leo stood. Though he didn't look forward to telling Chrishelle their breakup would shortly be in the news, he couldn't put it off any longer.

"Chrishelle, can you spare a moment?"

Surprise illuminated her expression, but she nodded. She glanced at Prince Timeo. "If you'll excuse me."

"Of course. I'll meet you in the grand salon later."

Chrishelle nodded.

Leo escorted her from the dining hall and outside onto the terrace. Storm clouds hung overhead, and the scent of rain carried on the breeze.

Leo crossed to the concrete balustrade to give them some distance from the guard posted by the door. "There's something I need to talk to you about."

She lifted her eyebrows. "Don't tell me you're having second thoughts about our breakup."

"No, but it's likely our breakup is about to hit the press," Leo said. "I'm sorry."

She stared at him for several seconds. "You were with Princess Annabelle today."

"Nothing happened, but there were several photographers nearby when we left the event. I put my hand on her back—"

"And you think the press will make it seem like you were cheating on me."

"Yes."

"It's not like this hasn't happened before," Chrishelle said. "What's different this time?"

The answer to that question was instant. Never before had the woman beside him been Annabelle. Focusing on Annabelle's business rather than their longtime friendship, Leo said, "You're probably aware that Annabelle is about to launch her new cosmetics company."

"Yes." Understanding dawned in her eyes. "You're afraid negative press about her will hurt her company."

"She's been working toward this for years. I don't want her to suffer because she did a favor for my family."

Chrishelle sighed. "There's something else you should be aware of."

"What's that?"

"Timeo invited me to leave with him Monday."

The use of the prince's first name without his title caught Leo's attention. "Are the two of you dating now?"

"No, but I'd like to know whether that possibility exists without worrying about how it would look for me or for him and his family." She rolled her eyes. "I can see the clickbait now: 'Chrishelle Montgomery on the hunt for a new prince.'"

Leo couldn't deny it. The press could be ruthless, and Chrishelle's current circumstances would make her an easy target.

"Maybe I should stay here like we originally planned," Chrishelle said. "I could see if Timeo can arrange for my job interview to be online instead."

"Job interview?" Leo asked. "What job?"

"There's an opening as an assistant events coordinator at a ski resort in Crovacia. It would be about a two-hour drive from the palace."

"Looking at another long-distance relationship, huh?"

"Possibly, but at least we'd be in the same time zone."

Leo pondered their dilemma. "You know, we never gave any official statements when you arrived. It wouldn't be difficult to spin a story that will be advantageous for both of us."

"What kind of story?"

"We say that while we were dating, you became good friends with my sister. Your visit here was to see her and help with her wedding plans."

She tilted her head. "Since we hadn't seen each other for six months, we could let people think we broke up then instead of yesterday."

"And I did ignore you for the first part of your visit." Leo still felt bad about that.

"Which means no one would doubt that we were no longer a couple." She nodded. "It could work."

"I'll call Sebastian. I think I can get him to leak a story for us that will head this off before it really gets started."

"Thank you, Leonardo." Chrishelle put her hand on his arm. "I know you don't like to fuel the media, but I appreciate you doing this."

"You deserve to be happy, without the press's interference."

She leaned in and kissed his cheek. "So do you."

- - -

Annabelle waited beside the window until Chrishelle returned inside. Annabelle expected Leo to follow, but instead he pulled his phone from his pocket and made a call.

Not wanting to intrude, Annabelle waited until he hung up before she stepped outside. "Is everything okay?"

"Yes. Everything is good actually." He pocketed his phone. "Well, it would be good if our dock incident was behind us."

"I'm starting to wonder if we'll ever have that behind us," Annabelle said.

"We will. It's only been four days. Investigations take time."

"I know." She'd lived through situations like this before.

"You've been amazing through all of this."

Annabelle lifted her hand to Leo's forehead as though to check his temperature. "Are you feeling all right?"

"Yes. Why?"

"Then who are you, and what have you done with Prince Leonardo?" At his confused look, she continued. "First, you compliment me and Tayla at dinner. And now you're praising me again. This isn't like the Leo I know."

"You aren't exactly the same person I'm used to either. Before when you'd come to visit, you were always riding my favorite horse without asking or spending hours on Tayla's hair and makeup while I had to go through archery practice alone."

"Doing Tayla's hair and makeup never took more than thirty minutes. It's not my fault your sister used me as an excuse to avoid archery."

"I should have known."

"And if you didn't always choose the best horses to call your own, I wouldn't borrow yours."

Leo narrowed his eyes. "You rode Calypso when you went out with Tayla and Chrishelle, didn't you?"

Annabelle couldn't help but smile. "He's a magnificent animal."

Leo laughed. "Yes, he is."

A comfortable silence fell between them, both enjoying the cool evening breeze and the scent of the storm on the horizon. Even though she knew she shouldn't pry, Annabelle asked, "Who was that on the phone?"

"Sebastian. I asked him to leak a story about me and Chrishelle."

"She was okay with that?"

"Yes, but we did decide to stretch the truth a bit," Leo said. "We're announcing that the two of us broke up six months ago and that she's here to help my sister with wedding plans."

"The helping with wedding plans is true enough. She's been amazing."

"I'm afraid her help is coming to an end soon. She plans to leave with Prince Timeo and spend a few days in Crovacia."

"Really?"

"It seems there's a promising job opening in one of their ski resorts."

"I really like her. I hope everything works out."

"Me, too." Leo leaned back against the balustrade. "Of course, you realize what this means, don't you?"

"What?"

"Those photos of us together will no longer look like I was cheating with you."

"Thank goodness. I don't need those types of rumors swirling around."

Leo slid his hands into his pockets. "Yes, but how are you going to feel about people believing you and I are dating?"

"What?" She shook her head. "No one will believe that for long. Everyone knows we've been friends since childhood."

"Yes, but it makes a better story if the press believes the reason I didn't announce my breakup with Chrishelle was because I was secretly in love with someone else."

Someone else. Like her. "Leo. You didn't."

"It was Sebastian's idea."

"And you could have said no." For the majority of her life, Annabelle had happily stayed out of the press with the exception of her participation in official events. She had no interest in having her love life—or pretend love life—making headlines. She motioned toward his phone. "Call him back. Tell him to leave me out of it."

"He isn't going to name you specifically."

"Even if he doesn't, by announcing you have a secret girlfriend at the same time you were seen with me, everyone will jump to the same conclusion."

"Would it be so terrible for people to think we were dating?"

Memories of him holding her after the bomb went off pushed to the forefront of her mind. That spurt of attraction was just a fluke. It didn't mean anything.

Choosing her words carefully, she said, "I'm sorry the press is always invading your personal life, but I've never had to deal with that. Not really. You can't blame me for wanting to stay out of the spotlight."

"No. I can't." A kind of resignation came over him. "I'll make a statement that you were simply accompanying me to the charity event as a longtime friend."

"I appreciate that." Annabelle's phone rang, and she pulled it free from her clutch. "It's my brother-in-law."

"Which one?" Leo asked.

"Levi." She hit the Talk button. "Hey, there."

"Where are you right now?" Levi asked.

"I'm on the terrace with Leo. Why?"

"I have an update for you, but I'd rather not discuss it over the phone when there are guards around," Levi said.

Suspecting the news was something that would involve both her and Leo, she said, "We'll call you back when we're in my rooms."

"If Prince Leonardo is coming with you, take Rocco too."

"Why?"

"Because photos have already leaked with you and Prince Leonardo together today," Levi said. "We don't need rumors spreading that you two were alone in your suite."

"Fine. Give us ten minutes," Annabelle said. "We'll talk to you then." She ended the call. "We have new intel coming in. I thought you might want to hear it firsthand."

"Yes." Leo nodded. "I would."

CHAPTER
21

LEO HADN'T BEEN IN ANNABELLE'S rooms in years, not since he and Tayla had sat around her kitchen table on a rainy day playing spades with Tayla's governess. The carpeting had been upgraded since then and the walls freshly painted, but nothing else had changed. Well, except that Annabelle was no longer a thirteen-year-old girl who hadn't yet outgrown her awkward stage.

"Have a seat." Annabelle motioned to the couch and headed for her bedroom. "I'll be right back."

Rocco secured the door.

Annabelle returned a moment later with her laptop. She set it on the coffee table and sat beside him. Then she opened a videochat program similar to the secure communications network Leo used when working with Alameda's intelligence service. Within seconds, King Levi appeared on the screen, a credenza visible behind him along with a stunning painting of the Sereno coastline.

"Okay, so what was it that you couldn't tell us on the phone?" Annabelle asked.

The king looked past Annabelle and appeared to focus on her guard. "Rocco, can you give us a minute?"

"Yes, sire." Rocco bowed slightly. "I'll just be in the suite's kitchen."

As soon as her guard left the room, Annabelle asked, "Well?"

"We did an extensive search for Gonzalo but couldn't find any evidence of him leaving Alameda."

"We already suspected he was still in the country," Leo said.

"Yes." Levi held up a file folder. "But did you suspect he was also dead?"

"Dead?" Annabelle and Leo asked in unison.

"Prince Leonardo, I'm sure you're aware that a body was discovered at the gold mine in your northern country."

"Yes. It was discovered a few months ago when we were putting in safety enhancements at the mine." The man was believed to have been killed a couple years earlier, his body buried where it would likely never have been found had it not been for the safety upgrades.

"I suspect the body was never identified because the victim was believed to still be alive," King Levi said. "I took the liberty of having Gonzalo's dental records compared to the unidentified body." The king paused briefly. "They matched."

"Gonzalo is dead?" Annabelle asked.

"Yes."

Leo's mind was spinning. "How did you even think to check the dental records?"

"The time of death of the body found at the mine corresponded with when Gonzalo was supposed to have been transported to prison."

"So someone killed him and then made it look like he was in prison," Leo said. "Why?"

"That's the million-euro question," King Levi said. "Why would anyone want to make it look like he was in prison instead of dead?"

"I'm sure Tayla will sleep easier knowing he can never bother her again," Annabelle said, "but I can't think of anyone who would want him dead and then want to hide it."

"Me neither."

"There's something else," King Levi said. "We tracked down the bomb-maker behind the luggage explosion."

Leo straightened. "Do you know who hired him?"

"Yes, but I'm afraid that brings us to another dead end," Levi said. "It was Julian Benitez."

"You think the two deaths are connected," Annabelle said.

"I do." The king held up the file folder again. "The ballistics match."

Leo tapped a finger on his thigh. "So someone managed to kill Gonzalo, modify the transport and prison records to make it look like he was still alive, and then hired Benitez to try to kill my sister."

"In all likelihood, Benitez is the person who modified those prison records," King Levi said. "Whether he killed Gonzalo and was later killed with his own gun or if his killer committed both murders . . . that's all speculation."

"Regardless, our top suspect behind the bombing is dead," Leo said.

Annabelle sighed. "We're back to square one."

Leo nodded. "I'm afraid so."

"There is one other item we need to discuss," King Levi said.

Leo was afraid to ask what other news the king would have to offer. He'd already turned their working theories upside down.

Annabelle also remained silent.

King Levi continued. "My wife and I talked about it, and we think the two of you should date."

"What?" Annabelle asked.

"Excuse me?" Leo asked at the same moment. It was one thing for him to let the press misread the situation, but having a foreign head of state suggest a relationship between him and Annabelle was beyond unexpected.

"The photos are already circulating online, and the potential for negative press leading into the launch of Sereno Cove Cosmetics is high."

"Won't the two of us being seen together only make things worse?" Annabelle asked.

"Actually, we believe rumors of a real relationship will help settle the media down," King Levi said.

"You want to use me as a marketing ploy?" Leo didn't like the sound of that, although he could hardly complain since he'd planned to use his association with Annabelle in a similar way.

The king's eyebrows rose, and he stared at Leo. "You were going to let the press assume the two of you had secretly been dating."

"How did you know—"

King Levi held up a hand and cut him off. "My wife and I are simply suggesting you allow the press to believe the two of you are a happy couple, now secure enough in your relationship to share it with the world."

"This would be a nightmare," Annabelle said. "Instead of me being in the news to promote my new company, all anyone will care about is where Leo and I ate dinner."

"Consider this damage control," King Levi said. "You appear to be a happy couple, we leak a few photos of the two of you together to the media, and when the time comes, Prince Leonardo and his family can release a supportive statement of your new company."

"I'm sure my sister would have offered an endorsement anyway," Leo said.

"Then it's settled," King Levi said before Annabelle could argue further. "I'll be in touch if we receive any more intel regarding the bombing."

"Thank you," Leo said.

The screen went blank, and Annabelle closed the laptop.

"I can't believe Levi and Cassie want us to pretend to date."

Replaying her earlier words, Leo said, "Dating me will be a nightmare, huh?"

"That's not what I meant," Annabelle said. "It's the dating with the press watching I don't look forward to."

Mollified, Leo considered their situation in a new light. "Then we don't let the press dictate the terms of our relationship," Leo said. "We could go out sailing, away from the paparazzi."

"Prince Leonardo, are you asking me out on a date?"

Though Leo had never anticipated doing such a thing, he nodded. "I think I am."

CHAPTER

22

SHE HAD A DATE WITH Leo. Annabelle still wasn't sure what to think of that particular detail, nor had she dared look at the news online. Today was Sunday. In her mind, that meant church and a day of rest. More precisely, it was a day to let the world and its judgments fade away.

Leaning over, she fastened the strap of her favorite sandals. Then she checked her hair in the oval mirror on the wall in the living room and headed for the door. Church services today would be held in the private chapel in the palace, with only the royal family and a few select guests. Technically, she fell into the guest category, but it was hard to consider herself as such after spending so much time visiting here.

She silenced her phone and slipped it into her clutch before heading into the main hall. Tayla caught up to her at the top of the stairs and held up her phone. "Did you see the photos of you and Leo online?"

Annabelle held up a hand to stop her. "It's Sunday."

"Yes, but—"

"No checking online. No articles. No photos."

"You know you're just postponing the inevitable."

"By tomorrow, the photos will be a thing of the past." At least they would be if Leo and Levi didn't have plans to fuel the rumors. She put her hand on the banister. "Come on. We don't want to be late for church."

"You know the preacher won't start until we're all there, right?"

Annabelle supposed that was one advantage of having private worship services. "That doesn't mean we should keep him or your family waiting." She glanced over her shoulder, half expecting Leo to walk down the hall behind them. "Is everyone else already in the chapel?"

"I didn't check with anyone besides Isaac," Tayla said. "He said he'd meet me down there. He went to meet his mom at the palace gate."

"I don't think I've met his mother yet."

"You did once, at my birthday party. And Sunday or not, be ready to talk wedding plans today." Tayla started down the stairs. "Isaac's mom has a lot of ideas."

"She's not going to try to undo all the decisions you've already made, is she?"

"She can try, but I'm not going to let her," Tayla said. "I love the place settings Chrishelle helped us with."

"Did you hear she's leaving tomorrow?"

"Yes. I'll be sad to see her go."

"She's been a good friend." And she'd spent far more time with Tayla than Annabelle had over the past week. "You should invite her to the wedding."

"I was thinking about that, but I didn't know if it would be awkward for Leo."

"I don't think it would be. From what I witnessed Friday night, they parted as friends."

Tayla stopped walking. "You were spying on my brother?"

"No." Annabelle tugged on Tayla's arm to put her back in motion. "I went out to check on Leo, and Chrishelle was with him. From what little I heard, I'm quite certain they both only want the best for each other." Now Annabelle stopped walking and lowered her voice. "Speaking of which, your cousin is going to leak the story that Chrishelle and Leo broke up months ago so that any photos of me won't look like your brother was cheating."

"Then why would she be staying here at the palace?"

"To visit you."

"Ah." They started walking again. "I need to play make believe again."

"Just roll with the story anyway."

"I guess I can do that." Tayla stopped beside the entrance to the chapel. "With the way my mother has been arranging all the wedding appointments here at the palace, I doubt I'll be talking to the press anytime soon anyway."

A little pang of guilt tugged at her, and Annabelle ignored it. The misconceptions they were creating for Tayla were for her own good.

Tayla led the way into the vestibule where muted prelude music carried from the organ in the front of the chapel. Isaac and an older woman stood beside a marble statue of two children at the Savior's feet.

"Princess Annabelle." Isaac bowed his head. "May I present my mother, Nora Vega."

"I believe we met at Tayla's birthday party," Annabelle said. "It's lovely to see you again."

Isaac's mother curtsied before accepting Annabelle's offered hand.

They exchanged pleasantries for a few minutes until King Josep and Queen Eva arrived with Leo.

"Shall we?" Queen Eva motioned toward the chapel.

The polite command was enough to encourage everyone inside. Chrishelle and Prince Timeo already sat in the third row of the padded pews.

Annabelle waited for the king and queen to choose their seats before she opted for a spot behind them. Leo sat beside her.

He leaned close. "Have you looked at the news yet this morning?"

"It's Sunday. I don't look at the news on Sundays."

Leo cocked his head to the side. "Why? That's the day when most of the world gets caught up on all the events they missed during the week."

"Everyone else can get caught up. I prefer to enjoy peace and quiet on the sabbath."

The preacher approached the pulpit, and Leo settled back in his seat. When he stretched his arm along the back of the pew, his hand resting lightly on her shoulder, Annabelle turned toward him.

She lowered her voice to a whisper. "What are you doing?"

"Getting comfortable," he whispered back. "Pastor Rojas can get long-winded when we have visitors."

"Your sister and parents are going to think we're really a couple."

"Fine." Leo withdrew his arm and straightened in his seat. "Better?"

"Yes."

Then the pastor stepped forward and began his sermon. "Today, I would like to talk about honesty."

Annabelle looked at Leo instinctively.

He leaned close. "Some secrets are necessary."

Annabelle nodded. Some secrets were necessary. She glanced at where Tayla and Isaac sat across the aisle. But which ones were necessary, and which were secrets of convenience? At this point, Annabelle wasn't sure she could distinguish between the two.

- - -

Had Leo not known better, he would have sworn Pastor Rojas was preaching directly to him. Even as he spoke of the importance of honesty, Leo debated the preacher's words in his mind. The white lies, or rather the lack of information, being shared with Tayla was justifiable. She was healthy now, both mentally and physically, and no one in the family wanted her to experience a relapse.

Even the deception about the timing of his breakup was for Chrishelle's good more than his own.

Despite his surety of those thoughts, he couldn't stop the guilt from rising within him, and it had nothing to do with his sister or ex-girlfriend. No, his guilt about telling white lies was directly related to the woman beside him.

Annabelle may not have seen the photos or the articles in the news, but he had, and hiding from them wouldn't make them any less real. Rumors were flying about him and Annabelle dating, but the public response online wasn't anything like what he'd expected. Rather than the typical "How long will this one last" or "Will Prince Leonardo cheat" headlines, the public outcry was largely positive. People seemed to want him to succeed in his relationship with Annabelle. The comments ranged from "Prince Leonardo may have met his match" to "It's about time" to "What a great couple."

Not one headline suggested Leo had cheated on Chrishelle, but he wasn't sure if that was because of the story Sebastian leaked or if it was due to Annabelle's reputation. No one believed she would be involved with someone who had a boyfriend, so it followed that he hadn't cheated.

What had he been thinking in suggesting they pretend to date? What had King Levi and Queen Cassandra been thinking? When the world inevitably discovered they weren't a couple, even if that detail came wrapped in a fictional breakup story, what would happen to Annabelle's reputation? Would she be dragged through the mud like so many of his other past girlfriends? Or would she simply suffer his typical fate of being hounded by the paparazzi as they tried to discover whom she was dating next?

When the church service finally ended, Annabelle leaned close. "Well, that was decidedly uncomfortable."

Leo didn't disagree.

In front of him, his parents stood. As expected, they departed first, followed by Leo and Annabelle and then Tayla and Isaac. Within minutes, everyone was seated at the table on the terrace where the staff had prepared brunch. The only exceptions were Chrishelle and Prince Timeo, who had opted to take a ride into town. And although Leo was grateful that he hadn't experienced any lingering tension with his ex-girlfriend, he could admit that it was nice to have a meal without her and the visiting prince.

"I love that your family has Sunday brunch too."

"It's hard to believe you were still in Sereno this time last week," Leo said, struggling to comprehend how much had occurred over the past six days.

"I know. Last Sunday I was having brunch with my family." Annabelle glanced down the table to where his father had already placed a bit of ham and cheese on his plate before she reached for the bread basket. "We still have brunch every week." She looked out over the Mediterranean. "Of course, our terrace doesn't have a view of the water."

"Tayla, what is on the agenda this week?" his father asked.

"We have a cake testing tomorrow, and the first caterer will bring samples on Tuesday."

"I believe the rest of the week will be filled with food prepared by various caterers," his mother said.

"I understand the caterer we're previewing on Wednesday is quite popular," Isaac's mom said.

"Isaac, will you be able to attend all these tastings?" his father asked.

"I have to prepare for my next case, but I brought the files with me here to the palace," Isaac said. "If I get up early and work late, I'll be able to take a few hours off each day."

"And this is why I didn't want to study law. The hours are insane." Leo glanced at his future brother-in-law. "I'm glad you can represent the family in that field."

"Law is an important aspect of ruling," his father said. "It's important all kings have a firm understanding in the field."

"Then we're fortunate Tayla is marrying well, since I clearly didn't choose the right education to be king," Leo said, a hint of sarcasm running through his words.

"I may have the education to be king." Isaac nodded toward Leo's father. "But I'll never have the bloodline."

"Thankfully, our children will never have to worry about such things," Tayla said, "assuming my brother ever finds a woman to marry."

"I'm not yet thirty," Leo reminded her. "I have plenty of time to find a wife."

"Leo, what do you have planned this week?" his father asked, thankfully diverting the attention away from his marital status.

"Besides making sure Tayla puts something chocolate for dessert on the menu?" Leo asked.

His father chuckled. "Yes, besides that."

"Annabelle and I talked about going sailing sometime this week."

"I'm afraid the weather isn't likely to cooperate for a few days," his mother said.

The tone of her voice suggested she had already looked into the possibility of going out on the water herself.

"We may need to postpone those plans until the weekend," Annabelle suggested.

"Maybe we can all go out on Saturday," his mother suggested. "We could all use a nice distraction."

Just what Leo needed—his family joining him on his first date with Annabelle.

"That could be fun," Tayla said.

Annabelle nodded, keeping her gaze diverted from him. "Yes, it could be."

The conversation turned back to the upcoming tasting appointments, and Leo leaned close to Annabelle. "You realize my family just invited themselves on our date, right?"

"But we aren't really dating, are we?"

"I don't know," Leo whispered, "but taking a crowd out with us isn't going to help us find out."

- - -

Annabelle carried two plates down the hall to Leo's office, each one laden with six different kinds of cake and a dessert fork tucked in the center. She didn't know what had prompted Leo to miss the cake testing—beyond his typical aversion to talking about weddings—but the lemon raspberry and the red velvet cakes were too good not to share. She considered herself lucky the red velvet had even been included since Tayla didn't eat chocolate.

Marcus looked up from his computer and stood. "Good afternoon, Your Highness." He motioned toward Leo's closed office door. "You can go right in."

"Thank you." She handed one of the plates to Marcus. "This is for you."

"Thank you, Your Highness."

"You're welcome." Annabelle knocked on Leo's door twice before she opened it.

Leo looked up from where he sat on the sofa beside the window. He stood as she entered, and his gaze lowered to the plate. "You brought me cake?"

"We may need your vote to break the tie. Tayla's future mother-in-law is quite fond of the coconut with passion fruit."

Leo instantly wrinkled his nose. "Who would do that to a cake?"

Fully aware of his aversion to coconut, she handed him the plate. "Don't worry. I gave that one to Marcus. These are all my favorites."

"Thank you." He reached past her and closed the door before he returned to the couch and motioned for her to join him.

Once they were seated, he passed her a file and picked up his fork.

"What's this?"

"The intel your brother-in-law sent over." Leo took a bite of the red velvet cake. He rolled his eyes heavenward and wagged his fork at her. "Oh, that's a winner."

"It's a top contender." Annabelle held up the file. "Are there going to be gruesome photos of the body in here?"

"No, King Levi spared us of those. But the report leaves little doubt as to the identity of the remains found. The dental records match, and there's evidence of a broken leg, which is consistent with Gonzalo's medical records."

Annabelle opened the file and skimmed over the report. The DNA records wouldn't be ready for several weeks, but everything in the report from the time of death to the broken leg to the dental records matched the identity of Tayla's stalker.

"We really are back to square one." Annabelle set the file on the coffee table. "Someone we know is responsible for trying to kill your sister."

Leo held up his empty fork. "The even scarier thought is whoever is behind this will likely be on Tayla's guest list for her wedding."

"That is a scary thought." A killer among their friends. "What I still can't wrap my mind around is the idea that someone would want to kill Tayla in the first place. There's no logical motive."

"Let's focus on something a little more positive for a while." He pointed at the partially eaten samples of cake. "Which one was your favorite?"

"I narrowed it down to two."

"The lemon raspberry and the red velvet." Leo nodded. "But how do you choose between them?"

"I couldn't." She reached out and snitched a piece of the lemon raspberry.

Leo gave her a look of disbelief. "That wasn't very princess-like."

"If you'd offered to share, I wouldn't have had to use my fingers." Annabelle licked the icing off the pad of her thumb.

Leo laughed and scooped a piece of the red velvet onto his fork and held it out.

Annabelle leaned forward and accepted the bite. "Mmm. That really is good."

"Maybe they can do a layer of each."

"That's what I suggested, but I had some resistance. Isaac's mother also liked the lemon poppy seed, and she also had the vanilla as one of her top choices."

Leo shook his head. "Poppy seeds have a way of getting stuck in your teeth, and the vanilla is too boring."

"I'm afraid you may have to live with boring at your sister's wedding because the vanilla is one of Tayla's top choices too."

"Seriously?"

"Yes, but I think we can convince her to add our favorites as two of the layers."

"I'll text her and tell her which ones I liked. Maybe the two of us can out-vote the competition."

"Maybe, but in the end, it's Tayla's wedding, not ours."

Leo motioned toward the plate. "If it was ours, the choice would be easy."

Annabelle couldn't help but smile at the image of Leo getting married.

"What?"

"Nothing. It's just hard to imagine you settling down."

"No matter what the paparazzi thinks, I'm not planning on heading down that road for a while."

Annabelle narrowed her eyes. "The paparazzi?"

"You never looked at the media blitz we created, did you?"

"No. Why?"

"Apparently, we're quite popular as a couple."

"Oh, really?" She hadn't expected that. "And how do you feel about being paired with your sister's best friend?"

"It could be worse." Leo took another bite of the red velvet cake. "And you did bring me food, so that's a point in your favor."

"It's too bad none of your previous girlfriends recognized how easy it is to get on your good side."

"They tried." He shrugged. "It never lasted."

"Why do you think that is?" Annabelle asked, curious.

"None of them were the right girl."

"But you think you'll find the right girl someday."

Leo set his fork down, and his gaze met hers. For several seconds, he stared at her, his expression thoughtful and a little worried.

When he didn't respond, Annabelle said, "It's not a difficult question, Leo."

"It shouldn't be, but I've had a solid decade of the press commenting on who they think is and isn't good enough for me." He picked up his mobile from where it lay on the coffee table. "I don't want that to happen with you."

"It won't." She put her hand on his knee. "We won't let it."

His eyes darkened and lowered briefly to her lips. The intensity of his gaze caused the breath to back up in her lungs, and an unexpected thought rushed to the forefront of her mind. Was Leo going to kiss her? More importantly, did she want him to?

Her insides fluttered, her hand still warm on his.

Several more seconds passed in silence before Leo drew a deep breath and looked down at the file on the coffee table. "We should look through the list of your friends again."

Annabelle withdrew her hand and tried to clear her head. "I don't know what good that will do. Julian Benitez was the one who paid the bombmaker. That means it's far more likely that the attempt is coming from someone tied to him and Gonzalo Caballero."

"We need to do something."

"I agree, but you aren't going to like my suggestion."

"What is it?"

"We need to look into your family and the heirs to the throne."

"What good would that do?" Leo asked. "No one knew I was going to be at the docks besides my parents and Tayla, and we know none of them would try to kill me."

And the bomb required preplanning. "Then maybe we need to consider another possibility."

"What's that?"

Annabelle drew a deep breath and blew it out slowly. "Maybe I was the real target."

Leo instantly shook his head. "Someone going after you is as ludicrous as someone trying to kill my sister. Neither one of you have ever made an enemy."

"That was true until I announced the launch of my business," Annabelle said. "The president of Sandalwood Cosmetics wasn't happy to find out I would be infringing on their market share."

"I imagine they weren't the only ones." Leo tiled his head toward her. "I'm sure everyone knows your company will be a huge success."

The compliment both surprised and touched her. "What makes you say that?"

"Annabelle, you never do anything halfway. And no one knows your market better than you do."

Heat rushed to her cheeks, and her heart swelled with unexpected gratitude. "Thank you."

"You're welcome." Leo waved his hand in the air. "But I'm not sure your company is a real motive. Like you just said, Julian Benitez paid for the bomb. It doesn't make sense that he would be involved in both Gonzalo's escape and an attempted assassination on you."

"Unless he's someone who hires himself out for nefarious purposes," Annabelle said.

Leo's face paled slightly, and he picked up his phone. "We should talk to King Levi about the possibilities. He can tell us if anyone associated with your business rivals has visited Alameda recently. And maybe he can trace any unknown payments to Benitez."

"Wouldn't it be easier to go to your intelligence sources?" Annabelle asked. "After all, your people can run the reports of who has gone through passport control."

"Yes, but I suspect King Levi has the resources to help determine which names we should be looking for."

CHAPTER

23

SEARCHING FOR SUSPECTS AMONG ANNABELLE'S soon-to-be competitors wasn't any better than looking through lists of Tayla's friends. Both scenarios emphasized that someone Leo cared about was in danger.

He had spent all day Monday in meetings with Esteban and reviewing updates on the location of Tayla's friends. Annabelle's day had been filled with phone calls and video conferences with her executive board as well as both of her brothers-in-law as they explored the possibility of Annabelle being the target. Though they had touched base at lunch, Leo didn't particularly care for looking at suspects this way. He much preferred a united effort.

His phone vibrated with an incoming text. Annabelle. *You need to come to the kitchen.*

He checked the time. The meeting with the caterers wasn't supposed to start for another hour. *Why?* he texted back.

An image popped up in the next message: a tray laden with desserts, all of them chocolate.

Tempting, but he should stay and look over the latest construction estimates for the new bridge being built along the southern peninsula.

His phone buzzed again. *If you don't come now, I'm starting without you.*

Leo laughed. Leave it to Annabelle to give him an ultimatum to get him out of his office. He pushed back from his desk and headed out the door.

"Marcus, I'll be out for a while. Call me if anything important comes up."

"Yes, Your Highness."

When Leo walked into the kitchen. Annabelle already sat at the table, a spoon in her hand and a dish of chocolate mousse in front of her. Across the room, a half dozen people worked at the prep counter, and Duran stood beside a man wearing a white chef's hat. Besides their matching headwear, both men also wore identical scowls.

Leo crossed to the table and nodded in Duran's direction. "Let me guess: Duran is annoyed at having outsiders in his kitchen, and the caterer doesn't appreciate being supervised."

"You guessed that in one try." Annabelle spooned up a bite of chocolate mousse. "It's like you went to Harvard or something."

"It didn't take a doctoral degree to figure that out." He picked up a clean spoon from the place setting in front of him. "And what happened to waiting for me?"

"You were taking too long." She took a bite and let out an appreciative hum. "You need to try this."

"Careful. If Duran sees you enjoying someone else's food too much, he may ban you from the kitchen."

"Never." Annabelle furrowed her eyebrows as though she was considering if there was any truth to Leo's statement.

Leo took a bite of his own and hummed his approval too.

"You have to try the chocolate torte." Annabelle held up a plate that had one mini torte on it.

"You really didn't wait for me."

"I tried, but the caterer gave me a sample plate for two, and then you didn't respond to my text."

"The fact that you got me out of my office in the middle of the day is rather impressive."

Annabelle wiggled her eyebrows, pure delight shining in her eyes. "I know."

"Is distracting me from my work a new pastime of yours?"

"We've had too much serious lately."

"You're in a surprisingly good mood for someone who thinks someone may be trying to kill her."

"I talked to Alan a half hour ago," Annabelle said, referring to her sister Victoria's husband. "He's convinced there's no way I could have been the target."

"How can he be so sure?"

"I don't know, but he talked to Rocco again, and from what he described, Alan said the bomb had to have been triggered before whoever planted it would have known I would have been in the blast range."

"Which brings us back to Tayla."

Annabelle's mood sobered. "Or you."

"My cousins aren't trying to kill me, and no one I associate with would be aware of what kind of luggage you use."

"Then you're right." Annabelle picked up her napkin and wiped a crumb from her lips. "It has to be Tayla."

"Maybe after the tasting today, we can look over the latest intel reports together and compare notes."

"It's worth a try."

Leo lifted a paper cup filled with chocolate-covered mints. "You realize that when we go to the taste testing, we're going to be too full to try more of this."

Annabelle leaned close. "We'll just have a little bit."

"If you can have just a little bit, you have more self-control than I do."

- - -

Annabelle put a hand on her stomach as she led the way out of the kitchen. She shouldn't have eaten so much, but she hadn't been able to resist. "I now know that I have zero willpower."

"That makes two of us." Leo lowered his voice to a whisper. "We may have to confess that we've already been tasting."

"I'm not sure I want your mother to know I'm still sneaking into the kitchen when no one is looking."

"My mother won't be there today. She had some charity board meeting she didn't want to reschedule."

"Is that how you got volunteered to go to the tasting?"

"I had fully planned to be on an important phone call right now so I could avoid it."

"What changed?"

"You texted me the photo of the desserts."

Annabelle hooked her arm through Leo's. "It's a good thing I did. Tayla wouldn't be happy if you skipped out." Annabelle leaned closer. "And we may need reinforcements when dealing with Isaac's mother."

Leo glanced behind them as though to ensure they were alone. "I didn't agree with her taste in cake. Who knows what she'll like when it comes to other types of food. We may be doing the wedding guests a favor."

Annabelle couldn't agree more. She released Leo's arm and walked into the morning room where Tayla sat at a table, and a member of the catering staff stood beside the door.

Tayla looked up, her relief evident. "Oh good. You brought Leo." She motioned at the empty seat beside her. "We may need him to be our tiebreaker."

"Where are Isaac and his mother?"

"They should be along any minute." Tayla lifted two papers from a stack in front of her and handed one to each of them. "Here's the list of what we're sampling today."

They both took the offered menus, and Annabelle sat beside Tayla.

When Leo took the spot beside Annabelle instead of on the other side of his sister, Tayla leaned forward so she could see Leo. "How did Annabelle get you to come today?"

"Why do you think Annabelle had anything to do with me being here?"

"Because I know how much you hate this stuff." Tayla cast a knowing look at her brother before focusing on Annabelle. "You usually bribe one of us to bring you leftovers. Like yesterday."

"I didn't bribe anyone."

"That's true," Annabelle said. "I took him the cake samples voluntarily."

"I'm glad you did. The last thing I want is a coconut cake when half the family doesn't like it."

"I still think you should have considered at least one option with chocolate," Annabelle said.

"There wasn't any point since I don't like chocolate and Isaac doesn't eat it because of his acid reflux." Tayla tapped on the bottom of Annabelle's menu. "Be glad we're willing to add a dessert to cater to the chocoholics in the family."

"This chocolate torte does look good," Leo said, as though they hadn't already chosen that as their favorite.

Tayla's phone chimed with an incoming text. She read it and set her phone aside. "It looks like Isaac's mother is running a few minutes late, and Isaac has some fire he has to put out at work. He said to start without them."

The server waiting by the door stepped forward. "Shall we bring in the first selections?"

"Yes, please, but let the caterer know that we'll have two more coming a few minutes late."

He bowed his head. "Yes, Your Highness."

Annabelle lowered her voice and leaned forward. "Maybe if we're quick, we can make all the decisions before they get here."

"Isaac will be easy," Tayla said. "He likes almost everything."

"Except chocolate."

"Yes, which is surprisingly refreshing."

"You're both missing out," Annabelle said. Although with the way her stomach had turned queasy, perhaps overindulgence of chocolate wasn't advisable.

Sampler plates with appetizers came first. Annabelle took tiny bites of each one as the caterer described the various selections. After she, Leo, and Tayla noted their top choices, they moved on to the next set of options as the grandfather clock in the hall chimed the half hour. They were halfway through the breads when Isaac walked in.

"Sorry I'm late." He put his hand briefly on Tayla's shoulder before he took his seat. "What did I miss?"

"The appetizers and salads." Tayla slid a menu toward him.

Mrs. Vega entered in a rush. "I'm dreadfully sorry I'm late."

"It's okay, Mom." Isaac stood, as did Leo. "I only just arrived myself."

New plates were brought out for Isaac and his mother, first with the breads so they could all discuss the options together and then the appetizers and salads.

While Isaac and his mother discussed their favorites with Tayla, Leo leaned close to Annabelle. "Is it bad that I'm relieved to have a break from eating?"

"I feel the same way," she whispered back.

A fish course, then chicken and beef options. By the time the desserts were brought in, Annabelle wanted to go find a nice stretch of beach somewhere to walk off all those calories.

"These all look amazing." Tayla dipped her spoon into a red-and-white pudding concoction.

Annabelle lifted her spoon and put it back down again. If the non-chocolate desserts were anything like the chocolate ones, it wouldn't matter what Tayla and Isaac chose.

Beside her, Leo cut off a piece of a cheesecake square but didn't eat it. He leaned closer. "I can't eat another bite."

"Me neither."

Tayla pointed at her plate. "I like the cherry parfait and the cheesecake squares the best."

"I'm good with those," Isaac said.

"Great. If we add a chocolate option, that should work," Tayla said.

"Now that my part is done, I really need to get back to work." Isaac stood. "Will you all please excuse me?"

"Of course," Tayla said.

"I should be going too." Isaac's mother stood as well.

After the goodbyes were said and Isaac and his mother left, Tayla motioned to the chocolate delicacies in front of them. "Which one should we do?"

Annabelle and Leo looked at each other.

"The chocolate torte," Annabelle said.

"The chocolate mousse," Leo said in the same moment.

Annabelle widened her eyes and gave Leo a pointed look. "I thought you said you liked the chocolate torte the best."

"Oh, right. The chocolate torte it is."

Tayla leaned closer to Annabelle. "You haven't even touched your samples."

"Sorry, Tayla, but if I eat anything else, I'm going to be ill."

"Me too."

"Well, someone needs to try them."

Annabelle opened her mouth to confess that they already had, but the caterer spoke first.

"Perhaps we can ask the opinion of your royal chef. He would most certainly be able to make an educated suggestion."

Taking the lifeline the caterer had thrown her, she glanced at Leo. "That's not a bad idea."

Leo nodded. "We can do that."

The head caterer instructed one of his staff members to go to the kitchen to make the request for Duran to join them.

Moments later, Duran walked in, a scowl on his face. "You needed something?"

"Yes." Tayla motioned to Annabelle and Leo. "These two are too full to try the desserts. We hoped you would help us decide on the best chocolate one."

"I see." Duran narrowed his eyes.

For a moment, Annabelle suspected he was about to share the exact circumstances in which she and Leo had overindulged today. Instead, he sat beside Leo.

"Pass me the samples."

Leo slid his plate to him, and a staff member stepped forward with a fresh set of utensils.

He spooned a tiny bite of chocolate mousse from the glass dish and took a bite. He lifted his eyebrows, his only outward sign of approval. Switching to his fork, he cut off a bite of chocolate torte that was a third the size of what would be considered normal. This time, the sample earned a slight nod.

One by one, Duran proceeded to taste the other four items on the tray. Finally, he set his fork down. He pointed at the chocolate torte. "That one."

"Then that does it." Tayla pushed back from the table and stood. "Thank you, Duran. I appreciate you helping us."

"It was my pleasure." Duran stood as well, but he barely made it upright before he grabbed the back of his chair as though he couldn't quite find his equilibrium.

"Are you okay?"

"Yes, I—" That was as far as he got before he gasped for air.

"What's wrong?" Annabelle stepped forward.

When Duran dropped back into his seat, Leo shouted to the guard stationed at the door. "Call the doctor!"

Within minutes, one of the royal physicians rushed into the room.

Leo stepped back beside Annabelle.

Tayla pushed forward. "Is he going to be okay?"

Leo never took his focus off Duran. "I don't know."

CHAPTER
24

Leo stood at the edge of the morning room, Annabelle still by his side. Duran had already been transported by ambulance to the nearest hospital, the doctor accompanying him. The moment the doctor discovered how suddenly Duran became ill, the police had been called. Now the forensics team from the local police department were going through the food and silverware with great care, bagging and labeling each of their plates, the contents included.

Another team was currently scouring the kitchen for clues, while several police officers interviewed the catering staff as well as the kitchen and serving staff.

The whole scene could have been straight out of a crime show.

"They think he was poisoned." Annabelle's arms were folded across her chest, her hands gripping her arms.

"I know." That fact was far too apparent, as was the reality he didn't want to face. Had he not joined Annabelle in the kitchen before the tasting, he and Annabelle would be the ones in the hospital right now instead of Duran.

"You don't need to stay here," Leo said, his gaze still fixed on the forensics team in front of him. "You should go upstairs with Tayla."

"Tayla is with Isaac," Annabelle said. "He came back right after he heard what happened."

He looked at her now. "I don't want you to have to deal with this."

"That could have been us." Tears glistened in Annabelle's eyes.

His body stiffened. Hearing the words spoken aloud was way worse than thinking them.

"Do you want to take a walk?" She angled her head toward the gardens. "It would do us both some good to get fresh air."

What he needed right now was some time alone, time to process what had happened. Maybe this was all a big mistake. Duran could have had some sort of medical condition they were all unaware of. It might have even been a heart attack that didn't manifest itself in the expected ways.

"Leo." Annabelle reached up and touched his cheek. "Come on a walk with me."

Still not able to form words, he nodded.

Annabelle dropped her hand and signaled to her guard, who was standing nearby. Rocco escorted them out the door.

They stepped onto the terrace and continued down the wide steps to the path leading to the gardens and the ocean beyond. A police officer stood near the corner of the palace, and the number of guards outside had increased since this morning.

They continued into the gardens, Rocco trailing behind them at a discreet distance.

"How much time do you think passed between when we left the kitchen and when the caterer brought the desserts out to us?"

Leo cleared his throat in an effort to shake himself loose of the emotions clogged there. "I don't know. An hour. Maybe a little more."

"If Duran really was poisoned, that hour had to be when the poison was added to whatever dessert it was in."

Annabelle's logic was sound. "It couldn't have been earlier," he agreed. "Otherwise, we would have gotten sick."

"There's something else that's bothering me."

"I have a whole list of things bothering me right now."

Ignoring his comment, Annabelle pressed on. "Duran only sampled the chocolate desserts."

"So?"

"So Tayla doesn't eat chocolate. That's widely known among our friends."

"It's possible all of the desserts on my plate were poisoned," Leo said. "I didn't try any of them."

"Maybe, but that still proves my point. This poisoning appears to have been aimed at you, not Tayla."

Fear and frustration warred within him. "First a bombing attempt. Now someone tries to poison us," Leo said. "Maybe we've been looking in the wrong direction this whole time."

"How so?"

"What if another country is behind these attacks?"

"For what purpose?" Annabelle asked. "Your relations with all the neighboring countries are stable. You're the heir, not the king, so why go after you? And if the bomb was intended for Tayla, what would killing her accomplish?"

Though he couldn't comprehend the possibility of one of his cousins trying to eliminate him and Tayla to gain access to the throne, Leo could no longer ignore the possibility. "I need you to do me a favor."

"What's that?"

"Will you ask King Levi to conduct an investigation on my behalf?" Leo asked. "It would need to be done with great discretion."

Annabelle didn't ask who he wanted investigated. The look on her face indicated she already knew. "Levi has great skills in the art of protecting secrets. I'll call him when I go to my room."

"Thank you."

They continued to the far end of the gardens and stopped beside the rock wall that separated the gardens from the path leading to the Mediterranean.

Leo put his hand on the wall and stared out over the water. The tide washed up on the sandy beach below, waves crashing against the rocks a short distance down the shore. The peace and security the palace grounds always offered had been lost in that moment when the doctor had first mentioned poison, and Leo didn't know if he would ever feel safe again.

"How did your family do it?" Leo asked. "How did they find a way to feel safe again after your home was invaded?"

"It wasn't easy, but extra security and a lot of prayers can do wonders." Annabelle set her hand on the wall beside his. "More than anything, though, it takes time."

"Time won't solve anything if we don't find out who's behind these attacks."

"We'll find out who it is," Annabelle said. "Levi and Alan will help."

"Thank you."

She fell silent, and Leo's thoughts continued to race. The mere possibility of Sebastian or Rafael wanting him or his sister dead was far beyond the realm of comprehension. Guilt needled through him as he considered what he had asked Annabelle to do, but he couldn't go back now. He needed to know if there was any possibility his family could be involved. He needed to find a way to prevent this sense of invasion and the fear it invoked from ever reaching his home again.

Leo turned back toward the palace. "We should get back."

"You're probably right." Annabelle put her hand on his arm. "Just so you know, I'm glad you're okay."

"Thanks." He put his hand over hers. "I'm glad you're okay too."

- - -

Annabelle doubted her family would approve of her being alone with Leo in her private quarters, but the request he had made of her and her family was too confidential to risk even Rocco overhearing, and this was the only place she could securely contact Levi. Annabelle retrieved her laptop and set it on the coffee table. "Are you sure about this?" she asked Leo.

"We have to explore every possibility," Leo said grimly. "We can't afford not to."

"Okay." Annabelle sat on the couch. She hit the button to request a secure call with Levi. As soon as her brother-in-law came on the screen, Leo sat beside her.

"If you're hoping I have information about Duran, I'm afraid all I know so far is that they suspect cyanide poisoning."

"Cyanide?"

"The blood tests won't be back until tomorrow, but the police have already confirmed that cyanide was present in one of the items Duran ate."

"Do you know which item?" Leo asked.

"The chocolate mousse. Esteban should have the complete forensics report within the next few hours."

Chocolate mousse. A chill ran through Annabelle. Leo was right. He was the likely target.

"I'll check with him," Leo said.

"We actually were calling about something else," Annabelle said.

Levi instantly straightened. "Did something else happen?"

"No, but we need your discretion to do some research for us." Annabelle glanced at Leo.

She was giving him the option to move forward with his request or to withdraw it.

Leo took a deep breath. "Would it be possible for your intelligence service to conduct an investigation into my family, specifically Sebastian?"

"Do you have any reason to believe he might be involved?" Levi asked.

"No. We're simply trying to find a motive for why someone would want to kill either me or Tayla."

"You think today's attempt was directed at you."

Levi wasn't asking a question, but Leo responded anyway. "Yes."

"I'll put the request in, but can you tell me if he was at the palace today?"

"As far as I know, he hasn't been at the palace for the past three weeks."

"Can you have Esteban compile a list of everyone who was at the palace today during the time the poison could have been introduced?" Levi said. "If the person responsible wasn't present, then someone was paid to add the cyanide to the chocolate mousse."

"I'm sure he's already working on that."

"If you're willing to share those names, I'm happy to lend you extra resources to help in the investigation."

"Thank you," Leo said. "I'll let Esteban know."

"In the meantime, I'll look into your family," Levi said. "Discreetly."

"Thank you."

Annabelle ended the call and carried her laptop back to her room. When she returned to the living room, Leo stood beside the balcony doors, his gaze fixed on something in the distance.

Though she suspected she already knew the answer, she asked, "What are you thinking about?"

He didn't turn. "Remember when we used to play hide-and-seek in the gardens?"

"Yes. Your governess used to have a fit when she couldn't find us to come in for your lessons."

"We didn't have a care in the world except whether we would be able to play for another ten minutes."

"Someday your children will have the same luxury." She stared at the roses, remembering far too many times she had come too close to the thorns as a child. "All of this will be a bad memory that is nothing more than a reminder that the royal guard has a job to do."

"I don't know if we'll ever get to that point."

"You will." Annabelle stepped in front of him and put both hands on his shoulders. "I promise."

He lowered his gaze, and to her surprise, he pulled her into an embrace. Sensing his unexpected need for comfort, she drew him close and held on.

She inhaled the musky smell of his cologne and the underlying scent that was uniquely his. Leo's hand lifted to cradle the back of her head, and a shiver ran through her.

A knock sounded at the door, and Leo stepped back. He drew a deep breath as though gathering his strength. "I'll get it."

He opened the door, and Esteban entered.

"I'm sorry to disturb you, but I wanted to give you the latest update in person," Esteban said.

"How's Duran?" Annabelle asked.

"Alive. That's all I know so far."

Annabelle prayed he would stay that way.

"What have you learned?" Leo asked.

Esteban's already grave expression darkened. "The chocolate mousse was poisoned with cyanide."

Annabelle didn't mention her brother-in-law had already shared that detail. "Has there been any progress on identifying who gave the poisoned dessert to Leo?" she asked. "Someone on the catering staff must have been involved to make sure he was the one who received it."

"No, you don't understand," Esteban said. "It wasn't only Prince Leonardo's chocolate mousse that was poisoned." He paused and took a breath. "It was all of them."

"All of them?"

"Yes." He nodded. "The test of the remnants in the mixing bowl turned up negative for toxins, but every one of the dishes of chocolate mousse that was served at the tasting contained poison. The levels were high enough to be fatal."

"Duran only took a tiny bite," Leo said. "That may have saved his life."

And Annabelle's sweet tooth may have saved theirs.

CHAPTER

25

LEO APPROACHED HIS FATHER'S PRIVATE conference room, his guard joining the two already positioned in the hall. The early morning meeting request had come in the form of a text message, followed by a phone call from his father's executive assistant.

Leo entered to discover he wasn't the only one who had been summoned. Isaac and Esteban both already sat at the table, along with Rocco.

Everyone besides his father started to stand upon Leo's arrival, but he motioned for them to remain where they were. "Are we expecting anyone else?"

"No." His father gestured toward the door, and Leo closed it before taking his seat on the right of his father.

"Anything new from the hospital?" Leo asked.

"Duran is still in serious condition," his father said. "The doctors believe the next twenty-four hours will be critical."

Critical, as in determining whether their longtime chef and honorary family member would live or die. Leo's chest tightened painfully.

"I apologize for the last-minute request," his father continued, "but in light of yesterday's events, I've made some decisions concerning all of you."

The king looked at Leo first. "I believe it prudent to send you and Tayla away for a time, somewhere we can ensure your safety."

"If someone can get to us here, they can get to us anywhere."

"Which is why no one outside this room will know where you're going." The king focused on Isaac. "I realize going into hiding is not the ideal situation with your work, but I believe having you accompany my daughter will allow us to continue to shield her from the threats against her."

"Father, she was there when Duran collapsed yesterday. She knows something isn't right."

"I told her he had a heart attack," Isaac said. "I thought it best not to share the possibility that he had been poisoned."

"He was poisoned," Leo said simply. "And that poison was meant for me or Annabelle."

"Or Tayla," Esteban said.

Leo shook his head. "Anyone who knows enough about Annabelle to identify her luggage would also know that Tayla doesn't eat chocolate. And the only thing that was poisoned was the chocolate mousse."

His father lifted his hand. "That may be, but I'm not taking any chances. I want both of my heirs away from the palace until we can guarantee your safety."

"Where do you propose to send us?"

"Sereno," his father said.

Esteban looked from Isaac to Leo's father. "Perhaps it would be wise to separate Prince Leonardo and Princess Tayla."

"I could take Tayla somewhere on a private holiday," Isaac said.

"King Levi has put extensive security measures in place," Leo's father said. "I don't know of anywhere else that secure."

"What about Meridia?" Leo asked. "King Levi served as the chief of security at Prince Garrett's château for years. Surely, he could attest to whether the security measures would be up to your standards."

Rocco spoke now. "The château *is* where Queen Cassandra took refuge when her life was in danger several years ago."

His father fell silent, clearly contemplating. Finally, he nodded. "I will reach out to Prince Garrett about the possibilities." He turned to Leo once more. "As for you, you and Annabelle will depart tomorrow morning."

"What about you and Mother?" Leo asked. "We can't be certain you're safe here either."

"Esteban is putting extra precautions in place, and it will be easier for the royal guard to protect us when they are able to focus their efforts on only the two of us."

Though Leo didn't care for the directive, he asked, "What time does our flight leave?"

"A visit to the airport is likely to be noticed," his father said. "You mentioned going for a sail with Annabelle. That's exactly what you're going to do."

- - -

Exhausted after a sleepless night, Annabelle stood on her balcony, the sound of the surf competing with her sister's voice coming through the AirPods in her ears.

"Levi agrees with me. It's time for you to come home."

"The yacht isn't ready yet, and what if—" She swallowed hard. "What if the poison was meant for me?"

"Levi has already spoken to King Josep. He's making arrangements for you, Leonardo, Tayla, and her fiancé to sail tomorrow morning."

"We're sailing to Sereno?" Annabelle asked. "I've been on Leo's sailboat. That will be pretty tight quarters for a two-day journey."

"That can't be helped," Cassie said in her most regal voice. "Pack your bags. Rocco will load your belongings tonight. You'll have to limit yourself to a daypack for tomorrow morning."

"Fine." Sounded like a light makeup and ponytail kind of day. Another thought pushed to the forefront of her mind. "Are you sure that by me and Leo coming there, we won't be putting the rest of the family in danger? Maybe we should go somewhere else."

"No one will know you're here, but if it makes you feel any better, Alan and Victoria are going to stay at the resort for the next week or two to make sure we aren't all in the same place."

Protecting the heirs. Alan and Victoria would have to give up their apartment at the palace to protect the royal lineage of Sereno just as Leo traveling to her country would help preserve his family tree.

"Annabelle, everything is going to be okay."

"You can't be sure of that."

"I prefer to believe in the positive and expect it to come true," Cassie said. "The alternative is too dark a place to spend our time."

And Annabelle had spent far too many hours in the darkness, thinking about the what-ifs and pondering the what-will-happen-nows.

At least the directive from her sister had come with one bright spot. She wouldn't be returning home alone. "I'll pack my things."

"Good. Levi and I are looking forward to having you home."

"Thanks, Cassie. Love you."

"Love you too. Stay safe."

"I'll do my best." Annabelle squeezed the tip of one of her AirPods to end the call. She then removed both from her ears.

She wasn't sure how long she stood there, the wind tugging at her hair, before her attention strayed to the gardens and the man currently standing at the seawall beyond them.

Like her, Leo stared at the water, his need for solitude evident in his stance.

She should leave him alone, but she needed to talk to someone about her sister's plans. Maybe he needed to talk too.

- - -

Leo didn't know how he should feel. Or more precisely, he wasn't sure what he was feeling. He needed to talk to someone, but the only person who might understand his current dilemma was likely still asleep.

He glanced instinctively at Annabelle's balcony. It was empty, but Annabelle most certainly wasn't sleeping; she was walking toward him.

Leo blinked twice, certain he must be imagining things. "What are you already doing up?"

"It's seven thirty. I've been up for a while." She stepped beside him. "To be honest, I've been up all night."

"Me too." Leo leaned against the wall, his back to the sea. "You should have called or texted me. We could have gone for a walk or something."

"I was hoping you managed to sleep." She turned her gaze to the water. "I should have known better."

"Did you hear the new directive?"

Annabelle nodded. "I've been ordered to pack my bags. It appears we'll be going sailing after all."

"Yes. The arrangements are still being made for Tayla and Isaac. I think they'll end up at Garrett and Janessa's château."

"Meridia?" Annabelle asked. "I thought they were coming with us."

"Isaac had some reservations about all of us being together," Leo said. "I can't blame him. I'm not sure I want Tayla anywhere near me if I'm really the target." He shifted so he was facing her. "Come to think of it, I'm not thrilled with you being with me either."

She angled her body toward him and folded her arms. "You don't want me around?"

"Of course I want you around." The moment the words spilled out, he acknowledged the oddity of how true they were. "You've been surprisingly good company during your time here." His lips twitched upward when he added, "You must have outgrown your pesky stage."

"Or maybe you're the one who outgrew his annoying stage."

"Maybe." He shrugged. "That doesn't change the fact that I don't want you in danger."

"I don't want you in danger either, but like it or not, we still can't be sure who that poison was meant for."

"We know it wasn't intended for Duran."

Annabelle's brow furrowed.

"What?"

"Someone had to have gone into the kitchen after we left to put the poison in the chocolate mousse."

"We already figured that out," Leo said. "When I met with my father this morning, he told me they're putting the kitchen staff on extended leave, at least for everyone who was in the kitchen yesterday."

"Someone who wasn't working could also have slipped in. The staff members would easily be able to walk in without anyone thinking twice about it."

"That's true, but it's far more likely that it was a member of the catering staff," Leo said. "Everyone who works at the palace knows you come in early to sneak dessert. And I've been with you more often than not lately."

"So if they wanted to poison one of us, they could have done it when we were in the kitchen instead of when everyone else would be at risk." She shook her head. "And all of this brings us back to the question of who would want one of us dead."

"At least you know for sure it's not someone in your family who wants the throne." Just the thought of having his cousins investigated turned his stomach sour.

"Levi will be discreet."

"I know, and I truly can't imagine Sebastian wanting the throne, much less trying to kill me, but I'll be glad when we can eliminate him as a possibility."

"Let's not talk about this anymore."

"What do you want to talk about?"

"How about sailing?" Annabelle said. "Are you going to be the one at the helm, or am I?"

"Neither. At least not when we first set out," Leo said. "Saul is a worthy captain. He'll take the helm on our way out so we can be seen sitting on deck."

"Rocco can take a turn as well. All of our royal guards are adept sailors."

"It's certainly an advantage of living on the water."

"If our guards are taking on the responsibility of sailing us to Sereno, how are we going to spend our time?"

"I'll print out the reports on our current suspect list," Leo said. "Maybe we'll find something we've missed."

"We aren't going to spend our entire two-day journey staring at reports. What about bringing some games with us?"

"I'd say we could play backgammon, but you always cheat."

She arched both eyebrows. "How does one cheat at backgammon?"

"I don't know, but there's no other explanation as to how you always win." Leo leaned a hip against the seawall. "You must have loaded dice or something. No one gets doubles as much as you do."

"It's called luck," Annabelle said. "It just so happens I have a lot of it."

"After yesterday, I'd say we both do."

"You're right," Annabelle said. "I hope our good luck will last."

Leo reached for her hand instinctively and rubbed his thumb over the back of it. "Me too."

CHAPTER

26

ANNABELLE ANSWERED THE KNOCK AT her door, surprised to find Tayla on the other side of it instead of Leo, though why she would expect her best friend's brother instead of her best friend, she didn't know. After all, technically, she was here to visit Tayla.

Tayla strode into Annabelle's private quarters and closed the door behind her. "I want to know what's really going on."

Annabelle cringed inwardly. She didn't want to lie to her best friend, so she did her best to evade. "You were there. Duran collapsed, and he was taken to the hospital."

"The police don't come out for a heart attack." Tayla crossed to the seating area before whirling back around to face Annabelle. "And I'm not just talking about today." She held up her hand. "First, there was the fire at the dock, something that was supposed to be a minor issue, yet my father had me stay away from home for the night. And then you and Leo left early from the benefit, so early you didn't even get the chance to eat."

"How did you know that?"

"Because you didn't say a single word about the food," Tayla said. "And let's be honest, you love your food."

"Maybe you should talk to your parents about this. Surely they know more than I do."

"But you know something." Tayla dropped onto the sofa. "And they're not talking."

"I can understand your frustration." She'd experienced her own when Cassie had been shipped off to Meridia without her and Victoria's knowledge. Annabelle sat in the chair across from Tayla. "Have you considered that maybe your parents don't want to worry you?"

"I am worried." She sighed. "I know everyone is afraid I can't handle stress after what happened with Gonzalo, but I'm better now. Except for right after the false alarm with the intruders, I haven't needed to see my therapist for months."

"That's great."

"And you're changing the subject." Tayla leaned forward, her eyes pleading. "You're my best friend. Please, tell me what you know."

Annabelle wavered. Keeping Tayla in the dark had been easier than she'd expected, but only because she had spent so little time in her friend's presence.

"Annabelle, please." Tayla waved toward the ocean. "I'm being shipped off to Meridia tomorrow. It's only fair I know why."

"Tayla, I wish I knew more about what was really going on." That much was true.

"What happened to Duran?"

Annabelle lowered her gaze to the Aubusson rug at her feet and debated the crossroads before her. This was it. She could tell the truth and defy King Josep's directive, or she could lie.

"Annabelle," Tayla said. "Look at me."

Annabelle complied, the tension in her friend evident. She and Tayla's family were no longer protecting her. The lack of information was hurting her.

"We think he was poisoned."

"What?" Tayla stood. "Poisoned?"

"The tests showed there was cyanide in the chocolate mousse."

"Who would do such a thing?" Tayla paced the length of the room before turning back to face Annabelle. "If you or Leo had eaten that—"

"I know." Annabelle stood as well. "Neither of us got much sleep last night."

"And the reason you didn't eat at the charity event?"

"That may have been a false alarm," Annabelle said. "Security found an open door on the roof, and they didn't want to take any chances."

"Because something had already happened, hadn't it?"

Now Annabelle paced the room, only she moved to the balcony rather than the table. "Your father is going to kill me for talking about this with you."

"It won't be any worse than when we decided to take a detour to Rome and forgot to tell him."

"You're the one who didn't tell him about it," Annabelle said. "And your father expressly asked me not to tell you about—" Annabelle cut herself off.

"Tell me about what?"

She'd already violated the king's trust. Surrendering to Tayla's need for information, Annabelle forced the words out. "About the bomb that went off at the dock when I arrived."

"A bomb?" Tayla's eyes widened. "You've been here over a week and all this time you've been keeping this from me?"

"Yes, but partly because we thought Gonzalo might be behind it."

Her face paled. "Gonzalo's in jail. Isaac told me he was in jail."

"He can't hurt you," Annabelle quickly assured her. "But he isn't in jail. He's dead."

"When did this happen?"

"From what I've been told, the coroner thinks he was killed around the same time he was supposed to be transported to the prison," Annabelle said. "Then the person who we think made it look like Gonzalo was in jail was killed last Saturday."

Tayla lowered herself back onto the sofa. "All of this is making my head spin."

"Which is why no one wanted to tell you about what's been going on." Annabelle sat beside her. "We didn't want to worry you, and your family didn't want to risk you having more anxiety attacks."

Tayla put her hand on Annabelle's arm. "Thank you for telling me the truth. I needed to know." She shifted back on the couch. "And it makes me feel a lot better knowing you weren't trying to avoid helping me with the wedding."

"Of course I wasn't avoiding that," Annabelle said. "Leo and I have just spent a lot of time trying to figure out who might want to hurt one of us."

"I don't know why security would expect the two of you to be able to help with that."

Annabelle had given Tayla most of the facts, but sharing the possibility that someone close to them was a potential assassin was more than she could share. Rather than give more details, Annabelle said, "I think security was trying to distract us more than anything."

"Did it work?" Tayla asked.

"I'm not sure." Annabelle let her body fall back against the sofa cushions. "What am I going to tell your father when he finds out I told you the truth?"

"Maybe it's time to give him a taste of his own medicine."

"What are you talking about?"

Tayla shot her a conspiratorial smirk. "If we don't tell him, he'll never know."

- - -

Leo sorted through the printouts on his desk. Dossiers on the caterer and his staff, the latest security checks on the household staff here at the palace, yesterday's log from the gate.

All told, the printouts alone stacked six inches high, and that didn't include the latest updates on Annabelle and Tayla's friends, which were stored digitally on his laptop, or the report on his extended family, which he expected from King Levi in the next day or two.

He slid the files into the backpack he would carry with him when he boarded the sailboat tomorrow. He wasn't about to let this documentation be loaded onto the boat early and leave it unsecured.

Marcus entered his office. "Excuse me, Your Highness. Esteban wanted me to tell you the security team has completed the initial sweep of your sailboat. Federico and his dog will do another check before you depart tomorrow."

"Thank you."

Leo noted the time, already half past five. "You don't need to stay late. I'm nearly done here."

"Thank you, Your Highness." He bowed. "Enjoy your evening."

An evening spent packing for a journey of an indeterminate length, a journey Marcus falsely believed would only last for a matter of hours. "I'll touch base before I leave tomorrow."

Marcus nodded again and left the room.

Leo added his laptop and cell phone to his backpack, making sure he also packed the charging cords. Then he hefted the overly full pack onto one shoulder and secured his office.

He exited the outer office, trying not to dwell on the fact that he had no idea how long he would be away from home. His cell phone rang with an incoming call. He debated briefly whether it was worth it to dig his phone out of his pack but decided against it. He could return the call once he reached his apartment.

Taking a back staircase, he made his way to the family quarters. He turned into the main hall leading to his room and was surprised to find Annabelle standing outside his door, her guard at her side.

"What are you doing here?" Leo asked.

"You didn't answer your mobile or your office phone when I called, so I thought maybe you were here."

"You must have called right after I left."

"I need to speak to you." Annabelle glanced at Rocco before she added, "Privately."

He unlocked his door and held it open for her. As soon as they passed inside, he closed it, leaving their guards in the hall. Leo continued into the open space of his living room, pausing when he reached his favorite chair. Annabelle followed him as far as the sofa.

"I know this is an odd question to ask in lieu of all that's happened, but is everything okay?" he asked.

Annabelle linked her hands together in front of her. "Promise not to be mad?"

"Is this a 'I just broke your favorite toy' kind of question or a 'I got you in trouble without meaning to' kind of question?"

"Probably the latter." Annabelle lifted her gaze to his. "I told Tayla the truth."

"You did what?" Leo dropped his backpack onto his chair. "Why would you do that?"

"She knew something was wrong." Annabelle sat on the sofa. "I'm sorry, Leo. She came to my room asking for the truth. She'd already figured out that she was being misled about what happened to Duran, and she had guessed there was more she wasn't being told." This time when she lifted her gaze to his, there were tears in her eyes. "Tayla's my best friend. I couldn't lie to her."

"I'm the one who should be sorry." He sat beside her. "My family never should have put you in this position."

"For all we know, it could be someone trying to kill *me* who is putting your family in this situation."

The fact that she would think that after so many facts pointed to the contrary demonstrated just how rattled Annabelle was.

"We can't be sure of anything." Leo gestured to his backpack. "We have stacks and stacks of reports but nothing to prove who is behind this or why."

"Why does this keep happening to my family?" Annabelle asked. "First, Cassie. Then Victoria. It's like we're cursed."

"You're not cursed," Leo said. "And there's a reason why all countries go to extensive measures to protect their rulers. Inevitably, some crazy person thinks that eliminating someone at the top of the political structure will change their life for the better."

"Which is why none of this is making any sense."

And why Leo needed the report on his family sooner than later. Beyond them, he couldn't think of anyone who would benefit from his death. And no matter how hard he tried, he couldn't fathom a reason someone would want Annabelle dead. Surely a cosmetics line wasn't worth killing over.

"What exactly did you tell my sister?"

Annabelle replayed her conversation, right down to Tayla's promise not to tell their father.

"So now we're keeping secrets from my father about pretending to keep secrets from my sister." Leo shook his head. How had they come to this point? "Maybe it would be best to come clean with my father."

Relief shone in her eyes. "I was kind of hoping you would say that. I hate feeling like I'm lying to people."

"You never have been very good about keeping a secret."

"I think we've both done an admirable job at keeping secrets this past week." Annabelle tucked a lock of hair behind her ear. "Well, until today."

"Yes, until today." He stared at Annabelle, an odd kaleidoscope of the passage of time rushing through his thoughts. The little girl playing hide-and-seek in the rosebushes, the gangly twelve-year-old who wanted nothing more than to braid his sister's hair and play with makeup, the blossoming teenager who had attracted far too much attention from the boys her age, and now the lovely woman seated before him.

Something swelled inside him, as though his heart didn't quite have enough room in his chest.

"Leo?" Annabelle narrowed her eyes. "Why are you looking at me like that?"

"I'm sorry, but I have to do something." He lifted his hand to her cheek, her skin so soft beneath his touch.

Confusion lit her eyes. It shifted to awareness when he leaned closer.

"Are you about to kiss me?"

"I think so." He slid his hand around to cup the back of her neck. "Is that okay?"

"I don't know." The confusion was back, but she didn't move.

Several seconds stretched out, Leo giving her the opportunity to back away. Was he crazy to open himself up to her, to step into the unknown with a woman who was such an integral part of his life? He couldn't answer those questions, nor could he deny the attraction rising inside him.

When Annabelle remained where she was, their faces close, their breath mingling, Leo could no longer resist. He closed the distance between them, his lips pressing against hers.

He expected the jolt of attraction. After all, Annabelle was a beautiful woman, inside and out. With their long friendship, he might have even expected the rush of emotions. But when the jolt knocked him flat and the wave of emotions threatened to drown him, he didn't have any choice but to pull her closer and hold on.

CHAPTER
27

ANNABELLE'S BRAIN MIGHT VERY WELL explode. Every nerve ending tingled, and her stomach was riding a roller coaster with an unknown turn occurring every second. She was kissing Leo. She was kissing her best friend's brother.

She pulled back, her eyes wide, her face still close to his. She lifted her hand to his shoulder, unable to ignore his strength.

She blinked twice, searching for something intelligible to say, but before she could find words, Leo closed the distance between them again.

The second kiss rocked her even more than the first. It was as though the world was spinning so fast nothing else existed beyond the two of them.

Leo slid his free hand to her cheek, and a shiver worked through her. He changed the angle of the kiss, and a bevy of butterflies erupted in her stomach.

This time when he pulled back, his eyes clouded. He pressed his forehead to hers, and his breath came out in a rush. "Wow."

The fact that he could form any word was impressive. At the moment, her thoughts were an incoherent jumble of English, Spanish, and Italian.

Leo straightened, but his eyes remained on hers. He blew out an unsteady breath. "You are potent."

Something about his lack of composure settled her. "That's not something I've ever been accused of before."

"I—" Leo broke off. Then as though needing to draw upon her strength, he took her hand. "How did this happen?"

The confusion on his face would have been comical had she not been trying to sort out her own emotions. "Leo, you of all people know what happens when a man kisses a woman."

"But how did we get here?" Leo rubbed his thumb over the back of her hand, causing goosebumps to ripple over her skin. "When did you stop being my little sister's annoying best friend?"

When had things changed between them? Annabelle couldn't say when she had started to look forward to seeing Leo each day or even when being in his presence became a joy rather than a frustration, but she couldn't deny the connection between them when he kissed her, nor did she know what to do about it.

An errant thought pushed to the forefront of her mind. "You didn't break up with Chrishelle because of me, did you?"

"No." Leo laced his fingers through hers. "Chrishelle and I weren't right for each other. It wasn't until she was here that I realized that." He tilted his head toward the door, and his lips twitched into a half smile. "And Chrishelle never would have been able to get me to leave my office to eat desserts in the middle of the afternoon."

"Thank goodness I did." Annabelle shuddered. "I still can't believe we came so close to being poisoned yesterday."

"I'm surprised we haven't heard anything from the hospital yet."

"Maybe you should call," Annabelle said. Focusing on someone else would allow her time to sort out her feelings about what had just happened between her and Leo.

"You're trying to change the subject."

"I'd rather focus on Duran getting better than dwelling on what could have happened to the two of us had we eaten a second serving of chocolate mousse."

"That's not what I'm talking about." He lifted his hand to her shoulder and leaned in for another brief kiss. "What do we do about us?"

"I don't know. I never thought about there being an 'us' before this visit."

"I hadn't either." Leo paused. "At least not since we were teenagers."

"Wait." Annabelle leaned back. "You thought about dating me before?"

"Annabelle, from the time you turned fifteen, any guy with a pulse fantasized about going out with you." Leo rolled his eyes as though stating a fact she should have been acutely aware of. "You're gorgeous and sweet. And then you throw in that whole princess thing and you're quite the catch."

"But you hardly talked to me when I was a teenager."

"I was too old for you then."

"The age difference between us hasn't changed."

"No, but we're both adults now."

And the public would no longer condemn Leo for dating her. Annabelle didn't need him to say the words to know that thought would have been at the forefront of his mind, even when he was in his late teens. "The press has been so hard on you."

"Not lately. The public rather likes the idea of the two of us together."

"It isn't going to look good for my reputation when we sail off together and don't come back."

"Your safety is more important than your reputation." Leo squeezed her hand. "And if it will make you feel any better, I promise not to kiss you in front of any cameras."

He was expecting the opportunity to kiss her again. Did that mean he wanted the two of them to date for real? Even though she hadn't wanted to continue the relationship talk Leo had started, she needed clarity.

"How long do you expect this to last?" Annabelle asked. "Am I the Chrishelle sort, the type of woman who you'll date long enough to get the press buzzing about wedding bells, or are you expecting me to be another flavor of the month?"

"Annabelle, you will never be anyone's flavor of the month." He stood and drew her to her feet. "But maybe we should keep the changes between us to ourselves for a little while. I'm not sure I'm ready to tell my sister that I'm interested in her best friend."

"She can handle it."

"I know, but I'm not sure I can." He took both of her hands. "This is all new to me."

"What is?" She narrowed her eyes. "You've dated a lot of women."

"I know." Leo stepped closer and kissed her once more. "But none of them were you."

- - -

Leo escorted Annabelle into his parents' apartment, barely resisting putting his hand on her waist. An odd feeling had settled in his chest, like the warm anticipation of a little boy waiting for Santa Claus and then waking up on Christmas morning to discover all his wishes had been fulfilled and then some.

The scent of roasted chicken and vegetables carried on the air.

His father entered from the kitchen. "I was hoping that was you. Your mother said dinner will be ready any minute."

Leo focused on the table where six places were set. "Where are Tayla and Isaac?"

"Tayla's in the kitchen helping your mother. Isaac should be along shortly," his father said.

The lack of servants struck Leo, another reminder that their lives were not normal. His mother and sister cooking in the kitchen was proof enough of that.

Tayla entered carrying a platter with the chicken and vegetables on it.

His mother followed with a bread basket in one hand and a salad bowl in the other. "Dinner is served."

"Let me help you with that." Annabelle reached out and took the salad from his mother before clearing a spot in the center of the table so Tayla could put the platter down.

A knock sounded at the door, and Leo opened it to let Isaac in. "You're just in time."

Everyone took their seats, Leo positioned between Annabelle and his father.

"I'm sorry for the simple meal, but we haven't reopened the kitchen since Duran became ill." His mother dished some salad into her salad bowl.

"This looks wonderful," his father said, adding a roll to his plate.

"Has there been any news from the hospital this afternoon?" Tayla asked.

Leo's parents exchanged a worried glance. "Father, we all care about Duran. Please tell us how he is."

His father glanced at Tayla briefly before turning his attention back to Leo. "The doctors are optimistic, but Duran still hasn't regained consciousness except for a few brief moments."

"How much longer do they expect it to take for him to get better?" Annabelle asked.

"If he can start breathing on his own without the aid of a respirator, his prognosis is good." His father broke off a piece of his roll. "Unfortunately, only time will tell if he will recover fully."

A silence fell over them as the food was passed around the table.

Finally, Leo asked, "Have the final travel arrangements been made for Isaac and Tayla?"

"Yes. Tomorrow evening, they will be flown by helicopter from the palace to the airport in Marseille, where they'll be met by a private plane."

"Why wait until tomorrow night?" Leo asked.

Leo's father cast him a warning glance, a reminder that he was unaware of Tayla's recent knowledge about the attacks on their family.

Leo looked at Annabelle, silently asking permission to reveal the truth. He'd been prepared to address the topic personally, but Annabelle spoke first.

"King Josep, I need to ask your forgiveness."

"Annabelle." Tayla set her fork aside.

"It's okay," Annabelle said. "It's best we tell him the truth."

A faint scowl marred his father's face. "The truth about what?"

"Tayla came to my room today. She suspected Duran's condition wasn't a heart attack."

Now Leo's father set his fork down. "Exactly what did you tell her?"

"The truth." Annabelle shook her head slightly. "I'm sorry, Your Majesty, but not knowing was causing her so much stress, and I couldn't lie to her."

"I see."

"Don't blame Annabelle. I'm the one who pushed her to tell me everything." Tayla reached out and put her hand on her father's arm. "And I'm strong enough to know the truth."

The scowl on their father's face softened. "We were only trying to protect you."

"I know, and I know you thought I was in danger, but after yesterday, I think it's Leo we need to be worried about."

"Which is why he'll be leaving first," his father said. "And it will take a little more time to prepare for Tayla and Isaac's journey to Meridia."

"Why's that?"

"Prince Garrett insisted on sending his own pilots to bring Tayla and Isaac to their home," his father said. "It will take time for the helicopter to make the journey."

"Why aren't Tayla and Isaac flying directly from Alameda?" Annabelle asked.

"We wish to hide their eventual location from the media. The best way to do that is to have them flown to France first."

"Where everyone will assume they went for a holiday," Leo said.

"Precisely."

"What time do the two of you set sail tomorrow?" Isaac asked Leo.

"We'll leave at first light." Leo nodded at Annabelle. "Assuming this one can get up that early."

Annabelle lifted both eyebrows in the same way she always did when he teased her. "I'm sure I can manage."

"Good." He kept his tone casual, pleased that he had thus far managed to hide his changing relationship from his family.

His heart warmed at the thought they would spend the next two days together without the pressures of the outside world. Two whole days to explore what they wanted in their future and if that future included a relationship beyond friendship.

Tayla's voice interrupted his thoughts. "Annabelle, did you pack the backgammon game to take with you?"

Annabelle's eyes lit up. "As a matter of fact, I did."

"I'm doomed." Leo groaned.

Annabelle nudged his shoulder. "Yes, you are."

- - -

Annabelle couldn't remember the last time she'd been on dish duty, but she suspected it hadn't happened since the last time she and Tayla had used the daytime plates as bases when playing baseball in the yard with Leo and her sisters. She rinsed another plate and handed it to Leo. "I can't believe you volunteered to help with the dishes."

"Tayla helped make dinner." Leo dried the plate and set it on the counter. "I would have been asked to help if I hadn't volunteered."

Tayla walked into the kitchen carrying two glasses. "I think this is the last of them."

"Thanks." Annabelle loaded them into the soapy water. "We're almost done here. Did you want to talk wedding plans tonight? It may be our last chance to be together for a while."

"Thanks, but I think we're going to put a hold on making decisions until all of this craziness is behind us," Tayla said. "Isaac and I are going to go down to the theater room and watch a movie."

"Maybe—" Annabelle started.

Leo cut her off. "Have fun."

"Thanks." Tayla reached out and embraced Leo. "Be safe."

Leo held her close for a moment. "You too."

Annabelle dried her hands so she could give Tayla a hug too. "I'll miss you."

"We'll see each other again soon," Tayla said.

"I hope so." Annabelle released her. "And if you need anything, I'm sure Garrett can find a way for us to talk."

Tayla blinked rapidly as though fighting her emotions. She pointed at Leo. "Keep him out of trouble."

"I'll do my best."

Tayla turned and left them.

"Why did you interrupt me?" Annabelle asked. "I was going to see if we could join Tayla and Isaac."

"I know. That's why I cut you off."

"And your reason was . . . ?"

Leo set another dish aside and leaned close. "There's no way we'd be able to spend an evening with my sister without her noticing that we're—you know."

If he couldn't put a name on it, neither could she. Technically, Leo hadn't said he wanted to date her. "Actually, I'm not sure I do know." Annabelle washed the last glass and handed it to him. "You kissed me. I don't know what that means in your world." She shrugged. "It's not like I've dated that much."

"You had five different boyfriends during college."

"What? You were keeping track of my dating life?"

"Not intentionally." Leo opened a cabinet and put the plates in their proper spot. "You're my sister's best friend. She likes to talk about you."

Annabelle drained the sink and dried her hands. She waited until he put the rest of the dishes away before she asked, "So, what does it mean when you kiss a woman?"

"Typically, I don't kiss a woman until I start dating her."

"Are you telling me I'm an exception?"

"In more ways than I can count." Leo closed the last cabinet. "And technically, we are dating."

"How do you figure?"

"We went to the benefit together." He took a step forward.

"That was a favor to your father."

He took another step. "We've been spending a lot of time together."

"Looking for suspects in a bombing investigation."

He reached for her hand. "And I want to kiss you again."

"And that means we're dating."

"It depends."

"On what?"

"On whether you want to kiss me again too."

Her heartbeat quickened. She did want to kiss him again.

He leaned his head down, but before he could follow through with his intentions, his mother walked into the kitchen.

"Are you two about done in here?"

Leo stepped back. "We just finished."

"Thank you for your help." She crossed to them and kissed Leo's cheek. "We're going to miss you while you're gone." She kissed Annabelle's cheek as well. "Both of you."

"I hope to see you soon," Annabelle said.

They all walked into the living room.

"Father, will I see you in the morning?"

"No. I have a teleconference with the prime minister of Israel at six, but I thought we could go over some details on the mining enhancements tonight."

"Can it wait a bit? Annabelle and I were going to take a walk in the gardens."

That was news to Annabelle.

"I prefer to take care of it now," King Josep said.

"I'll see you tomorrow, then," Annabelle said. "Thank you for dinner."

"Safe travels," King Josep said.

Annabelle nodded and crossed to the door. Leo followed her. He reached for the doorknob but didn't turn it. Instead, he leaned close and whispered, "Just so you know, until you tell me differently, I'm going to assume you want to kiss me again too."

Annabelle couldn't quite suppress her smile. "I'll see you in the morning."

"At first light."

"I'll be there."

CHAPTER
28

LEO SLIPPED HIS BACKPACK STRAP over his shoulder and grabbed the small duffel with his other hand. His and Annabelle's luggage had been transported to his sailboat sometime during the night, and now he needed to look like he didn't have anything with him beyond sunscreen, a towel, and some snacks for their journey.

He walked into the hall where Saul already waited. "Are you ready?"

"Yes, Your Highness."

They made their way outside, the first fingers of light already breaking over the water. A steady breeze rippled the fabric of his T-shirt, the temperature low enough to make him grateful he'd tossed a jacket in his bag.

Saul led the way down the path toward the cove where the family's private dock was located. Unlike the spot where Annabelle's family's yacht was still moored, this dock was only large enough to accommodate the family's smaller personal vessels.

Trees lined both sides of the quarter-mile-long path, which was wide enough for the golf cart his father liked to use when traversing it. Leo should have borrowed the quicker form of transportation rather than following his usual pattern of walking.

Annabelle already stood on the dock when they arrived.

Leo stopped at the edge of the wooden planking and stared. Annabelle really was stunning.

Today, her hair was pulled back in a ponytail, a few loose tendrils framing her face. A sense of serenity exuded from her, though how she managed that in light of the events of the past week and a half was beyond him. "The security team should be finished momentarily," Saul said, apparently assuming that Leo had stopped to wait for them to complete that task before continuing forward.

Better his guard make that assumption than admit that the mere sight of Annabelle had stopped him in his tracks. "Thank you."

Annabelle turned, and her expression brightened.

Leo closed the distance between them. "Good morning." Unable to resist, he leaned down and kissed her cheek.

"What happened to not kissing me in public?"

"That wasn't a real kiss." Leo put his hand on her waist. "And there aren't any photographers around."

"No, but our guards are here."

"And it won't take them long to figure out we're a couple." He glanced at the oversized bag hanging from her shoulder. "I assume our luggage has already been stored belowdecks."

"Yes. I asked Rocco to double-check when we got here."

Federico and his dog appeared through the hatch leading to the sleeping quarters. They joined them on the dock.

"Everything looks good," Federico said. "Zeus didn't signal any problems."

"And we've had guards here since we stored your luggage," Saul added.

"In that case, let's set sail." Leo took Annabelle's hand to help steady her as she took hold of the standing rigging and stepped from the dock onto the boat. He followed her aboard.

"Your Highness, may I suggest you and Princess Annabelle go belowdecks until we clear the early morning boat traffic?" Saul said.

"Good idea." Leo opened the hatch for Annabelle.

As soon as they reached the living space, she sat at the table and set her bag down. "Do you want to play some backgammon?"

"As much as I know you're looking forward to beating me at that awful game, I thought we should look over the reports security gave us from the day Duran was poisoned."

"That doesn't sound nearly as fun, but we'll all feel better when we find answers."

"Agreed. There's just one thing I have to do first."

"What's that?"

An unexpected surge of nerves rushed through him, a sensation he hadn't experienced with a woman since his teenage years. Despite his unsteady footing, he took her hand in his. "I need to greet you properly." His gaze met hers, and he prayed his growing feelings for Annabelle were returned. He stepped closer, his gaze still on hers. "That is, if you don't mind."

She didn't speak for a moment, as though contemplating whether she was ready to step into the relationship he was offering. Then she tilted her chin up. "No. I don't mind."

- - -

Annabelle leaned back in the padded booth that surrounded the kitchen table and rubbed her eyes. For the past three hours, she and Leo had sat side by side, reviewing the various notes and reports regarding the bombing and the poisoning of Duran. And all the while the memory of their earlier kiss kept playing through her mind. Leo may have called her potent, but the term could easily be applied to him. And she was starting to realize she was very much in danger of falling for him.

Leo leaned his head back. "My eyes are going to fall out if I stare at this screen much longer."

"I know what you mean." She closed the file in front of her and slid out of the booth. "Do you want something to drink?"

"Sure." Leo pushed his laptop back. "I haven't found anything on the caterers. Not one hint of anyone who would want me dead, and if any payments were made, they hid them well."

"I'm having the same issue with my friends." Annabelle retrieved a bottled lemonade from the refrigerator for herself and an apple juice for Leo.

"Sounds like it's time to look at something else." Leo shifted the top file to the bottom. "Which do you want? The security logs from Tuesday or the file on Gonzalo?"

"I'll take the security logs." She handed him the juice and reclaimed her seat beside him. "Thinking about Gonzalo still gives me nightmares."

"Even though he's dead?"

"Especially because he's dead." Annabelle twisted at the top of her drink. When it didn't easily open, she handed Leo the bottle.

He took it from her, removed the lid, and handed it back. "Why would him not being around give you nightmares?"

"Just the thought that he was arrested, broken out of jail, and then killed is so outside the realm of normal that it scares me." She sipped her lemonade. "I mean, who would help him escape only to kill him? And then hide the body."

Leo shook his head. "If Tayla would have known Gonzalo was dead, she probably would have stopped having anxiety attacks way sooner."

"That's true, but it's not like anyone benefitted from her not knowing."

"And there was one bright side in all of this," Leo said. "Tayla wouldn't have met Isaac had it not been for his role in prosecuting Gonzalo. And thank goodness she did. He was a huge support for her when she was going through therapy."

Annabelle tapped a fingernail against the table. "Therapy that wouldn't have been necessary if it hadn't been for Gonzalo and the strain of having to testify against him."

"True, but talking about Gonzalo isn't going to get us closer to finding the truth." Leo pulled his phone from his pocket. "No service."

"Who did you want to call?"

"Esteban. I want to see if they have any updates on Duran or who poisoned him."

Annabelle waved toward the hatch. "You can use the radio."

"It's an open channel."

"Yes, but you can at least ask if they have anything new. No one will know the context of your question."

"It's better than nothing." Leo leaned over and gave her a quick kiss.

The simplicity of the gesture struck her. Only a day ago, he had kissed her for the first time, and now they were acting like a couple who had been together for years.

Leo headed for the stairs. "I'll be right back."

Annabelle waited until he left before she lifted her fingers to her lips. An almost uncomfortable sensation started in her chest, a yearning for something unknown.

She had loved Leo her whole life, but as a friend. Was it possible those feelings could expand into the kind of love her sisters had found?

She shook that thought away. Leo had kissed her a handful of times. That didn't mean he planned to offer her a happily ever after. And they had work to do.

After locating the log from the front gate, she scrolled through the list until she reached Isaac's name. He'd come late to the tasting, yet according to the log, he had arrived with plenty of time to not only be on time, but to be early. So where had he been?

Leo's earlier comment repeated in her mind. Had it not been for Gonzalo, Tayla and Isaac never would have met. And while Tayla had no interest in becoming queen, that didn't mean her intended husband hadn't found a way to give her that role so he could rise to a ruling position beside her. As the facts clicked into place, she scrambled out of her seat and rushed to the stairs.

She emerged above deck as Leo was heading toward her.

They both spoke at once, their words almost in unison. "We have a problem."

CHAPTER

29

LEO'S DISCOVERY THAT THE RADIO wasn't working took a backseat to whatever had caused the look of alarm on Annabelle's face. He turned away from the two guards to face Annabelle more fully. "What's wrong?"

"It's Isaac." Annabelle ignored Saul and Rocco and gripped Leo's hand. "Leo, he arrived over an hour before the tasting, but he was late."

The implications crashed over him. "You think he tried to poison me?"

"We kept looking at who would benefit if you died." She squeezed his hand. "Isaac is about to marry the person who is second in line to the throne."

"Second behind me." His insides withered as a new realization surfaced. "Isaac knew that I was picking you up at the dock."

"For all we know, he could have arranged for the meeting with his mother to happen at that exact time to make sure it was you instead of Tayla on the dock." Annabelle gestured to the radio. "We need to let your father know before Tayla and Isaac leave for Meridia."

"We can't. The radio is broken."

"Oh, no." Annabelle's eyes widened. "We finally have a solid suspect in mind, and now we have no way to contact anyone?"

Leo turned to Saul, who currently stood at the helm. "Turn about. We're going back to Alameda."

Saul complied, Leo and Annabelle assisting as he reversed course.

As soon as they were headed back toward his home Leo asked, "Was the radio working when we left?"

"We checked it yesterday when we did our initial security sweep," Saul said.

"What time was that?" Annabelle asked.

"Six o'clock." Rocco used a screwdriver to open the control panel.

"Was a guard posted at the dock at that point?"

"Only our usual guard at the top of the path and the coastal patrol out on the water," Saul said. "We didn't want to draw any attention to our preparations in case someone on staff was involved with the assassination attempts."

Assassination attempts. On him.

As though sensing where his thoughts had gone, Annabelle put her hand on his shoulder. "This will be over soon. Assuming we can prove our theory."

"We have a four-hour trip back," Leo said. "Now that we know what to look for, we have a much better chance at finding proof."

"I'll get started." Annabelle headed back below deck.

Several minutes passed, Rocco working on the radio without success. Finally, he looked up. "I'm sorry, Your Highness. It's no use."

"We have some handheld radios in the emergency kit," Saul said.

Rocco straightened. "Those won't do us any good until we're within thirty miles or so of another vessel."

And they had deliberately taken a route outside the typical shipping lanes to avoid being seen. Leo's sense of urgency competed with a sense of helplessness. He had to do something. "Grab them anyway." Leo took over the helm. "We can at least see if someone can relay to my father that our radio is down."

"I'll be right back." Saul disappeared below deck.

The wind shifted, and Leo adjusted the wheel. When the boat didn't respond as quickly as he expected, he turned the wheel further, adjusting his weight to compensate for the tilt of the boat.

Saul returned with a handheld radio. "I tried calling out. No luck."

"Keep trying." Leo signaled to Rocco. "Take over for me. I'm going to help Annabelle search for proof."

Rocco took his place.

"I left one of the radios with Princess Annabelle. We'll radio you if we get through to anyone."

"Thanks." Leo stepped back. "Also, the boat's slow to respond. Did you notice anything on our way out?"

"She was a bit sluggish when I came about, but that's the first time I noticed."

"There might be something off with the rigging. We'll need to have it checked out when we get back to port." Leo continued belowdecks and joined Annabelle at the table. "Any luck?"

"Yes, but not in the way I expected." Annabelle adjusted her laptop so he could see the screen. "Look at Gonzalo's bank account."

Leo skimmed over the deposits and withdrawals. A deposit every other week of three thousand euros and random purchases for typical items: groceries, restaurants, rent, mobile phone service, an occasional hotel. "I don't see anything unusual."

"According to the court records, Gonzalo was working as a freelance photographer."

"That sounds right."

"So why was he getting paid so consistently and always for the same amount?"

"Maybe he was only working for one client during that time."

"That was my thought too," Annabelle said. "And then I noticed when those payments started."

"When?" Leo pushed out of his seat so he could look over her shoulder.

"Three weeks before Tayla had her first run-in with Gonzalo." Annabelle pointed at the screen. "From that point on, he received regular payments, all the way through until he was convicted."

"Even after he was arrested?"

"That's right." Annabelle scrolled through the bank statements and showed him the final one. "He was in jail for five months awaiting trial, and that whole time, he was still receiving payments."

A stone dropped to the pit of his stomach. "Any idea where those payments came from?"

"A numbered account in the Caymans."

Now his chest tightened, and Leo clenched his fists. "Isaac and his mom go scuba diving in the Caymans a couple times a year."

"I don't know how hard it would be to prove who owns that account, but as absurd as it seems, I think Gonzalo was being paid to harass Tayla."

The stressful months of Tayla being stalked replayed through his mind. Gonzalo's initial harassment outside her favorite dance club, the disturbing notes left on her car, the messages taped to the door of her flat. All of those moments when Leo had felt helpless to protect his sister, and all of them had been caused by the man who was supposed to love her.

"These hotel charges. Check the dates against where you were on those days."

"That was over three years ago."

"Yes, but knowing you, you still have your old boarding passes and hotel receipts stored in the wallet app on your phone."

"It's scary how well you know me." Annabelle opened the app on her phone. "What's the first one?"

"February 19th."

"Tayla and I were in Austria. We went skiing with a few friends."

Which matched Gonzalo's hotel reservation. "How about March 7th and 8th?"

"I was in Paris."

"With Tayla?"

Annabelle looked up. "Yes."

Another match. "How about the week of March 20th?"

"That was spring break," Annabelle said.

"I'm guessing you and Tayla spent it in Vienna."

"Yes." She gestured at her laptop. "It makes sense that Gonzalo would have hotel charges on all of those dates. We knew he was following us around. That's what freaked Tayla out so much. Everywhere we went, he showed up."

"Yes, and if you look at these deposits at the end of every month, they're enough to cover all of Gonzalo's travel costs." Leo leaned back in his seat, the pit in his stomach now a gaping hole. "I think you're right; Gonzalo was being paid to stalk Tayla."

Annabelle's horror was reflected in her eyes. "And he wasn't caught until two weeks after Tayla met Isaac."

"My guess is that Gonzalo got caught on purpose to keep Isaac at the forefront of Tayla's attention."

"That's sick."

"Yes, it is." Leo's heart ached for his sister. "And the worst part is that it worked."

Sympathy shone on Annabelle's face. "Poor Tayla."

"Yeah. Poor Tayla."

- - -

The more Annabelle dug into Gonzalo's past, the more convinced she became. Everything in the man's background suggested he was a small-time photographer subsisting on whatever photos he could catch of the royal family. And as such, he was in the perfect position to know their habits and have contacts within the media network to gain whatever information he needed.

The photographs of the royal family discovered in his apartment after his arrest hadn't shown the expected outward obsession with Tayla, but rather had run the gamut of photos of Annabelle and Tayla together to long-range shots of Leo and his father to the queen at brunch with friends.

"As soon as we get back to the palace, I need to call Levi," Annabelle said. "I think he might be able to pull in a favor to find out who that offshore account belongs to."

"And while you do that, I'll make sure Tayla is well away from Isaac."

"What do you think Tayla's going to do when she finds out?" Annabelle asked.

"I don't know, but it may be a good thing you told her about the assassination attempts," Leo said. "I'm not sure she'd be able to handle this new information without knowing something was already going on."

"This is going to break her heart," Annabelle said. "She is so in love with Isaac."

"He fooled us all." Leo shook his head. "We were even making plans to go skiing together next winter."

"Making plans with the person he wants dead . . ." Annabelle couldn't imagine.

"I intend to be very much alive when ski season arrives, and by then, Isaac will be behind bars, Tayla will have survived another round of counseling, and the three of us can go skiing together."

But would they go skiing as friends, or was it possible she and Leo would be a couple six months from now? "How are we going to break the news to Tayla?"

"I don't know." Leo shook his head. "She's never had such a public relationship before. Spinning a story for the press that protects her isn't going to be easy, especially once everyone realizes that Isaac is behind bars."

"This is all making my head spin."

"Mine too." He shifted in his seat so he was facing her. "And I have no idea how she's going to feel about the change in our relationship." He furrowed his brow. "Maybe we can wait to tell her until we go on our next ski trip."

No longer able to hold back her thoughts, Annabelle said, "Ski season doesn't start for another six months. You really expect us to last that long?"

"Six months isn't that long."

"Leo, you've only had two girlfriends who lasted longer than six months. Chrishelle and Felicia."

"Felicia and I broke up months before the press got wind of it," Leo said. "She liked the idea of being my girlfriend more than she liked me."

"You're only emphasizing my point," Annabelle said. "I can't remember a time when you weren't a part of my life. I'd like to think that even if your feelings change for me, we'll still be friends, and that we'll find a way to make it so we aren't awkward around each other."

"Already planning our breakup?" Leo asked. "We've only been together for a day."

"I'm telling you you're important to me, whether you're my boyfriend or my best friend's brother. I don't want to jeopardize the past twenty-something years because of how things have changed over the past few days."

Leo pushed the laptop back on the table and shifted so he was facing her. "You know what's even scarier than my sister's fiancé trying to kill me?"

"What's that?"

"I can't see the end for us."

The tone of his voice indicated he was completely serious. The look in his eyes only confirmed Annabelle's assessment.

"Why is that scary?"

"I've always been able to see the end." He gestured toward the stairs. "Even with Chrishelle, even when everything was going well, I knew things would end eventually."

"Since you're the one who typically initiates your breakups, that's not surprising."

"Yes, but I can't imagine ever wanting to break up with you."

Annabelle cocked an eyebrow. "Is this a line you feed all your girlfriends?"

"It's not a line." Leo reached out and took her hand. "And I've never said that to anyone else."

The combination of Leo's words and the intensity of his gaze left her speechless.

He rubbed the back of her hand with his thumb. An overwhelming need to protect rushed through her along with an uncomfortable sensation that might be love. Not prepared to analyze her feelings, she leaned in for a kiss.

She should have expected the fireworks that shot through her every time her lips met Leo's, but the thrill was every bit as powerful as the first time he kissed her. She lifted her hand to his shoulder, vaguely aware of an odd hissing sound.

She pulled back to make sure they were still alone, and her gaze swept over the room.

Leo leaned in for another kiss, but before he could follow through with his intention, Annabelle looked toward the source of the sound.

Beneath the rear stateroom door, the carpet had darkened, and a trickle of water flowed into the room.

"Leo!" Annabelle pushed against his shoulder and pointed. "We're taking on water!"

Leo closed his laptop and hastily stacked the paperwork. "Tell the guards."

"What are you going to do?"

"I'm going to see how bad it is."

"Be careful."

He gave her a quick kiss. "I will."

CHAPTER

30

LEO'S SHOES SQUISHED AGAINST THE wet carpet as a steady stream of water seeped beneath the door. He opened his stateroom door and took in the scene before him. A half inch of water covered the entire room. A circle of wood about the size of a two-euro coin floated a short distance from him.

He plucked it up. It was several centimeters thick, and if he were to guess, he suspected the thickness was an exact match for the wooden hull of his boat.

Ignoring the wetness seeping into his shoes and socks, he moved to the side of his stateroom that followed the shape of the outer hull. He leaned down and ran his hand along the base of the wall, searching for a hole the size of the wooden plug he'd found. He barely started his search when a surge of water rushed into the room, another circle piece of wood shooting to the surface.

Leo hurried to the spot where it had appeared from and reached down to run his hand along the base of the wall again. It only took him a moment to find what he was looking for. A perfectly round, three-centimeter hole.

Sabotage. The word erupted in his mind. There was no way a hole like this could have occurred naturally, and certainly not more than one. Despite all their efforts to ensure his and Annabelle's safety, they had failed.

Rapid footsteps approached.

Annabelle's voice followed. "What can we do?"

Leo leaned down and tried to plug the wooden disk into the nearest hole, but the wood had already swelled too much to fit into the space. He spared Annabelle and Saul a quick glance. "Saul, check the other staterooms, and break out the life raft. Annabelle, grab me something to plug this hole."

They both disappeared. Annabelle returned a moment later and handed him a towel.

"How many holes are there?"

"I don't know." Leo stuffed the edge of the towel through the hole, plugging it the best he could. He straightened and held up one of the wooden plugs. "This is how big they are. We need to plug the holes and bail out as much water as we can."

Saul's voice carried to them. "Rocco, get down here!" He then rushed into Leo's stateroom. "The life raft has been shredded, and we're taking on water from both of the forward staterooms."

No life raft and taking on water. Leo's pulse kicked up another notch.

"I'll check my room." Annabelle slid past Saul.

Saul left, his voice carrying again, clearly speaking to Rocco. "Grab a bucket. We've got to get some of this water out of here."

Leo found a second hole. He pulled the comforter off his bed and shoved the corner of it into the hole. He kept going.

The water kept rising, now ankle deep.

The extra shirt from his bag plugged the next hole. His swim trunks the one after that. Another wooden plug popped to the surface.

Leo snatched a pair of socks and crossed to the spot where he suspected the new leak was coming from. With the rising water level, this one took longer to find. After several seconds, he located it and pushed one of the socks into the hole. When that didn't fully plug it, he added the other one.

Annabelle returned a moment later. "This isn't working. The fabric is slowing the leaks down, but it isn't stopping the water completely."

With a sense of urgency rushing through him, he waded out of his stateroom and entered the common area. Water covered the entire floor.

At the rate the water was rising, the paperwork and laptops on the table would be soaked within another fifteen to twenty minutes.

"Annabelle, get all of our files and take them abovedeck. Store them in the portside locker," Leo said. "And while you're up there, check our heading and see if you can raise anyone on the radio."

"Our files aren't going to matter if the boat sinks."

"We don't want to take any chances. Isaac could destroy the gate logs, and no one will ever know the truth."

"Fine." Annabelle grabbed her oversize bag and stuffed the files and their laptops inside.

Leo continued past the table to the forward compartments. Because they were so much smaller, only large enough to accommodate a single bunk, they were filling fast.

Rocco rushed past him with two buckets filled with water.

"How far are we from shore?" Leo asked him.

"At least three hours." Rocco continued past him and headed up the stairs.

"We have to find a better way to plug these holes or we'll never make it back to land," Saul said.

"I know." And if they didn't make it to shore, he and Annabelle would perish at sea before they ever had the chance to explore a life together.

Not willing to give up, Leo said, "Keep plugging the holes and bailing water. There has to be something we can use to patch these holes better."

Saul's voice was tight when he spoke. "I'll do my best."

- - -

Annabelle knew what Leo was doing. He was trying to send her to safety, but the evidence was clear. The water levels were rising, and it was only a matter of time before the boat would sink.

She stored her bag in the storage compartment, not bothering to right it when it tipped over, a lipstick and a tube of moisturizer spilling out of the inner pocket.

She quickly closed the lid and grabbed the radio off the control console, then checked their heading. They were still on course, or close to it, but if the water continued to rise, it was only a matter of time before the boat's electrical system would be affected, including the navigation and autopilot systems.

Rocco emerged from the hatch, a bucket full of water in each hand. He emptied them overboard and headed back downstairs.

Annabelle turned her attention to the emergency radio and issued a distress call in every frequency without any luck. With nothing more she could do topside, she headed back down the stairs.

In the few minutes she'd been away, the water had risen by at least two inches.

"It's not working," Rocco shouted from her stateroom.

Annabelle took off her shoes and held them up as she stepped into the water that now came up to her calves. She set the shoes on the table as she passed by and continued into her stateroom, where her suitcases were now on the bed, one of them open. Rocco held one of her shirts in each hand before he leaned down and used one of them to attempt to plug another hole.

"How many holes are there?"

"There have to be at least thirty of them in this room alone."

The evidence to his statement was punctuated by the circles of wood floating in her stateroom.

"Any luck with the radio?" Rocco asked.

"No. We're still too far out."

Leo splashed up beside her. "Annabelle, you should stay up top."

"No. I want to help."

"The water is getting too high. We can barely reach the holes without going under." Leo pushed past her and focused on Rocco. "I think I've plugged the ones in my room. Which way are you going?"

Rocco grabbed more of Annabelle's clothing and tilted his head to the right. "I started over there."

Annabelle stepped out of her room. If she couldn't plug holes, she could help bail water. She rushed into the kitchen and opened cabinets until she found a plastic water pitcher. A large bowl was her next best option. She leaned down and dunked both below water. Then she tucked the bowl into the crook of her elbow, gripped the handle of the pitcher, and climbed the stairs.

When she reached the top, she barely avoided colliding with Saul, who had taken over bailout duty from Rocco.

"Sorry." She stepped past him and dumped the water overboard.

Saul headed back down the stairs, and Annabelle hurried behind him. She followed him up and down six more times, her arms and legs burning with exertion, the water level rising, centimeter by centimeter.

She splashed back downstairs and dipped her bowl into the water, but this time, she caught a sock in the bowl along with the water.

A ripple of panic rushed through her. If the items they were using to plug the holes were coming loose, there was no way they were going to make it back to shore.

Annabelle slogged her way to her room where Leo and Rocco were still attempting to plug holes. "The water pressure is pushing the clothes back out of the holes. We need something else to push in there."

Leo turned, his tension evident. "See what you can find." He plucked a wooden circle off the surface of the water and tossed it to her. "We need something that will fit in that without coming loose."

Annabelle glanced around the room, but the little desk was bare, and she knew from previous outings with Leo and Tayla that the built-in dressers and cabinets would be empty.

She unzipped her largest suitcase, pawing through her clothing. Maybe something with a large button would work. She grabbed a dress with oversized buttons up the front. "Try this. You might be able to use the button to help keep it in place."

Leo reached down, plunging the dress below the surface. He was barely able to keep his chin above water as he did so.

Annabelle kept looking. The dress pushed back to the surface.

"It's not working." Leo turned to Rocco. "Try the radio again."

Rocco nodded, the gravity of their situation evident on his face. "Don't let the water get above your waist before you come up."

"We won't." Leo grabbed the dress and tried again, this time ducking beneath the water's surface.

Annabelle shoved her case aside and unzipped the next one. More clothes. Her gaze dropped to her extra case. Her makeup case. Maybe . . .

She quickly unzipped it.

Leo surfaced, the dress popping up right beside him. "It's no use. The deeper the water, the higher the water pressure."

Annabelle grabbed one of her samples of moisturizer and held it up to the wooden plug. The cap was a couple centimeters wider, but the tube was pliable enough; it just might work.

"Where's your snorkeling equipment?" Annabelle asked.

"In the starboard-side locker."

Annabelle turned as Saul came down the stairs, empty buckets in hand. "Saul, grab masks and snorkels for us. I have an idea."

The guard nodded. He filled his buckets and hurried up the stairs.

Annabelle turned to Leo and held up a tube of moisturizer. "I think we can shove these into the holes."

"I'm willing to try anything." Leo didn't wait for the snorkeling equipment. He ducked back beneath the water, his air bubbling up beside him. He surfaced a moment later, hope shining in his eyes. "How many of these do you have?"

"About a hundred."

"I'm not going to ask why you have so many with you."

Nor was Annabelle going to explain that she'd brought enough to share samples with their friends at Tayla's engagement party that was supposed to take place next week. She simply handed him several more tubes.

Saul waded toward them, masks and snorkels in hand. "I have the equipment. Rocco said no luck on the radio."

Leo took a snorkel and mask from him. "Have him keep bailing. Annabelle, tell Saul what to do."

Leo quickly put on the mask and snorkel and ducked back beneath the surface of the water, tubes of moisturizer in hand.

Annabelle lifted a case that contained two dozen tubes and handed it to Saul, trading it for a mask and snorkel. "We're using these to plug the holes. If you shove it in with the narrow side first, it should let you push it in far enough to keep it from coming back out."

"I'll start in the forward compartments. You take the prince's stateroom. We need to work both sides at the same time or the boat will start to list."

Annabelle nodded and grabbed a case of product for herself. As she headed for Leo's compartment, she prayed this would work and they could move fast enough to keep the boat afloat.

CHAPTER
31

ANNABELLE'S IDEA WAS WORKING, BUT they had yet to plug enough holes to keep the water from rising. Leo slid another tube of makeup in place, surfaced to clear his snorkel, and pulled his body back down to feel for the next hole.

Rocco had turned off the power grid to protect them from possible electrocution, but while he appreciated that foresight, he didn't particularly like working in the dark. Currently, the window of Annabelle's stateroom was almost entirely underwater, in part because of the water in the boat and in part because the boat was currently heeled in that direction.

He plugged three more holes before surfacing to replenish his supply.

Annabelle appeared in the doorway at the same time. Her hair was drenched, her mask pushed up on top of her head, her snorkel dangling beside her mouth.

Though Leo wanted to ask how many she'd already plugged, there wasn't time for words. Instead, he handed her a box of makeup and grabbed another six tubes for himself.

He took a breath, slid his snorkel back into his mouth, and squatted down to search for the next leak to be stemmed.

He plugged four more holes before he reached the inner wall that separated Annabelle's stateroom from his.

He surfaced and grabbed more tubes, wading as quickly as he could into his room.

Annabelle was already upright, reaching into the box on his desk. "I'm almost done in here. Go help Rocco with the bailing. We have to get more of this water out of here."

Though it pained him to do so, Leo left her amidst the rising water and pushed into the living area. He spotted the water jug and bowl floating beside the table and grabbed both. These would hardly remove much water, but it was better than nothing.

Saul emerged from one of the forward staterooms.

"Have you finished with both?" Leo asked.

"Yes." Saul gave a quick nod. "There weren't as many up here."

Rocco came down the steps. He held out both buckets. "If you two are done with the repair work, I say we start a relay system to get this water out of here. It will be better than us fighting our way past each other on the stairs."

"I'll take down here," Leo said.

"You take the top," Saul told Rocco. "I'll get them up to you."

Leo filled the first bucket and handed it to Saul who had taken position halfway up the steps. He carried it up a few steps to Rocco before coming down to take the next one.

Empty buckets were passed down, full ones passed up.

The splashing behind him alerted Leo to Annabelle's presence before she reached his side. "I can help too. Where do you want me?"

"Go up top and take the helm. Steer us toward the shipping lanes."

"That isn't the fastest way back."

"I know, but if this doesn't work, it will give us a better chance of radioing for help."

"Okay." Annabelle waited until they were passing empty buckets back down to slide past Rocco and climb topside.

Leo kept bailing, his arms and shoulders tightening as he did so. He didn't want to think of the weariness the two guards must be experiencing. They had both taken turns hauling water up, two buckets at a time, by themselves.

Rocco reached for the next bucket and slipped, barely righting himself before tumbling down the steep stairs.

"Do you want to switch places?"

"I'm okay."

Leo dunked the bucket into the water to fill it, the back side of the bucket connecting with the floor. He handed the bucket up to Rocco before glancing behind him. He couldn't be sure, but it was possible the water level had finally lowered.

"I think it's working," Leo said, accepting the next empty bucket. "Let's go for another five minutes, and then we'll take a break."

"I don't know if we can afford to take a break," Saul said.

"Okay, you and Rocco can take turns at the helm, and Annabelle can take your place."

"You're going to have the princess bail out the water?"

"I think it's more accurate to say I'm not going to stop her from helping."

- - -

Annabelle dumped another bucket of water over the railing. After all three of the men had taken a rest, she'd convinced them that the process would go faster if they let her carry the water from the top of the stairs to the railing. They'd all been too weary to argue.

For more than an hour, they had worked steadily, the buckets now coming up only half to three-quarters full.

Only another ten minutes passed before Rocco stepped back from his spot at the top of the stairs to let Saul and Leo walk out onto the deck.

Leo rubbed at his right shoulder. "I say we call it good for now."

"How much water is still down there?"

"It's back to about ankle deep, but it's too hard to try to bail it out, and it's probably good to keep the water above the tubes of makeup since they seem to be holding." Leo put his hand on the railing to steady himself against the tilt of the boat. "That was brilliant, by the way."

"That was desperation." Annabelle adjusted her weight as the boat leveled. She glanced up. "We need to trim the sails. We're losing our wind."

Leo took the lead, ordering everyone on what was to be done. They adjusted the sails enough to increase their speed again, but the robust wind they had enjoyed earlier that morning had faded to a gentle breeze.

"Do we dare try engaging the motor?" Rocco asked.

"No. The water reached the battery panels. We don't want to risk it, especially with so much water still down there."

"What's our speed?" Annabelle asked.

"We're barely at three knots."

"At this rate, we won't get back to Alameda until after Tayla and Isaac leave."

"If Isaac's motives are what we think they are, Tayla's not in any danger."

"She might not be in any physical danger, but every minute she spends planning her future with him is another hurt she's going to have to endure when she finds out the truth."

"Annabelle, there's nothing we can do now."

Her gaze lowered to the buckets still on the deck by the hatch. They had survived a sabotage attempt, just as they had survived a bombing and the poisoned chocolate mousse.

"What now?" Annabelle asked. "Do you want me to keep trying the radio?"

"Yeah. Go ahead and do that." Leo motioned for Rocco to take the wheel. As soon as he did so, Leo moved to the storage compartment at the stern. He opened it and pulled out a cloth hammock. "Saul, go ahead and string this up downstairs. Then use it to take a rest."

"Perhaps you or Princess Annabelle should take a turn first."

"No. We didn't haul nearly as much water up those stairs as you and Rocco did." Leo grabbed a second hammock.

Annabelle stepped forward and held out her hands. "I'll hang this one downstairs for Rocco."

"I can do it."

"It's okay. I want to see how bad it still is down there," Annabelle said. "Besides, you're better at navigating than I am."

Leo handed the hammock over. "Thanks."

She carried it downstairs, the scent of seawater heavy in the humid space. Water rippled below, but with the light spilling in through the windows and skylights, she could now easily see the floor.

She held the hammock up to make sure it didn't get wet as she waded through the water that came just beyond her ankles. Since Saul had already taken his hammock into the forward stateroom, Annabelle stepped onto the couch and hooked the hammock into the two hooks that were mounted above it for just such an occasion. Or rather, for when an extra sleeping space was needed. Never in her wildest imagination had she expected to have something like this happen to her.

Suspecting she would spend the better part of their journey abovedeck, she waded through her room in search of sunscreen. She entered her stateroom, the evidence of the sabotage glaring at her in the form of makeup tubes sticking out of the bottom of the wall in twenty-centimeter increments.

She picked up one of the wooden pieces of the hull that had been carved out and ran her finger along the edge of the circle. She didn't know how long it must have taken to drill all these little circles and then secure them back in place, but one thing was certain: Isaac was brilliant in his efforts. Had it not been for his fiancée asking Annabelle to bring extra samples to share with their friends, she and Leo would be floating somewhere in the middle of the Mediterranean with little likelihood of ever being found.

CHAPTER

32

LEO SAT AT THE STARBOARD-SIDE helm, Annabelle at his side. She had donned a still-damp, gauzy, long-sleeved shirt to protect her arms from the sun, and a wide-brimmed hat covered her head. The two guards remained downstairs, hopefully sleeping, as the afternoon sun lowered in the sky.

The wind picked up a bit, and Leo adjusted the wheel to take advantage of it. He checked their speed. Four knots. Finally. Leo checked the compass, checked his navigation chart, and then checked his compass again.

"How's our position?"

"We should be good, but without the navigation system working, I can't be sure how close we are to the regular shipping lanes."

"As long as we're heading toward shore, I'm happy." Annabelle tipped the brim of her hat and looked up at the sails. "Of course, I'd be happier if we could pick up more speed."

"We're up to four knots. That's better than it was."

"It's still not fast enough."

"I know." The thought of his sister flying off in a helicopter with a murderer sickened him beyond description. He glanced at his watch. Only four more hours until she and Isaac were scheduled to depart.

Annabelle stepped behind him and put her hands on his shoulders. She leaned forward and kissed his cheek. "I'm sorry. I know you're as worried as I am."

"We both have reason to worry." He looked up at the sun on the horizon. A few more hours, and it would be dark. Once they lost the light, he wouldn't be able to use his knowledge of the coastline to get them home.

Annabelle rubbed at the tension in his shoulders, and Leo couldn't help but lean his head forward as she kneaded his tight muscles.

"That feels so good."

"It's supposed to." She massaged his shoulders for a minute longer before she moved back to his side. "I keep thinking about how much time it must have taken to drill all those holes in the side of the boat."

"It wasn't just creating the holes," Leo said. "It was making sure they stayed in place while we set out. Isaac must have used some sort of adhesive that wouldn't hold up long beneath the pressure of the water."

"Which is why we got so far away before we noticed a problem."

"My guess is he used his scuba gear and an underwater drill last night after dinner."

"But how did he get the equipment onto the palace grounds? When I was looking through the gate log, I didn't see him leaving at all after Duran was poisoned."

"Maybe he had an accomplice."

"After seeing what happened to Gonzalo, whoever that accomplice was should be worried he or she won't survive the next few weeks," Annabelle said. "From everything we've seen, it looks like he eliminates anyone who could possibly point a finger at him."

"No witnesses."

"Technically, we still don't have any witnesses," Annabelle said. "The only thing we have a chance at proving is that the payments to Gonzalo came from him."

And even that was a longshot. Circumstantial evidence. That's what Isaac would call it. And he had the legal knowledge and experience to twist the story to suit his purposes. "Do you think Tayla will believe us, that Isaac was behind all of this?"

"I don't know." She sat in the second captain's chair. "She absolutely adores him. He was the person she trusted when her whole world was falling apart."

"And now we know he set her up to have her world fall apart." Leo shook his head. "I always thought I was a good judge of character, but I never suspected a thing."

"None of us did." She leaned back in her seat and pulled her feet up to the edge of it, her arms looped around her knees. "I think we were all so grateful someone could be there for her that we saw what Isaac wanted us to see."

"That's exactly what happened." Guilt welled inside him. "I didn't want Tayla's problems to interrupt my life, so I was more than happy to let someone else be her sounding board when she needed one."

"Don't beat yourself up. I did the same thing," Annabelle said. "I could have tried harder to get my sisters and brothers-in-law to support me coming to Alameda that summer after Gonzalo was arrested."

"They wanted you home where you were safe."

"Yes, but I would have been safe here."

"Maybe, maybe not." What would Isaac have done if Annabelle had come to visit and gotten in his way? He shuddered to think about it. "We can't change the past, but we can make sure Tayla doesn't step into her future without knowing the truth."

"I hope she doesn't hate us for digging all this up."

"Isaac didn't give us much choice," Leo said. "He tried to kill both of us."

"And we still don't know how Duran is doing."

"He was alive when we left. The doctors seem to think they can keep him that way."

"I hope so." Annabelle held up a finger. "And no, it's not just because he makes the best crema catalana."

Leo looked out over the Mediterranean, no land in sight. "We're going to be at least a couple more hours. Do you want to trade places with Rocco for a while?"

"No. It will do both him and Saul good to get as much rest as they can. You know they'll insist on taking over when it gets dark."

"I'm really hoping we make it back before then."

"Me too." She stood. "I'm going to grab a water bottle. Do you want one?"

"Yes, please."

Annabelle disappeared through the hatch and returned a moment later, two water bottles in her hand, one of them already half empty. She held the full one out.

"Thanks." Leo took it from her, but she was focused on some point on the water beyond him.

"Annabelle?"

"Where are your binoculars?"

He motioned toward the storage compartment beside the radio.

She quickly dug them out and lifted them to her eyes. She pointed with her free hand. "There's a ship!"

Leo grabbed the radio and immediately started relaying a mayday call. He went through six frequencies before another voice sounded.

Relief flowed through him. He motioned to Annabelle. "Get Saul and Rocco."

Annabelle nodded and hurried back to the hatch.

If Leo had his way, she would stay out of sight until they were sure that whoever was on the approaching boat was really willing to help them or if they posed a new danger.

- - -

Annabelle dangled on the rope ladder, her foot pressing into the piece of wood fitted between the strips of rope as she used her hands to climb slowly and steadily upward.

From beneath her, Leo's steady voice encouraged her. "Keep going. One rung at a time."

Annabelle didn't share her sister Cassie's fear of heights, but she couldn't say she was particularly fond of standing on nothing more than wooden planks held together by strings of twisted fibers.

She placed her foot on the next rung before sliding her hands upward. She repeated the process until two men reached down, their firm grips encircling her arms as they pulled her over the ship railing. She was barely upright when they released her and turned to help Leo.

On the sailboat below, two of the freighter's crew connected a tow line so the evidence of what had been done to Leo's vessel wouldn't be lost, even though it would be taken first to Meridia, the freighter's current destination.

Leo reached her side and adjusted the straps of the backpack he had stored their files and laptops in while they climbed aboard. "We need to use your radio."

The burly man to their left—likely the captain—nodded. "This way, Your Highness."

Annabelle knew Leo was often photographed, but she hadn't expected him to be recognized here. She fell into step with Leo, Rocco on her other side and Saul trailing behind them. When they reached the bridge, the captain grabbed the radio. "We're on an open frequency."

"Is there any way to make a secure call?" Annabelle asked.

"Assuming you know what number you need to call, we have a satellite phone."

"Who do we call?" Annabelle asked. "Your father?"

"No. Both of my parents have assistants who answer their phones. We can't risk someone telling Isaac we're still alive."

"Levi." Annabelle reached for the phone. "He answers his own calls, and he's close friends with the Meridian royal family."

"Please tell me you know his phone number by heart."

Annabelle reached for the phone and, with the captain's help, made the call.

The phone rang five times and went to voice mail. "Levi, it's Annabelle." She paused, searching for the words to explain her situation. "Call me back at this number, and don't tell anyone you heard from us. Someone tried to kill me and Leo."

She ended the call.

"Try again." Leo motioned toward the phone. "He might not have answered because he didn't recognize the number."

Annabelle called a second time. Again, no answer. "Let's see if the third time will be the charm."

She dialed again. Relief whooshed through her when Levi answered with a gruff hello.

"Levi, it's Annabelle."

"I thought you were supposed to be underway by now."

"We were, but someone sabotaged Leo's sailboat." Even though the identity of that someone burned on her tongue, she couldn't bring herself to say Isaac's name in front of the captain and the two crewmembers present. "We were picked up by a freighter, and we're heading to Meridia now."

"But you're okay?" Levi asked.

"Yes. We're all fine."

"I'll contact King Josep and let him know your status. He may want to divert Princess Tayla and her fiancé to stay here since you're bound for Meridia. You can swap places."

"Actually, we have reasons we'd prefer that doesn't happen." Annabelle paused and turned to the captain. "What's our position?"

The captain grabbed a piece of paper and jotted down the longitude and latitude for her.

"I have an idea, but it will require some deception on Prince Garrett's part."

"I'm listening."

"Remember that helicopter that's supposed to transport Tayla and Isaac?"

"Yeah?"

"I think it needs to make an unplanned stop before going to Alameda." Annabelle described her idea.

Finally, Levi said, "I think that can be arranged."

CHAPTER
33

LEO SAT IN THE BACK of the helicopter, Annabelle beside him and their guards positioned in the seats beside the doors. A headset protected his ears from the noise but also made communication with everyone else impossible. The last thing he or Annabelle wanted was for their voices to be picked up on the frequency the pilot was using for fear they might alert someone that they were no longer in the middle of the Mediterranean. They especially didn't want to take the chance of Isaac learning they were still breathing and on their way back to Alameda.

While Leo would like to think the man really loved his sister and wouldn't do anything to hurt her, Isaac's actions had been less than honorable from the beginning.

The pilot's voice came over the headset. "We're cleared for final approach."

Leo looked out the window at the palace grounds below. From this view, it could have been straight out of a fairy tale, complete with the conical spires and manicured grounds. They circled to the north side of the palace where Federico and Zeus stood beside a stack of luggage, undoubtedly Tayla's and Isaac's belongings.

To think this latest nightmare had begun with a bomb hidden in a suitcase.

Annabelle must have entertained a similar thought because she reached out and gripped his hand. He laced his fingers through hers, giving and receiving comfort at the same time. If Federico and Zeus were there, clearly the luggage had already been inspected.

The helicopter lowered onto the wide lawn, the aircraft bumping against the ground as it landed. The pilot shut down the engines, the rotors slowing, the deafening noise fading.

Leo took off his headset as Annabelle and the others did the same.

Rocco pulled out his phone and dialed. Almost instantly, Federico pulled his mobile from his pocket.

"Have you informed the royal guard?" Rocco asked. He paused and then spoke again. "We'll wait for your signal." He hung up and twisted his body so he could see Annabelle and Leo. "The princess and Isaac are on their way out. We'll all wait in here until Princess Tayla is protected by her guards and Isaac is in custody."

Leo regretted that he hadn't been able to speak with Tayla directly, or even his parents for that matter, but his parents' unavailability today combined with the possibility of Tayla tipping Isaac off to their plan had forced his hand.

Annabelle leaned forward and pointed. "There they are."

Even though they were surrounded by guards, Isaac kept his hand on Tayla's waist. The show of affection—or perhaps it was control—was unlike him.

"This isn't going to be as easy as we hoped," Leo said.

"We have two choices," Saul said. "We have the royal guard pull the princess from Isaac's grip or we let them continue to the helicopter. Once Princess Tayla climbs aboard, the guards can take Isaac into custody."

"Tayla has already been through so much," Annabelle said. "I vote for the second option."

Though Leo hated letting Isaac get that close to Annabelle, he nodded. "I agree. Pass the word."

Saul made the call.

"Your Highnesses, come to this side of the helicopter." Rocco motioned for Leo and Annabelle to join him on the bench seat running along the side closest to where Tayla and Isaac were approaching. He focused on Leo. "We don't want your sister to see you right away."

Leo unbuckled, and he and Annabelle slid into the spot beside Rocco. Saul shifted as well, moving to stand on the other side of the door.

Leo's hands fisted as his sister's fiancé drew closer.

The guard nearest the helicopter waited until Tayla and Isaac were right beside him before he opened the door. Though Leo had expected Isaac to release Tayla so she could climb aboard first, he shifted his grip to her arm and started to enter the helicopter beside her.

Leo leaned forward so his guard could see him. Leo nodded toward Isaac and put a hand on Rocco's back to signal him into action.

"Now!" Leo shouted.

Moving in tandem, Rocco grabbed Tayla's arm and pulled her into the helicopter while Saul kicked his foot directly into Isaac's chest to stop Isaac's forward motion.

Tayla cried out, and Leo reached for her, pulling her even deeper into the helicopter.

"Leo?" She looked past him. "Annabelle? What are you doing here?"

"Saving you." Leo shifted forward, nudging Tayla into the spot between him and Annabelle.

Isaac, who had been knocked to the ground, stood up. Instantly, two guards moved forward and gripped his arms. "What's the meaning of this?"

Leo followed Saul out of the helicopter, leaving Rocco to protect Annabelle and his sister.

Isaac's eyes widened when he spotted Leo. "What are you doing here? I thought you were sailing to Sereno."

"Oh, we tried." Leo stepped forward, leaving only a meter of space between them. "That was before you tried to kill me."

"What? I did no such thing."

"Just like you didn't try to poison me or try to blow me up."

"Of course I didn't do any of those things."

His sister's voice carried behind him. "Let me out of here." Tayla emerged from the helicopter and gripped Leo's arm. "What are you doing? Isaac hasn't done anything wrong. He was with me when the bombing happened."

"But he wasn't with you when his accomplice was killed."

Tayla's face paled. "What?"

"The man who helped arrange for Gonzalo to disappear was found murdered last week." Adrenaline rushed through Leo, and he had to remind himself that Tayla didn't know everything he and Annabelle had learned. Leo gestured toward Isaac, who was still held in place by the two guards flanking him. "Ironically, the murder occurred the same night Isaac decided not to stay at the palace."

"That doesn't mean he's a murderer," Tayla insisted. "Even I know you need proof."

"Proof." Leo balled his fists. "Like the payments being made to Gonzalo from the person who hired him to stalk you, payments that continued right up until Gonzalo disappeared."

"What are you talking about?" Tayla asked.

"Isaac wanted to be part of your life. What better way than to create a crime against you and then arrange to be the prosecutor who was constantly a source of information and support?"

Instantly, Isaac slumped his shoulders, and he looked away.

Leo took another step toward Isaac. "You know we can trace the payments to your account in the Caymans." Leo hoped they could find that proof.

Isaac clamped his mouth shut, and the muscle in his jaw twitched.

"Leo, there has to be some mistake. Isaac would never hurt me. He loves me."

"I do love you," Isaac said, his focus entirely on Tayla.

"And you made sure she would have plenty of opportunities to fall in love with you during Gonzalo's trial," Leo said, the details of those days coming back with full force. "All of those continuances that you didn't fight, all of those visits to the palace to help Tayla prepare for her testimony." Leo stepped forward until he was practically nose to nose with Isaac. "It was brilliant, really. And it would have worked if you hadn't gotten greedy." Leo waved toward his sister. "You couldn't stand the idea of only being married to a princess, not when getting rid of me would make her the future queen."

"That's enough, Leo!" Tayla grabbed Leo by the arm and pulled him back several steps. "I don't know where you got these crazy ideas, but Isaac didn't do anything wrong."

"He has the education of a king," Leo said, repeating words Isaac had spoken only a few days ago. "Marrying you and killing me meant he would get the chance to step into that role."

Before Tayla could protest further, Annabelle edged forward and put her hand on Tayla's arm. "None of us want to believe this could be true, but Isaac arrived at the palace nearly an hour before he arrived in the morning room for that tasting."

Leo took a step toward Isaac until only a half meter of space remained between them. "Plenty of time to stop by the kitchen and slip some cyanide into the chocolate mousse, the dessert you knew Tayla wouldn't try."

"I stopped to go to the bathroom and then went to the dining room by mistake," Isaac said.

Leo turned to face his sister now. "Isaac was also one of the only people who knew we were planning to sail to Sereno. The boat would have had to be sabotaged that night."

"How long were you and Isaac together after dinner?" Annabelle asked Tayla.

"We started to watch a movie, but then he received a call and said he had something he needed to take care of." A new awareness spread across Tayla's face. She turned to face Isaac. "Did you do any of this? Did you try to kill my brother?"

"I swear, I didn't."

"But you did hire Gonzalo."

Something flashed in Isaac's eyes. And while his expression was far from an admission of guilt, it was enough to convince Leo they had the right man.

Tayla must have sensed it too. She took a step back. "How could you be so cruel?"

Isaac tried to step forward. "Tayla, I love you."

"Don't ever say that to me again." Tayla's body trembled, but Leo didn't sense fear in his sister; he sensed anger.

Isaac turned his attention to Leo. "I swear, I didn't try to kill you."

"If not you, then who?"

"None of these assassination attempts had anything to do with me."

"I'm sorry, but I don't believe you." Leo nodded at Saul. "Turn him over to the authorities."

"Yes, Your Highness."

"No!" Isaac tried to break free of the guards holding him, but they held him firm. "Tayla, you have to believe me. I didn't try to hurt your brother."

Tayla lifted her chin, and she took a step forward. "Even if that's true, can you deny that you hired Gonzalo?"

Isaac pressed his lips together but didn't speak.

Tayla blinked hard, and Leo suspected she was fighting tears. She drew a deep breath. "I didn't think so."

Leo tilted his head, signaling the guards once more.

They pulled Isaac away from Tayla and toward the front of the palace. Beside him, one of the other guards called the local police chief.

Leo put his hand on Tayla's back. "I'm so sorry, Tayla."

That's as far as he got before Tayla rushed into his arms.

CHAPTER
34

RELIEVED TO BE BACK IN Alameda, Annabelle sat on the sofa in Tayla's quarters and handed her friend another tissue. The tears had been constant since they reached her apartment, Annabelle accompanying her while Leo went to give his parents the latest updates, both on the sabotage of his boat and the fact that Isaac had been taken into custody.

"I'm so sorry." Annabelle put her arm around Tayla.

"I feel so stupid." She blew her nose and discarded the tissue in the wastebasket Annabelle had set beside the sofa. "I thought he really cared about me." She swiped at her eyes. "We had so many plans. Where we were going to visit on our holidays, where we planned to live, when we would start a family." She sniffled. "We were going to have our happily ever after. Now I know I was just a pawn."

Annabelle couldn't begin to understand the emotional turmoil Tayla must be suffering right now, so she offered the small amount of truth she had at her disposal. "I know it doesn't help any, but I think he really does love you," Annabelle said. "He just wanted more than what would ever rightfully be his."

"I can't believe he tried to sink Leo's boat. Did he really think I would be able to go through with the wedding if I lost my brother and my best friend?"

"He helped you through a rough time before. He probably assumed you'd adjust to us not being here by the time you reached your wedding day."

"I don't even want to think about the two of you not being here." Tayla took another tissue and wiped her nose. "And I'm so sorry for everything Isaac put you through."

"You had no way of knowing," Annabelle said. "Leo and I were fooled too. So were your parents."

"And the private investigator my father hired when we first started dating."

"Isaac looks great on paper," Annabelle said.

Tayla wiped at her eyes again. "I must look terrible."

"Not at all." Hoping to make light of the moment, Annabelle tilted her head to the side. "And there is one good thing."

"What?"

"You've proven my waterproof mascara can hold up to tears."

Tayla rolled her eyes. "This isn't the kind of testing I'd hoped to do for you."

"I know," Annabelle said. "I had to do my own impromptu demonstration to prove how durable my moisturizer containers were by shoving them all into the holes in Leo's boat."

Tayla straightened. "That's how you kept from sinking?"

"It is. Thank goodness you asked me to bring the samples and that Rocco automatically packed them on the boat for me."

Tayla rubbed both hands over her face, holding them in place for a moment before lowering them.

"Can I make you a cup of tea or anything?" Annabelle asked.

"No." She shook her head. "I need some time to process all of this."

Recognizing her cue that it was time to give Tayla some time alone, Annabelle stood. "Call me if you need someone to talk to, anytime, day or night."

"Thanks, Annabelle." Tayla stood. "I think I'm going to take a long shower and go to bed. Maybe I can sleep and pretend this day never happened."

"Good luck." Annabelle gave Tayla a hug. "I'll see myself out."

Annabelle left Tayla's apartment, pleased to see two guards posted in the hall of the residential hallway. She only had to go across the hall to reach Leo's private apartment.

Annabelle knocked lightly on his door, and Leo opened it a few seconds later. He had changed into fresh clothes, and his hair was damp, suggesting he'd recently showered.

He ushered her inside. "How's Tayla doing?"

"She's feeling like her entire world just got ripped out from under her." Annabelle stopped inside the door. "I feel so terrible for her."

"I know. Me too." Leo pulled her into an embrace, and Annabelle couldn't resist wrapping her arms around him. "This whole day feels like a nightmare that we should be able to wake up from any minute."

"Tayla said practically the same thing. She said she's going to shower and go to bed so she can pretend this whole day was a nightmare."

"You have to be starving. I had some dinner sent up."

"From the kitchen?" Annabelle asked. Even though it had been two days since the poisoning attempt, she still couldn't shake the uneasiness that had plagued her since then.

"Yes, it came from the kitchen, but Federico tested the food and oversaw the preparations."

"Why was Federico on kitchen duty?"

"Because he insisted Rocco take some time off." Leo took her hand and led her into the dining room.

Three taper candles were positioned in the center, all of them already lit. On one end, two place settings had been arranged with a pitcher of lemonade and fresh bread in the center.

"How did you even know I would come over after talking to Tayla?"

"I was hoping." Leo leaned down and pressed his lips to hers. "And I guessed Tayla would want some time alone after she talked everything out."

"This looks wonderful. Thank you."

"I'll heat up our plates." Leo headed toward the kitchen.

Annabelle followed. "How did your parents take the news?"

"My father has determined that we now need a secure communication relay for situations such as these." Leo took the cover off one of the two plates on the counter and slid it into the microwave. "He wasn't happy that we coordinated my sister's rescue and Isaac's arrest through two different countries' royal families."

"Tayla didn't exactly need rescuing. We just needed to make sure she was away from Isaac."

"Same thing." He shrugged. "It's a good idea, regardless, especially since he and Mother are notorious for screening all of their calls through their assistants."

"What's the latest on Duran?" Annabelle asked.

"He's improving," Leo said. "They expect he'll be released from the hospital in another day or two."

"Thank goodness." The microwave dinged, and Annabelle handed Leo the second plate. "Maybe we can visit him at the hospital tomorrow."

"Do you really want to leave the palace grounds after all we've been through?"

Annabelle tried to picture it. "Maybe not."

The second plate finished in the microwave, and Leo and Annabelle carried their dinner into the dining room.

After they sat down, Leo reached for her hand. "I know you only planned to stay for another week or two, but is there any way you would consider extending?"

"Honestly, the thought of getting on a boat or a plane right now makes me want to curl up in a ball and hide."

"I'd rather hoped you'd have a reason to stay besides avoiding those two things." He leaned closer and pressed his lips to hers. "Like staying here with me."

The butterflies in her stomach were back. "That thought had crossed my mind."

"Good." He settled his lips more firmly on hers.

Annabelle fell into the kiss, certain her growing feelings might swallow her whole.

She pulled back as an uncomfortable thought broke through the magic of the moment. "Oh no."

"What?"

"We're going to have to tell Tayla." Annabelle's gaze lifted to meet Leo's. "What terrible timing."

"Maybe we should give her a few days before we have that conversation."

She let out a sigh. "Maybe so."

CHAPTER
35

LEO HADN'T REALIZED HOW MUCH Duran's health had been weighing on him until his chef walked through the palace doors. Leo had volunteered to be the greeting committee, and Annabelle had insisted on joining him. Now, here they were, a week to the day from when Duran had ingested the poison meant for him, and they were finally making steps to regaining a sense of normalcy.

"Welcome home." Leo stepped forward.

"Greeted by the prince himself." Duran shook his head. "Don't think this means I'm making chocolate mousse anytime soon."

"I think I need to find a new favorite dessert," Leo said. "Words can't express how sorry I am—"

Duran held up his hand to stop him. "You did nothing wrong, and your family made sure I had the best care possible. You owe me nothing."

"Not even that fancy new mixer you've been asking for?"

"Okay, maybe I'd take that."

Leo shook his hand. "It's good to have you back."

"We should get you to your room." Annabelle looped her arm through Duran's.

"I can walk on my own."

"I never said you couldn't, but it won't hurt for us to walk with you," Annabelle said.

Giving up on that particular battle, Duran started toward the servants' quarters. "What's the latest on Isaac?"

Leo should have known Duran would have heard the news about his would-be killer. Over the past five days, multiple versions had circulated in the news about why Isaac had been taken into custody. "The first hearing was yesterday," Leo said. "The judge agreed that there's enough evidence to go to trial."

"How long will that take?" Duran asked.

"The date hasn't been set yet, but the prosecutor believes it will be expedited because of the involvement of the royal family," Leo said.

"I don't know how I missed him coming into the kitchen last week. He's one I thought I would have noticed."

"He certainly played it cool by leaving before anyone ate the chocolate mousse," Leo said.

"He couldn't risk giving himself away," Annabelle said softly.

"It's a good thing you were too full to eat more or you wouldn't still be here," Duran told Leo. "I've seen how big of a bite you take when you try things."

"You mean, he would have finished the whole serving," Annabelle said.

"Typically, yes." Duran nodded. "From what the doctor said, though, a single full-size bite was enough to kill a grown man, even one of my size."

"We will forever be grateful that you didn't ingest more of that poison," Annabelle said.

They reached Duran's room, and Leo opened the door.

"I can take it from here." Duran stepped through the doorway.

"I'm sure my father has already told you this, but take as much time as you need to recover."

"He did tell me that." Duran nodded. "And the doctor said I can be back in the kitchen by Thursday." He jerked a thumb toward Annabelle. "This one must be going through withdrawals after not sneaking into my kitchen for a full week."

Annabelle nodded. "It's true, but I'll gladly suffer for a few more days until you're back to full strength."

"I'm fine, and I'll be back in the kitchen on Thursday."

Annabelle reached out and gave him a hug. "We really are glad you're back."

"It's good to be back." Duran gestured toward Annabelle but spoke to Leo. "You should take this one out to dinner. It would be good for people to see you out and about."

"Security hasn't been terribly fond of the idea of us leaving the palace grounds."

"I suspected as much, but the public needs to know you're okay," Duran said. "Rumors are never a good thing, especially in times like these." He put his hand on the door. "Now, if you'll excuse me, I'm going to rest and enjoy sleeping in my own bed."

"Let us know if you need anything," Annabelle said.

"I will." He closed the door between them.

Leo hooked his arm around Annabelle's waist. Was Duran right that the increased security at the palace was creating anxiety among their citizens?

"What do you think about Duran's suggestion? Would you like to go into town for dinner tonight?"

"Are you ready for that?" Her eyebrows lifted. "Going out, away from the palace?"

"Are you asking that question because you're ready to escape the palace grounds or because you're afraid to?" Leo asked.

"A little of both."

He couldn't deny he felt the same way.

Annabelle glanced toward the nearby guards. "Do you think it's safe?"

He wanted it to be safe, and he was ready to spend time with Annabelle away from the confines of his home. "Isaac is locked up, and no one will expect us in town."

"It would be nice to get away for a bit." Annabelle lifted her chin toward the residential wing. "It's been rough spending every night listening to Tayla go over every moment with Isaac, trying to analyze how she missed the signs of who he really was."

"Do you think she's ready to know about us?"

"We should give her a couple more days."

"The sooner the better." Leo dropped his arm from Annabelle's waist. "It's not easy pretending around her."

"I know," Annabelle said. "And whether she's ready to hear about us or not, maybe this will give her something else to think about."

"I just hope she doesn't hate me for stealing her best friend away from her."

"She's more likely to hate you if you break my heart."

"I already plan to avoid that."

A little smile surfaced on her face. "I'm glad to hear it."

- - -

Annabelle felt like she was getting ready for a first date. In a way, she was. Nearly a week had passed since that first kiss with Leo, since they had discovered the simmering attraction between them and the feelings that went so much deeper.

They had enjoyed walks in the gardens, movies in her guest suite, lunches in his office between his meetings and hers. And every one of those moments together felt like a stolen piece of time that they couldn't share with Tayla.

She hated how much Tayla was hurting right now, especially when her own heart was so full of joy it was nearly bursting. And even though tonight would give her a brief glimpse of what dating Leo could really be like, she needed to be able to share her good news with Tayla, even if Tayla was still fighting the demons that came from breaking her engagement.

Annabelle applied a fresh coat of lipstick and slipped the tube into her purse.

A knock sounded at her door, and she checked her watch. Leo was early. Maybe he was as eager to get out and experience a real date as she was.

With her purse in hand, she crossed to the door and pulled it open. To her surprise, Tayla stood on the other side instead of Leo.

Tayla's eyebrows lifted. "Are you going somewhere?"

She could lie. Who was she kidding? No, she couldn't. "Yes, actually. I'm going out to dinner."

"Without me?" The hurt in her voice spoke volumes.

"I'm sorry. Of course you can come too. It's just—it's sort of a date."

Understanding bloomed on Tayla's face. "And you didn't tell me because Isaac and I broke up."

Annabelle grabbed onto the excuse Tayla handed her. "Yes." She set her purse on the table by the sofa. "I'm sorry, Tayla. I know how much you're hurting right now."

"That doesn't mean you should stop living your life." Tayla closed the door. "I'm sorry I made you feel like you couldn't talk to me."

"It's okay." Annabelle reached out and drew Tayla into a hug. "You've been going through so much. Honestly, I don't know how you're doing it."

"Having a therapist in my favorites list doesn't hurt." Tayla held her close before releasing her. "Are you going to tell me who the lucky guy is? Anyone I know?"

"He is." This wasn't how Annabelle planned to tell Tayla, but she couldn't avoid the truth, not without straight-out lying. "I'm going out with Leo."

"Leo?" Tayla took a step back and furrowed her eyebrows. "Leo, as in my brother, Leo?"

"Yes, that Leo."

Annabelle studied her friend for any sign of what emotions she was experiencing at learning the truth, but Tayla's expression didn't go beyond pure shock. "You and Leo. When? How?"

"We spent a lot of time together helping with the bombing investigation. Then after he and Chrishelle broke up, we spent more time together."

"Are you the reason he and Chrishelle broke up?"

"No, not at all," Annabelle said. At least, she was pretty sure she wasn't. "I mean, I guess spending time with me may have helped Leo realize that he and Chrishelle weren't a good match, but it wasn't like he was really interested in me at that point."

"Annabelle, they only broke up last Friday."

"I know, but even I could tell something wasn't quite right between them when I first arrived."

"You know my brother dates a lot, that he rarely lasts with anyone for long," Tayla said, her tone filled with caution.

Annabelle didn't want to think about the women Leo dated before her, but with Tayla laying it out, she didn't have a choice. "I know what Leo has been like in the past, just like I know the paparazzi are good at exaggerating the truth."

"That doesn't change the fact that he isn't the sort who's likely to settle down anytime soon."

"I'm not looking to settle down. Not right now anyway." The moment the words were spoken, Annabelle tensed. Tayla had been hoping to settle down before another year passed. "I'm sorry. I was afraid this would be difficult for you, seeing me dating someone new, especially when that someone is your brother."

"I love you both. I just don't want to lose either of you."

"You won't. Leo will always be your brother. I will always be your best friend," Annabelle said. "And no matter what, even if Leo and I don't last, when you find the right guy, we are both going to be at your wedding."

"It's hard to imagine planning a life with someone else."

"I know, but too many people say that time heals all wounds for it not to be true."

"Time is one thing I have plenty of right now."

"You could always spend some of it helping me with my marketing campaign. My new company launches in three months."

"I suppose I could do that," Tayla said. "After all, you risked your life to save me from making a huge mistake with Isaac."

Another knock sounded.

"I assume that's Leo." Tayla opened the door.

Leo looked at his sister, glanced at Annabelle, and looked back at Tayla. "Um—"

"Don't worry." Tayla grabbed her brother's arm and pulled him into the suite. "Annabelle already told me."

"She did?" He looked at Annabelle again, a combination of relief and surprise on his face. "You did?"

"Yes." Annabelle nodded. "And I think she's nearly over the shock of our
news."

Tayla stepped in front of Leo so his focus would be on her. "All I can say
is, you'd better not break her heart."

"She said the same thing earlier today." Leo nodded at Annabelle. "Have
either of you considered that Annabelle might break my heart instead of it being
the other way around?"

Annabelle had never thought about that. Leo was always the person who
initiated his breakups.

"I'm just telling you what you should already know." Tayla motioned
toward Annabelle. "Annabelle's a keeper."

CHAPTER
36

LEO SLID BEHIND THE WHEEL of his Porsche convertible. "Tayla is right, you know."

"About what?"

"About you being a keeper."

"You're sweet." Annabelle leaned in and kissed him. "And thank you for tonight. I'm looking forward to going on a real date with you."

"Are you ready for what will happen if we're spotted together?" Leo asked, a surge of protectiveness welling up inside him. "I'm sure we can go in the back door to avoid being spotted."

"The whole idea of going out tonight is to be seen so that your people will feel safe."

"My whole idea was to spend time with my girlfriend."

"Your girlfriend. That sounds so weird."

"Yeah, well, I think it's a bit too quick to jump to fiancée."

Annabelle laughed. "I should think so."

He started to reach for the button to put the top down but thought better of it. Annabelle probably wouldn't want to mess up her hair.

Annabelle laughed. "You can put the top down."

"Are you sure?"

"I have a hair tie in my purse, and we could both use the sense of freedom that will come from driving along the coast in a convertible."

"I'm not going to argue that point." He hit the button and waited for the top to fold into the back of the car. Once the process was complete, he started the engine.

He pulled out of the expansive garage, following the vehicle that Saul was driving with Rocco in the passenger seat. A second car fell in behind them, two royal guards seated inside.

Annabelle opened her purse and pulled out what looked like a coated rubber band and pulled her hair back into a ponytail.

Leo passed the guard house and pulled onto the main road. He only had to drive a few hundred meters before the Mediterranean came into view, the rays from the lowering sun shimmering across the water.

"Where are we going, anyway?" Annabelle asked, raising her voice to be heard over the rush of air flowing over them.

"Riccardo's."

"That's my favorite."

"I know." He increased his speed. "You and Tayla go there every time you visit."

"I've never had a first date with someone who knows me so well."

Leo shifted gears. "We're way past a first date."

"In some ways, but this is the first time we're stepping out in public as a real couple."

It was the first time they were going out in public since the last threat against them. Or rather, against him. Tension rose inside him, and he had to remind himself that Isaac was safely behind bars and all his known associates were dead.

Known associates. Surely he didn't have anyone else working with him.

Annabelle lifted her face as though soaking in the last rays of the sun. A strand of her hair pulled free of her ponytail and whipped into her face. She ignored it.

A smile tugged at his lips. He rather liked how Annabelle looked when not every hair was in place. Was it possible she was even more perfect than he'd first thought?

They reached the village, and he reduced his speed. People walked along the main street, locals and tourists alike. It only took a moment for the first mobile phones to raise, for the first photos to be taken.

"You're going to be all over social media with your hair messed up," Leo said. "That's not going to be a problem for your image, is it?"

"My hair isn't messed up." Annabelle winked at him. "It's windblown."

"It's definitely that." Leo pulled into an open parking spot a short distance from their intended destination.

"And it's easily fixed." Annabelle pulled the band free, combed her fingers through her hair, and shook her head. "How's that?"

Her eyes bright, her makeup perfect, her hair now cascading loosely over her shoulders as though she'd spent hours styling it. His mouth went dry. She truly was beautiful.

Unable to resist, he put his hand on hers and leaned in for a kiss. "You're stunning."

Her gaze locked on his with an intensity that surprised him. Her response came in a mere whisper. "Thank you."

He hit the button and put the top up before he checked his guards' positions and climbed out of the car. He circled to Annabelle's side, opened her door, and took her hand to help her stand.

Still hand in hand, Leo and Annabelle entered the restaurant. Candles flickered on the occupied tables, the last of the evening light spilling through the wide windows that overlooked the Mediterranean. Potted palms were situated throughout to create an air of privacy, and muted music carried over the overhead speakers.

Leo inhaled the delightful scents of melted butter, cooked shellfish, and herbed bread.

The maître d' bowed when they entered. "Prince Leonardo, Princess Annabelle, what a delight to have you join us again."

"Thank you, Wilhelm," Leo said.

Wilhelm retrieved two menus from the rack beside his stand. "Please follow me." He led them to a table on the far side of a leafy palm and pulled out a chair for Annabelle. "Your Highness."

"Thank you."

She and Leo sat, and Wilhelm handed them each a menu. "Your server will be with you shortly."

Annabelle opened her menu and flipped to the dessert page.

"Trying to decide how much room you need to save for dessert?"

"Maybe." She shot him a mischievous grin. "Of course, if you want to be a really great boyfriend, you'll let me choose two and we can split them."

"That's an easy request to grant," Leo said. "After all, I'm still breathing because of the last time you picked out my desserts."

"Let's not think about that tonight. Right now, we get to be a regular couple." She set her menu down. "One that isn't going to have chocolate mousse for dessert."

- - -

Annabelle crossed her fork and knife on her plate to signal she was done with her main course even though half the salmon remained on her plate. "That was so good."

"You really are saving room for dessert."

"I am. That berry parfait looks amazing." She set her napkin aside. "If you'll excuse me, I need to use the ladies' room."

Leo scooped up another bite of his shrimp scampi. "Don't be long. If dessert arrives before you get back, you can't hold me responsible for what happens."

"Duly noted." Though with as much dinner as he still had on his plate, Annabelle suspected she would return to the table in plenty of time to keep Leo from eating her share.

She slipped past the large planter to her right and headed toward the back of the restaurant where the toilets were located. After she used the restroom, she moved to the sink to wash her hands. The door opened, and she glanced at the newcomer. Annabelle blinked several times. Nora, Isaac's mother, stood in front of her.

Though stunned to see the older woman here, Nora shocked her even more when she reached into her purse and lifted a pistol.

"Don't scream. Don't say anything," she said calmly as though holding someone at gunpoint wasn't a big deal. "If you do what I tell you, no one will get hurt."

Annabelle focused on the gun—the very deadly gun—in Nora's hand. Though the question of what the woman wanted with Annabelle formed in her mind, she couldn't quite get the words to come out.

"When I tell you, we're going to walk out of here and leave through the back door."

"Why?" Annabelle finally managed to ask. "Why are you doing this?"

"For my son."

"I don't understand."

"You don't have to." Nora lifted the gun a little higher. "You simply need to walk out with me without your guards noticing."

Panic pushed through Annabelle's shock. "There's a guard at the exit."

"There *was* a guard at the exit."

Annabelle let that implication sink in. Had Isaac's mother killed the guard? Even as she prayed that wasn't the case, another startling thought rushed into her mind. Had Nora killed before? Or tried to?

Isaac had been late to the taste testing, but so had his mother. Annabelle didn't remember how much time had passed between when the two of them had come through the main gate, but a new suspect now stood beside her hold-ing a gun.

Nora grabbed Annabelle's arm and jerked her toward the door.

Water dripped from Annabelle's hands, a reminder that she had not yet dried them, and she didn't think to grab her purse from the counter.

"We're going out together. Nice and steady."

Annabelle's thoughts continued to spin. "Isaac wasn't the one who tried to poison the prince, was he?" Annabelle asked.

Nora cracked the door open and peered out. Then she tugged on Annabelle's arm again. "Remember." She shoved the gun into Annabelle's side. "Don't say a word."

Annabelle swallowed hard and forced her legs to move. She walked through the door, Nora blocking her from view of anyone near the hallway leading to the toilets. Annabelle glanced behind her, catching a brief glimpse of Rocco's shoulder as he stood facing the main part of the restaurant. He was trying to protect her from any possible threat from within, but he had no idea he was looking the wrong way.

They reached the door, and Nora pressed the gun more firmly against Annabelle's side. "Open it."

Annabelle did so. They emerged into the alley behind the restaurant, and Annabelle spotted the prone figure at the base of the short set of stairs leading from the back door.

They reached the street level, and Annabelle started to lean down to see if the guard was still breathing. Before she could reach his side, Nora jerked her toward a car parked beyond the dumpsters.

She opened the driver's side door and shoved Annabelle toward it. "You drive."

Annabelle climbed into the car, her gaze remaining on the gun as Nora closed her car door and kept the pistol aimed at Annabelle as she circled to the passenger side. All of the royal guards' precautions, all of the security measures put in place by her brothers-in-law and Rocco, and a single trip to a public toilet had undermined them all.

Nora nodded toward the front of the car. "Now drive. Take a right at the end of the alley."

"Where are you taking me?" Annabelle asked.

"It's a beautiful night for a walk on the beach. Your boyfriend will be join-ing us shortly."

CHAPTER
37

Leo didn't know what was taking Annabelle so long, but if she didn't get here soon, the berry parfait would be a distant memory before she ever got to taste it.

He picked up a spoon and took a bite. He could always order another one.

The maître d' approached, an envelope in hand. "Excuse me, Your Highness. This message was just delivered for you."

"Thank you." Leo opened the message and read the contents.

> *If you ever want to see your princess alive again, bring Isaac Vega and two million euros in unmarked bills to the Royal Vista Yacht Club, pier one, at ten o'clock tonight. Come in your convertible with the top down. Come alone.*

Leo read the note a second time and pushed out of his seat. He stepped past the palms that had shielded him from view and scanned the interior of the restaurant. Rocco stood by the hallway leading to the restrooms and the kitchen, Saul positioned a few meters away.

Saul stepped forward. "Is everything okay, Your Highness?"

Leo passed the note to his guard and rushed to Rocco. "Have you seen Annabelle?"

"She's in the ladies' room."

"Not according to the note I just got." Without thought of how it might look to others, Leo ran the short distance to the ladies' room and knocked on the door twice. Then without waiting, he opened the door. "Coming in!"

Leo stepped into the empty room, his gaze drawn to Annabelle's handbag perched on the edge of the counter. "Annabelle?"

No answer.

Leo quickly checked the stalls, all of them empty. Panicked, he grabbed Annabelle's purse and ran back into the hall. Looking both ways, he evaluated the most likely exit for a kidnapper. With no way Annabelle could have been taken past both Rocco and Saul, he turned the other direction.

He thrust open the back door.

"Your Highness, wait!" Saul called after him.

Leo didn't wait. He stepped outside and instantly spotted the guard lying on the ground. Leo scanned the empty alley before rushing to the man's side.

Saul and Rocco rushed outside behind him.

Leo looked up. "He's still breathing. Call an ambulance." Leo stood and peered down the darkening alleyway. "And call the police." He swallowed hard before forcing the words out. "Annabelle has been kidnapped."

- - -

Never had Annabelle prayed so hard, nor wanted so badly to be recognized. Unfortunately, if anyone noticed she was the person behind the wheel of the simple sedan, they didn't do more than take a photo and put their mobile back in their pocket. The fading light wasn't working in her favor either.

What would Levi or Alan do in this situation? Who was she kidding? They never would have allowed themselves to be taken captive, especially not by a middle-aged woman.

"Why are you doing this?" Annabelle asked. "Your son was about to marry into the royal family."

"My son was about to be next in line for the throne." She lifted the gun slightly. "I can't sit by and watch him rot away in a prison."

When she didn't continue, Annabelle added for her, "Especially for something he didn't do."

"Isaac would never hurt anyone."

"No, he wouldn't." Annabelle could see that now. "He has a tender heart, and he loved Tayla."

"They were the perfect couple."

"The perfect couple to rule Alameda," Annabelle said, hoping to keep Nora talking. Maybe if she understood her, she could use that to reason with her. "I don't understand why it was so important to get rid of Prince Leonardo now, though. I would think you would have wanted to wait until after Isaac and Tayla married."

"When else would I have been invited to the palace?" Nora asked. "And then the prince was given his grandmother's ring. It was obvious he was about to propose to someone."

"But he had already broken up with Chrishelle when you poisoned the desserts."

"He hadn't broken up with you." She shook her head. "It was clever bringing his old girlfriend here to make it look like he wasn't already interested in you."

Annabelle's blood chilled, and her jaw dropped. "You didn't care if I died with Leo because you thought I might marry him and produce an heir?"

"You aren't the sort of woman a prince would casually date." She rested the gun in her lap and pointed with her free hand. "Turn right at the next road."

"Now that Tayla and Isaac broke up, why come after me now?"

"Like I said, I can't sit back and allow my son to remain in jail."

"You could tell the truth." Annabelle glanced at the gun briefly before turning her attention back to the road. "If you turn yourself in, Isaac would be free."

"My son has worked in the legal system long enough for me to know there aren't any guarantees. He doesn't have an alibi for Julian Benitez's murder. He could be named an accomplice."

"How do you know he doesn't have an alibi?" Annabelle asked.

Nora didn't respond.

Annabelle made the turn and glanced at her again. Pieces of the puzzle began to fall into place. If Nora was the person who had killed Benitez, there was only one way she could be positive her son didn't have an alibi: he was there when the murder took place.

- - -

Leo circled through the waterfront district a second time with no luck. Annabelle was gone, and he had no clue where she was or who had taken her.

Who had taken her? Or more specifically, who would benefit from Isaac's release? Isaac, certainly, but since he was still locked away in the local jail, he must have an accomplice to have pulled this off.

His mobile rang, and the automated voice in his car announced the caller was Saul. He hit the button on the steering wheel to connect the call.

"Anything?" Leo asked.

"No, Your Highness. We need to go back to the palace and determine our best way forward."

Even though the crown's policy was to ignore ransom requests, with Annabelle's safety at stake, that policy no longer mattered. "There's only one way forward," he said. "Tell the police to keep looking, and I need you to go to the jail."

"Are you saying—?"

"I'll be asking my father to release Isaac and gather the ransom money." Without waiting for Saul to express his opinion of Leo's plan, he said, "Just get over to the jail. I'll be in touch."

"Yes, Your Highness."

Leo ended the call and turned toward the palace. Though he rarely took advantage of the speed his Porsche was capable of, tonight, he had no time to waste. The moment he cleared the town limits, he pressed the gas, zipping up the winding road to the palace without any concern about speed limits.

He honked as he made the final turn to the main entrance, slowing only enough to make sure he didn't hit the gate as the guards raised it.

He skidded to a stop by the family entrance where Tayla already waited.

His sister took one look at the empty passenger seat, and panic bloomed on her face. "You didn't find her."

"No."

He rushed past her to the door, Tayla following right behind him. He only made it as far as the stairwell before his father appeared. "Saul told me what happened." He ushered him into the library.

Tayla closed the door. "How could Isaac do this? He's in jail."

"He must have had an accomplice," Leo said.

"I checked with the jail," his father said. "According to their records, Isaac hasn't spoken to anyone besides his attorney."

"Then his attorney must be passing messages," Tayla said.

Impatience bubbled inside Leo. "Regardless of how this happened, we need to release Isaac, or at least make it look like we're releasing him."

"You know our policy on hostage negotiations."

"But, Father—" Tayla began.

Leo put his hand on his sister's shoulder. "Annabelle isn't just a visiting royal. I love her." The three little words startled him, and he corrected himself. "We all love her. She's part of our family."

"No one is debating how much Annabelle means to us, but we can't let you go rushing into a hostile situation."

Leo's phone rang, the king of Sereno's number lighting up his screen. Guilt swept through him, and Leo answered. "We're doing everything we can to find her."

"I have some information that may help." King Levi's voice carried with it a surprising calmness along with the expected tension.

Leo hit the speaker button. "I'm putting you on speaker with me and my father. Tayla is here too."

"I had some friends searching the banking information for Julian Benitez. It was obvious someone fronted him the money to pay for the bomb."

"Why are we talking about this right now?" Leo asked. "Our focus needs to be on finding Annabelle."

"It is. The money was transferred to Benitez out of an account in the Caymans."

"That makes sense. The man who was stalking Tayla was also paid from an account in the Caymans."

"Yes, but the payment to Benitez came from a different account in that same bank," King Levi said. "The payments to Gonzalo did come from an account belonging to Isaac Vega."

Tayla gripped the back of the nearest chair.

"And the payment to the bombmaker?" Leo's father asked. "Was that from Isaac too?"

"No." Levi paused. "It was from Nora Vega—Isaac's mother."

"What?" Facts shifted in Leo's mind. "Are you sure?"

"Positive. My source sent me the ID photos of the account holders."

"Why would Nora try to kill Leo?" Tayla asked.

The conversation about Isaac's education played through Leo's mind. "She wanted her son to be king."

Tayla's eyebrows shot up. "They planned this together?"

"Who planned what doesn't matter," Leo said. "How do we make sure we get Annabelle back home safely?"

"What exactly did she ask for in the ransom note?" King Levi asked.

"Isaac's release and two million euros."

"If we're going to pay the ransom, we'll need to get the bank to open after-hours," his father said.

"We need to take some control of the situation," King Levi said. "How much cash can you gather without going to the bank?"

"A quarter million euros."

"Put together a hundred thousand euros, two hundred thousand tops," King Levi said. "That's how much you'll take with you to the meet."

Leo's dad shook his head. "I can't allow my son to put himself at risk."

"Father, I'm sorry, but I'm going," Leo insisted. "I have to."

"King Josep, if you are willing to release Isaac Vega, I believe we can work together to ensure the safety of your son. Or at least greatly increase the chances of success. I can teach your son what he needs to know when he goes to negotiate Annabelle's release."

Leo's father stiffened, and he looked at Leo before turning his attention back to the phone. "I'm listening."

CHAPTER
38

ANNABELLE'S WRISTS CHAFED AGAINST THE handcuffs as she walked along the dock, Nora gripping her arm tightly. Her gaze darted to every vessel they passed, but this particular dock appeared to cater to simple speedboats and fishing vessels, not the sort that people lived aboard. Come morning, the area would likely be alive with activity. Whether she would still be breathing at that point, she had no idea.

Her throat closed at that thought. She'd found so much happiness over the past week with Leo. That it could end so abruptly in such an unexpected and permanent way was unfathomable.

The beam of the lighthouse shone like a beacon in the distance. The structure had been built to prevent disaster. She needed to find a way to do the same, only instead of warning ships of the potential danger, she needed to warn Leo.

"This way." Nora guided her past the line of boats to a small structure at the end that appeared to be a storage shed.

"It was you who killed Julian Benitez, wasn't it?" Annabelle asked, hoping someone, anyone, might be nearby to hear the conversation.

"He didn't give me a choice," Nora said. "Can you imagine him trying to blackmail me? I mean, he's the one who killed Gonzalo."

Annabelle suspected that even if Benitez had pulled the trigger, Nora had ordered him to do it. "Did Isaac know what you were doing?"

"He didn't need to know anything beyond that Gonzalo was creating a perfect opportunity to get close to the princess."

She cared about the title, not the person. That thought brought with it a healthy dose of fear.

"What are you going to do with me?" Annabelle asked.

"That depends entirely on whether your boyfriend follows directions." Nora opened the door to the windowless structure. She pulled the string attached to an overhead light that was nothing more than a bare lightbulb inside a simple fixture. Oxygen tanks lined the one wall, and scuba equipment was organized on a row of shelves on the other side. A collapsible camp chair was situated in the middle, an open crate beside it.

"Have a seat." Nora pushed her into the chair, and Annabelle got her first glimpse of the contents in the crate. She didn't have nearly the same exposure to explosives as her brothers-in-law or the royal guards had, but even she recognized the block of C4 with the detonator attached.

Instinctively, Annabelle tried to push out of the chair, but Nora gripped her shoulder to hold her in place, the pistol in her other hand now pressed to the side of Annabelle's head. "Oh, no. You stay right there."

Annabelle forced herself to remain seated. "Is this your plan? To lure the prince here and kill us both?"

"I'm willing to be persuaded to let you live." Nora pulled a second set of handcuffs from her pocket. She secured one side to Annabelle's wrist and the other to the chair.

When Nora didn't continue, Annabelle asked. "What kind of persuasion are you looking for?"

"I only want the chance for me and Isaac to start over somewhere, to create a comfortable life for both of us."

"You know they'll never stop looking for you if you kill either of us."

"They would have to find us first."

"You're assuming they'll let you get away in the first place," Annabelle said. "Let me go, and everything will go much easier for you."

"Spoken like a true diplomat." She shook her head, almost as though scolding a small child. "Surely, you don't think me so naive as to try to sail out of here without a plan of how to do so without being followed."

Annabelle glanced at the bomb again. Was she going to blow everyone up when they tried to save her and hope she and Isaac could escape in the chaos?

Annabelle swallowed hard. "What are you planning?"

"You needn't worry yourself about that. For now, we simply need to wait."

- - -

Leo had done everything he could, but would it be enough? King Levi already had a special forces unit in the air heading their way, but Nora had chosen her timeline a little too well. The reinforcements wouldn't arrive until twenty minutes after Leo was scheduled to meet with Annabelle's kidnapper.

In the meantime, the top two snipers from the local rapid response team were moving into position near the yacht club, and Alameda's coastal security force had positioned two vessels nearby, one beyond the lighthouse and the other at Royal Cove, a five-minute ride from the meeting spot.

After spending thirty minutes talking to King Levi about different hostage negotiation tactics, Leo had also taken the time to retrieve his pistol from the gun safe beside his bed. Annabelle's kidnapper may have said he had to come alone, but he wasn't going in unarmed.

Now, with less than an hour left before the deadline, Leo paced the library, only his sister still present, while they waited for the final authorization to release Isaac into Leo's custody.

"This is all my fault," Tayla said as she paced opposite him. "If I hadn't fallen for Isaac, none of this ever would have happened."

"This isn't a time for blame," Leo said, even though he was experiencing a healthy dose of what-if's tonight. If they hadn't decided to go out to dinner, if Annabelle hadn't come to visit, if they had sent her home after the first attempt on his life . . . His family never should have asked her to stay. He shouldn't have given her a reason to stay.

His chest tightened painfully. The thought of losing her, of not having the possibility of a future together, was simply unbearable.

His father rushed into the room. "It's done. The police will have Isaac waiting for you when you arrive at the jail."

"Thank you." Leo hugged his father and hurried toward the door.

"Leo, wait," Tayla called after him. "I'm coming with you."

"No," Leo and his father said in unison.

Before Leo could protest further, his father took Tayla by the arm. "I'm not risking the safety of both of you. It's bad enough that Leo insists on going himself."

"Then let me at least go with Leo to pick Isaac up from the jail," Tayla said. "He might give me more information than any of you will be able to get from him."

Desperate to take advantage of any edge they could get, Leo turned to his father. "You can send a guard with us to bring her back after I pick up Isaac."

His father wavered for several seconds. "I'll agree on one condition."

"What's that?"

"We let one of the guards drive your Porsche. I want the two of you inside one of the armored limos until you arrive at the prison."

"Fine," Leo agreed. "Come on, Tayla. Let's go."

- - -

Annabelle sat in silence, her gaze scanning the small space while Nora stood beside the partially opened door and peered into the darkness. Nora looked at her watch for what had to be the fifth time in the last few minutes.

Annabelle suspected that whatever was going to happen was expected soon. Somehow, she needed to find a way to free herself, or at least put some distance between herself and the bomb.

As far as Annabelle could tell, the bomb wasn't active. She'd prefer not to be anywhere in the vicinity of it if—or when—that changed.

Annabelle looked down at her wrists, her right wrist cuffed to her left, and her left hand cuffed to the chair. Two pairs of handcuffs, but only one was keeping her in place. And as far as she could tell, her chair wasn't affixed to anything in the shed. If Nora left her alone, she might be able to walk out of here, chair and all.

Drawing on the simplest solution of how to remove herself from this shack, Annabelle said, "I need to use the toilet."

"Sorry, Princess." Nora spared her a quick glance. "That's not going to happen."

She checked her watch again.

"I'll be back." Nora lifted her weapon, aiming it at Annabelle for several long seconds. "Don't try anything, or I *will* kill you."

The look in the older woman's eyes brought a chill to Annabelle's blood, despite the lingering heat inside the shed.

Isaac's mom left the shed, and the rattle of a lock clicking into place sounded.

Annabelle considered following Nora's instructions for a fraction of a second. That's all it took for her to come to her senses. If Annabelle didn't do something, she was as good as dead anyway.

CHAPTER
39

LEO CLIMBED OUT OF THE back of the vehicle, Tayla following him. Rocco parked Leo's Porsche along the curb, as did Saul, who was driving a second royal guard vehicle.

Rocco and Saul escorted Leo and Tayla inside, where they were immediately shown to a sterile room with a table, six chairs, and Isaac.

The moment Isaac spotted Tayla, he stood. "Tayla." Isaac took a step toward her, and Leo immediately moved between them.

"Leo, it's okay." Tayla put her hand on his shoulder and shifted to his side. "We need Isaac to tell us what he knows."

"About what?" Isaac asked.

"Someone kidnapped Princess Annabelle. Besides the request for a large amount of money, the primary demand in the ransom note was for you."

"Me?" Confusion illuminated his face. "I thought when the guards brought me my clothes that you'd found the real killer, that I was being released." Isaac paused. "That Tayla was willing to forgive me."

"I'm here to ask for your help," Tayla said. "It's the least you can do after everything you put me through."

"I'm sorry. I never meant for things to get so out of hand—"

What little thread of patience Leo still had snapped. "We don't have time for the two of you to sort through your personal drama. I need to know how to get Annabelle back from your mother."

"My mother?" Isaac's confusion disappeared, and his face went ashen.

With the way Isaac's face had paled, Leo suspected Isaac had put the pieces together about his mother's involvement.

"Your mother paid for the bomb that nearly killed me and several others. We already know she hired Julian Benitez to plant it." Leo crossed his arms. "Was it your idea to kill him after he finished his task, or was it hers?"

"I didn't hurt anyone." Isaac pressed his lips together as though trying to keep from saying anything more.

At his wit's end, Leo stepped forward. "Two men were killed in cold blood. You're telling me you didn't have anything to do with it?"

"I didn't."

"But your mother did."

The muscle jumped in Isaac's jaw.

"How do I get your mother to release Annabelle unharmed?"

"I don't know."

Tayla put her hand on Leo's arm before she moved to stand directly in front of Isaac. "We know how important your mother is to you, but she's in danger if she doesn't release Annabelle."

Isaac's eyes widened. "What kind of danger?"

Leo looked at him, bewildered. Did he not understand that the authorities would do anything necessary to rescue Annabelle, that when someone had a gun, it was likely the police would shoot back?

"We don't want the police to hurt your mom, so we need your help. How do we get her to let Annabelle go?" Tayla looked back at Leo. "And how do we make sure she doesn't hurt Leo?"

"Give her what she asked for," Isaac said. "She only wants me to be safe and happy."

The woman might want her son to be safe and happy, but she had also killed two people to try to give her son opportunities that weren't rightfully his. If Leo's suspicions were correct, she was also responsible for the holes that had been drilled in his boat. Not exactly the way he would have expected her to utilize her scuba training.

"I need your word that you'll do everything possible to keep her from hurting anyone else."

Isaac nodded. "I'll help you if you make sure the judge knows I cooperated."

Saul tapped his watch. "It's time to go."

"I'll take Isaac in my car," Leo said. For Isaac's benefit, he added, "You escort Tayla home. The note said I need to come alone."

"That's not wise, Your Highness," Saul said as though they hadn't already planned for him and Rocco to follow at a discreet distance.

"Isaac's right. Our best bet of ending this whole thing safely is for me to follow the instructions."

Saul nodded. "Call us as soon as you're safe, and we'll escort you home."

Tayla hugged Leo. "Be careful."

Leo held on for a long moment. "I will."

- - -

Annabelle stood as far as she was able, the chair forcing her to lean down slightly because of the second set of handcuffs. Outside, waves rushed against the dock, rising and receding with the tide. Annabelle pulled on the fabric arms and folded the chair the best she could, holding it with one hand as she moved to the wall of shelves.

She searched the lowest shelf first, able to dig through the regulators and buoyancy control vests while letting the weight of the chair rest on the floor. When she didn't find anything useful, she lifted the chair and searched the next shelf up. Fins and weight belts.

Reaching onto her toes, she looked at the contents of the top shelf. Masks and snorkels. Nothing more. Was it too much to ask for her to find a dive knife or, even better, a set of handcuff keys?

The distinctive sound of a key sliding into a lock carried to her over the gentle rise and fall of the sea. Annabelle quickly opened the chair and dropped into it just as the door opened.

Nora looked around the room as though expecting Annabelle to have disturbed something. Apparently satisfied, she crossed to the shelves and retrieved two weight belts. She then stepped behind Annabelle and leaned over.

"In case you have any crazy ideas of escaping, this should keep you grounded."

"What are you doing?"

"Just making sure you don't go anywhere." After securing the weights at the base of the chair legs, she stepped back in front of Annabelle and took off the scarf from around her neck. She put the scarf in Annabelle's mouth, pulling it tight enough to force the fabric between her lips. "We don't want you causing any complications."

Annabelle moaned, trying to force the scarf out of her mouth, but Nora tied it tightly to keep it in place.

She struggled against it again, turning her head back and forth.

"Relax. It won't be much longer." Nora reached up and pulled the string to turn off the light. Then she left the shack, closing the door and leaving Annabelle in the darkness.

CHAPTER
40

LEO DROVE ALONG THE HIGHWAY that bordered the coast, the top down, Isaac at his side. To anyone passing by, they would look like a couple of friends on their way home from whatever event they had chosen for the evening. How much Leo wished that was the case.

"How involved were you in your mother's activities?" Leo asked.

Isaac remained silent.

Leo had tried a dozen variations of the same question, but Isaac had apparently regained his composure enough to avoid incriminating himself any further.

Leo slowed as he approached their turn.

His phone rang, the call coming from an unfamiliar number. Though he normally didn't answer calls from anyone he didn't know, tonight he wasn't taking any chances of missing out on information on Annabelle. He hit the button on his steering wheel to answer.

"Hello?"

"Is my son with you?" Nora asked.

"I'm here," Isaac said.

Without acknowledging Isaac, his mother said, "I'll meet you at the Aguas Profundas Scuba Club. You have ten minutes. Now give your phone to my son."

A change of location, away from where the snipers were set up, and now he was supposed to let Annabelle's kidnapper have a private conversation with Isaac?

"You can talk to both of us," Leo said.

Nora's voice darkened, her words evenly spaced. "Give the phone to my son or the girl dies."

Unwilling to risk Annabelle's safety, Leo shifted in his seat so he could pull his phone from his pocket. He handed it to Isaac.

Isaac flipped through the settings and disconnected it from the car's audio system. "It's me."

Leo couldn't hear much over the car's engine and the wind, but after less than a minute, Isaac lifted the phone in the air and tossed it onto the road behind them.

Leo hit the brakes. "What are you doing?"

"Keep going," Isaac said, his voice remarkably calm. "We only have eight and a half minutes left."

Leo shifted his foot from the brakes to the gas pedal. His phone was probably broken anyway. He could only hope that Saul and Rocco would figure out where they were heading. Otherwise, he and Annabelle were on their own.

- - -

Only a sliver of light pierced the darkness of the storage shed. With the way the light dimmed and brightened at regular increments, she could only guess the source was the nearby lighthouse. She had no idea how soon Leo would get here, but the lack of light in the shed and Nora's decision to keep Annabelle quiet indicated she didn't have much time.

Though she would give anything right now for an unencumbered breath of air, getting out of here had to take priority. Annabelle tugged her arms as far as they would go, putting as much pressure as possible on the aluminum pole that extended from the arm of the chair to the base of it. It was no use; the handcuffs weren't going anywhere.

Annabelle pushed to her feet, leaning down to keep the metal cuffs from putting pressure on her wrists. She tipped the chair over and sat on the floor so she could use her feet to free the chair of the weight belts Nora had placed at the base of the legs. Once she had accomplished that, she stood, the chair in her hand.

A beep sounded, and a new light source glowed beside her. She turned toward it. Digital numbers illuminated the mechanism beside what Annabelle assumed was the detonator. She read the numbers. Nineteen minutes, forty-nine seconds. In less than twenty minutes, the bomb would go off.

Panic streaked through her. Had this been Nora's plan all along? To lure Leo here to kill him? And her too?

With no time to waste, she carried the chair with her to where the chink of light was coming in at the back corner of the shed.

She explored the gap between two planks of wood that had warped slightly. With a prayer in her heart, Annabelle sat beside the narrow opening, pressed her feet against the boards, and pushed both feet outward. The board bent slightly but didn't break. She scooted closer, her hands still cuffed together, the chair she was cuffed to lying across her lap. Again, she bent her legs, placed them on either side of the opening, and pushed.

A nail pulled free from the horizontal board the others had been nailed to. The gap opened wider, but not enough for her to squeeze through, especially not while attached to a camp chair. Annabelle tried again. And again.

She tried to pretend she was in the exercise room at home working on her quads, but tonight the burning in her thighs wasn't an indication of success but rather failure.

Taking a deep breath, she pushed again. A board cracked.

Energized, she tried again. This time, the board broke in half, the bottom portion dangling from the single nail that still held it in place.

With her wrists still encumbered, Annabelle used her feet to push the board the rest of the way free.

The hole was less than a third of a meter wide, but it was enough for the folded chair to fit through. Annabelle prayed it was wide enough for her to fit through too.

She slid the folded chair through the hole and then crawled out, headfirst. Her leg caught on one of the exposed nails as she climbed the rest of the way outside, and she gasped in pain.

Almost immediately, the lock clicked open, followed by the door.

"What!?" Nora cried out.

Annabelle's heart pounded, and she struggled to her feet. She stumbled away from the shack and headed toward the wooded area a short distance away. She only made it a few meters before a gunshot echoed through the air.

Nora's voice followed. "Stop right there, or the next time, I won't miss."

- - -

Leo heard the gunshot an instant before he pulled into the parking lot.

He bolted out of the car and caught sight of Isaac's mother pulling Annabelle around the side of a shed at the edge of the dock. "Annabelle!" Relief poured through him, and he barely remembered his passenger.

Isaac was already out of the car. Though Leo was tempted to draw the weapon he had holstered at the back of his waistband, he used his size to cut Isaac off before he could continue forward.

"Not so fast. We have more we need to take to your mother." Leo motioned to the trunk. "Open that for me."

"But—"

"I wasn't asking." Leo stood firm, fighting to stay focused on the man in front of him instead of the two women twenty meters away. Leo hit the button on his key fob to open the trunk. "Get the duffel out of there."

Isaac complied, gripping the duffel in one hand.

"Now, nice and easy." Leo grabbed Isaac's arm. "You stay at my side until your mother hands over Annabelle. Got it?"

"Yes."

They moved forward, and Leo finally let himself really look at Annabelle and Nora. Isaac's mother held Annabelle's arm, and a gag was tied around Annabelle's mouth. Something was gripped in Annabelle's hand. In the darkness, it almost looked like a collapsible chair.

"We're here." Leo continued a few steps forward. "Now let Annabelle go."

"Did you bring the money?"

"Isaac has it."

"All of it?"

"Two hundred thousand euros is all the cash I could get on such short notice." Leo kept his grip firm on Isaac's arm.

"That's not what I asked for."

Remembering the lessons King Levi had taught him, Leo lifted his chin slightly. "This isn't a negotiation," he said with steel in his voice. "If you want your son back, I suggest you take the deal."

"Isaac, bring the money here," Nora said.

"Not until you release Annabelle," Leo insisted.

Nora lifted her pistol more fully into view and pressed it against Annabelle's head. "I suggest you do what I tell you," she said evenly. "Isaac, now."

"Isaac, no. We had a deal."

"I'm sorry." Isaac jerked free of Leo's grip and hurried forward. He glanced backward as soon as he was out of Leo's reach and cast an apologetic look at him. "She's my mother."

Leo debated for a fraction of a second. He could draw his weapon, but that could put Annabelle in even more danger. He kept his hands at his sides. "Just let Annabelle go."

"I thought about letting her go until she tried running away." She waved her gun toward Leo. "I can't risk either of you following me, so I'll be taking the princess along for insurance."

"No!" Leo took another step forward.

"Stay where you are." She held her gun against Annabelle's head again. "As soon as we're on the boat, I'll let her go."

Annabelle tried to say something, but her words came out in an incomprehensible mumble.

Leo took a step forward, and Annabelle shook her head. Even in the darkness, he couldn't miss the panic in her eyes. He also knew the coastal border service would be able to intercept the boat once they were underway. All he had to do was make Isaac and his mother believe they'd won. And pray they didn't hurt Annabelle before he could get word to the patrol boats about where to intercept them.

CHAPTER

41

SECONDS TICKED BY IN ANNABELLE'S head. There couldn't be more than five minutes left before the bomb would go off, and Leo was right next to the shed.

He had survived multiple assassination attempts, all so Isaac could marry a future queen. And now, after that entire plot had been revealed, when Leo's death would serve no purpose, he was going to die anyway. Not if Annabelle could help it. She tried to stop her forward momentum, but Isaac took her other arm and forced her to continue.

They reached the narrow planking that ran between a fishing vessel and a sleek speedboat.

"Climb aboard," Nora said.

Annabelle looked down at the chair still cuffed to her arm. An unlikely plan formed in her mind, one that was every bit as dangerous as standing next to a bomb. She looked back at Leo, who still stood by the shed as though hoping to somehow run to her rescue. But he was in far more need of a rescue than she.

Gathering her courage and with the folded chair still gripped in her right hand, Annabelle lifted both arms. She grabbed the standing rigging at the back of the boat with her free hand, placed her first foot on the side of the boat, and then the second.

As soon as Annabelle stepped over the safety rope, Nora said, "Isaac, you go next."

Isaac moved forward to comply.

Annabelle planted her feet shoulder-width apart and waited until Isaac was most vulnerable, with one of his feet on the boat and the other leaving the dock. Then she threw her weight forward to cause the boat to rock.

Isaac maintained his grip on the standing rigging, but his other arm flailed as he fought for balance.

Not giving him the chance to recover, Annabelle swung the chair at him. The folded chair struck him in the chest, but instead of Isaac falling into the water, he managed to fall forward onto the boat.

Annabelle turned to swing the chair again, this time toward Nora, only to find Isaac's mom aiming her pistol at Annabelle.

A gunshot fired, and Annabelle's heart skipped a beat. For a split second, Annabelle thought she had been shot, but no pain registered.

When Nora ducked and turned, Annabelle caught a glimpse of Leo, gun in hand.

Isaac's mom returned fire at Leo, and he dropped out of sight behind a speedboat.

"No!" The word came out in a muffled moan against the gag still in her mouth. Terrified that Leo had been injured, Annabelle swung the chair out again. This time the legs connected with Nora's back.

Nora grunted and stumbled forward a few steps. Annabelle fought to regain her balance and glanced toward where she had last seen Leo. She managed to right herself and lifted the chair again to strike at Nora, but Isaac pushed her from behind. Annabelle's foot caught on the safety rope, and she grabbed it to keep from continuing overboard, but the weight of the chair kept her sliding toward the edge.

She clung to the rope, the metal handcuffs digging into her flesh, the chair dangling between the boat and the dock, and her feet splashing into the water. She tried to cry out, but no words could form against the wretched scarf still caught in her mouth.

Annabelle tried to lift her other hand to grip the rope too, but the weight of the chair was more than she could manage. The rope burned against her palm and fingers as her grip faltered. Within seconds, she lost her hold completely and splashed into the water, the weight of the chair pulling her under.

- - -

Leo heard the splash and peeked around the edge of the speedboat in search for the source of the sound.

Isaac was still on the boat, his mother on the dock. Where was Annabelle? Surely Isaac couldn't have taken her belowdecks that quickly.

Nora squeezed off another shot, and Leo ducked.

More splashing and a panicked moan carried to him. It only took a second for the terrifying reality to click in his mind: Annabelle must have gone overboard. Handcuffed and gagged. Even if she could prevent being crushed between the boat and the dock, she would drown if someone didn't help. And he was the only someone present who cared about her survival.

He gripped the pistol in his hand and tried to pretend he was shooting at a target rather than a woman. With a quick intake of breath, he popped up and took aim, squeezing the trigger twice in quick succession.

Nora's body jerked backward, and she cried out.

Isaac turned toward the dock. "Mom!"

His mother remained upright and took aim again.

"Drop it!" Leo shouted. When she didn't comply, he fired twice more. This time her body jerked, and she fell onto the wooden planking.

"No!" Isaac quickly stepped off the boat, the boat swaying violently as he did so.

As Isaac rushed to his mother's side, Leo deserted his hiding place and raced forward. Isaac hadn't proven himself to be violent, but Leo didn't want to find out what would happen if Isaac reached his mother's gun first.

Isaac only had a few meters to cross to get to Nora's side. Leo had traversed half of the twenty meters between them when Isaac leaned down and picked up the gun.

Leo had a choice: Take cover and risk Annabelle drowning before he could get to her or keep going and risk not reaching Isaac before he could shoot.

Leo kept going.

Isaac lifted the weapon, but his grip indicated he wasn't familiar with how to handle a firearm.

Rather than try to shoot at such a close distance, Leo dove at Isaac, wrapping his free arm around Isaac's waist.

Isaac grunted as Leo's forward momentum knocked both of them to the dock just beyond where Nora lay.

Flat on his back, Isaac pushed at Leo's shoulders, managing to free one hand. His fist connected with Leo's jaw, but their proximity prevented Isaac from putting much power behind it.

Another moan sounded from the nearby water. Annabelle!

Isaac punched Leo again, this time in his midsection.

Leo retaliated with an elbow to Isaac's ribs. He shifted his body, so he still had his torso across Isaac's chest and leaned up enough to bring his weapon into Isaac's view.

"Don't make me shoot you, Isaac."

"You shot my mother."

"And you'll be bleeding right beside her if you don't help me." Leo jerked his head toward the nearby shed. "Go get the life buoy. As soon as we get Annabelle out of the water, we'll call an ambulance."

Isaac hesitated.

Leo pressed the gun to Isaac's head. "This is your only option."

Isaac nodded weakly.

Leo stood and let Isaac up.

"Now go." Leo motioned toward the shed.

Nora spoke with a weak voice. "No, Isaac. Don't."

Ignoring her, Leo pointed again. "I said go."

Isaac nodded and ran toward the shed, his mother protesting yet again.

CHAPTER
42

SHE'D LOST ANOTHER PAIR OF shoes. Annabelle's thighs burned as she kicked her legs enough to put her head above water. She gasped in another breath, the wetness of the scarf forcing her to swallow water as she did so. Her efforts were only enough to keep her mouth above water for a few seconds before she sank back down again.

If she could only use her hands to help her tread water, or if she could at least rid herself of the chair that was dragging her down, she might be able to reach the dock. She might be able to warn Leo of the danger. The bomb was too close to where she'd seen him last, his vulnerability far too great.

She let her air out slowly, trying to relax her body as much as possible as she kept her legs kicking to keep her near the surface.

Needing another breath, she increased her kicking again to push herself upward. But this time, her face didn't break through the surface. She inhaled water and tried to kick herself upward again. When she again failed to reach air, panic closed over her.

She wasn't going to make it. Another minute or two, and she would sink permanently to the bottom of the harbor.

Something entered the water next to her, and she instinctively reached out. A strong hand gripped her arm and pulled her upward.

She sputtered when she reached the surface and gasped for air.

"It's okay." Leo pulled her closer, hooking his arm around her waist. "I've got you."

She tried to speak, to warn him, but she couldn't.

"Let's get you up onto the dock, and we'll get that gag off you."

Annabelle shook her head, fear pulsing through her. She shook her head again.

"Annabelle, it's okay."

She tried to form the word *bomb*, but it came out in another incoherent mumble.

Leo pulled her to the back of the sailboat where an aluminum ladder was affixed to the side. He started to help her up, but she shook her head yet again. "Bomb," she mumbled again, the word still not recognizable.

"See if you can hold onto the ladder," Leo said. "I'll try to get this off of you."

She grabbed the bottom of the ladder, ignoring the welts from where the handcuffs had cut into her wrists.

Leo worked at the knot in the damp fabric until finally, the scarf came free.

"A bomb," Annabelle said hoarsely. "There's a bomb in the shed."

"Oh, no." Leo grabbed the ladder and shouted, "Isaac! Come back!"

A deafening sound erupted, the flames from the bomb spearing through the air overhead, only the dock and the boat protecting them from the blast. The boat rocked violently, and Annabelle struggled to hold on.

Nora cried out, her wail like that of an injured animal.

Leo lowered himself back beside Annabelle and grabbed her arm to keep her from going underwater.

The rumble of a distant motor competed with the sound of the flames, growing louder with each passing second.

"I say we climb onto the boat and wait there until help gets here," Leo said.

"I'm not sure I can," Annabelle said as a shiver worked through her.

"You're freezing." Leo pulled her close. "There's this thing called the huddle method."

"I've heard of it, but it's a lot easier to do when I don't have handcuffs on and a chair dragging at me."

Leo grabbed the chair, holding it so the weight of it no longer pulled at her. "Help is coming." He kissed her forehead. "It won't be long."

- - -

Leo sat on the sofa beside Annabelle as the royal physician tended to the gash in her leg and the wounds on her wrists. The special tactical unit King Levi sent had arrived within minutes of seeing the bomb go off and had coordinated with local emergency services to bring in a medical transport and the coroner.

The bullets that hit Isaac's mother hadn't hit any vital organs, and she had survived her wounds, but Isaac had been too close to the bomb when it went off. Nora's attempts to give her son a better life had ultimately killed him.

The doctor taped off the last bandage. "We'll need to change the bandages tomorrow, but for now, your best cure is pain medicine and rest."

"Thank you, Doctor," Annabelle said.

He nodded. "I can see myself out."

Leo waited until the doctor left Annabelle's suite before he reached his arm around her.

Annabelle snuggled against him.

Love welled inside him as terrifying moments of tonight replayed through his mind, reminding him of what he had almost lost, emphasizing how important Annabelle truly was to him.

Leo leaned down and kissed her forehead. "I never want to go through anything like this again." He touched her cheek. "Thank the Lord your injuries weren't worse."

"Oh, I already have." She held up both hands. "I was so terrified that bomb would go off while you were next to the shed." She straightened. "Has anyone told Tayla about Isaac?"

"My parents did." Had it not been for the necessity of sharing the news with his sister, Leo suspected he and Annabelle would have been swamped with attention when they arrived back at the palace. "They're with her now."

A knock sounded at the door, and Leo stood. "I'll get it."

He opened the door to Duran. "What are you still doing up at this hour?" Leo asked.

"The doctor said Princess Annabelle needed something to eat before she takes her pain medicine." Duran held up a silver tray with two servings of crema catalana. "I thought you might want to join her."

"This will certainly brighten her mood." Leo motioned for him to enter.

Duran shook his head. "I don't want to intrude, and I need to be up early in the morning. Those croissants don't make themselves."

"Thank you, Duran."

He bowed his head and passed the tray to Leo. "I'll have breakfast sent up in the morning."

Leo left the entryway and returned to the living room.

"Was that Duran's voice I heard?" Annabelle's gaze lifted to the tray. "He didn't."

"He did." Leo passed one of the desserts to Annabelle. "He must have made this after he found out you'd gone missing so he'd have it ready when you returned."

"I love his optimism." She took a bite and rolled her eyes in appreciation. "You realize that if he keeps making this for me, I may never leave."

"Do you promise?"

"I have to go home. You know that," Annabelle said, but it was with obvious regret. "My company launches in three more months."

Leo set the tray on the coffee table. Rather than lift his dessert, he reclaimed his seat beside her. "I know you're supposed to go home next week, but I don't want to have that much distance between us. I want to give us a chance to see where this thing between us can go."

"Then come to Sereno with me."

"What?" Leo hadn't considered that possibility. "I have duties here, responsibilities."

"I have responsibilities too."

This conversation was far too much like the one he'd had with Chrishelle before he left the United States to move back home. But this time, an emptiness filled him he had never before experienced. "I don't think I can last months away from you."

"I'm not crazy about the idea either."

Leo stood and paced across the room, his mind whirling. "Could you delay your departure for another two weeks?"

"Maybe, assuming my production manager can keep things running smoothly," Annabelle said. "But what difference is two weeks going to make?"

"It will give me time to delegate some of my responsibilities with the safety inspections on the gold-mine enhancements," Leo said, a plan forming. "We could then go to Sereno together, spend a few weeks there while you set things up to establish a second office here in Alameda."

"You want me to work here."

"I want to be with you." He took her hand again. "For as long as you'll let me."

"I suppose if we both find ways to work remotely, we might be able to go back and forth for the next few months."

"And after that?"

"I don't know." Annabelle put her hand on his. "I guess we'll have to wait and see."

EPILOGUE

Three months later

SHE'D DONE IT. ANNABELLE HAD survived the launch party of her new company, and already the feedback was amazing. Nearly every celebrity and royal who had been invited had come to Sereno for the event, many of them taking samples with them with the promise of endorsements.

And even more improbable, she and Leo had somehow managed to juggle their busy schedules to spend the majority of the past three months together.

The last of the guests filtered out of the royal ballroom, escorted by her sister Victoria and brother-in-law Alan.

Cassie had made a brief appearance after feeding her newborn son, who was nearly six weeks old.

Annabelle's heart swelled as she considered her growing family. Before the month ended, Victoria would give birth to her niece.

Leo approached from the terrace and leaned in to kiss her cheek. "You were amazing tonight."

"All I did was mingle with our guests and pray everyone would like the makeup samples we handed out."

"The press alone is going to put you on the map, but I heard Tayla talking with a few of the actresses who came in from the UK. The buzz is all positive so far."

A new tingle of excitement sparked inside her. "That's wonderful to hear." Annabelle looked around the now-empty room. "Where's Tayla?"

"She headed up to her room. I think she needed a break after being around so many people."

"I can't believe she's doing as well as she is considering all she's gone through."

"This was good for her," Leo said. "She's finally starting to live life again instead of dwelling on everything she went through with Isaac."

"She deserves to be happy."

"I agree." Leo took her hand. "I have a gift for you."

"You didn't have to get me anything."

"Oh, but I did." Leo led her to the stage where three boxes about the size of a shoebox were wrapped in gold. He handed her the first one. "Open it."

Curious, Annabelle tore the paper from the package. It *was* a shoebox. She lifted the lid and pulled back the tissue paper. A pair of pink pumps lay inside, similar to the pair she had lost the night Isaac was killed.

"You bought me shoes?"

"You lost a few pairs when you were visiting Tayla in May."

Annabelle laughed. "That's very sweet." She opened the next one to reveal a pair of black sandals. "Oh, these are cute."

"You like them?"

"I do." She leaned forward and kissed him. "Thank you."

"You're welcome." He handed her the last box. "One more."

She peeled back the wrapping paper and pulled off the lid. This time, when she pushed aside the tissue paper, a pair of white heels lay inside, along with a blue square ring box that was nestled between the two shoes.

A ring? Annabelle's eyes lifted to meet Leo's.

"Is this—" She couldn't quite form the question.

Leo took the shoebox from her hand and set it aside, pulling out the ring box. "My father gave this to me in the hope that I would someday find the woman I would want to marry, a woman who would make me as happy as my mother has made him." Leo took her hand. "At the time, I didn't think that was possible. I was wrong."

Annabelle's throat closed up, and tears formed in her eyes. She couldn't deny she had never been happier than during these last few months with Leo, but part of her had always worried he would tire of her.

Leo opened the ring box to reveal a stunning emerald encircled by diamonds. "I had no idea I already knew the woman who would capture my heart." He dropped to one knee and held up the ring box with one hand, his other still clasping hers.

"Annabelle, I love you more than I ever thought possible, and it would be my honor and privilege to spend the rest of my life with you."

He loved her. And she loved him. That thought was still circling through Annabelle's mind when Leo drew a deep breath. With uncertainty shining in his eyes, he asked, "Will you marry me?"

Marry her best friend's brother, the man who had been part of her life for as long as she could remember. The man who knew her better than anyone, who had completely and utterly captured her heart. Nothing would make her happier.

Annabelle nodded, unable to speak past the lump in her throat.

"Yes?" he asked, as though needing a second confirmation.

She gave him a watery smile. "Yes."

Pure joy illuminated Leo's face, and he slid the ring into place on her finger. He straightened and pulled her into his arms. "I love you so much."

"And I love you." She tipped her chin up. "And I promise to love you forever."

"Forever. That sounds perfect." Then he leaned down and kissed her.

ABOUT THE AUTHOR

Traci Hunter Abramson was born in Arizona, where she lived until moving to Venezuela for a study-abroad program. After graduating from Brigham Young University, she worked for the Central Intelligence Agency, eventually resigning in order to raise her family. She credits the CIA with giving her a wealth of ideas as well as the skills needed to survive her children's teenage years. She loves to travel and recently retired after spending twenty-six years coaching her local high school swim team. She has written more than forty best-selling novels and is an eight-time Whitney Award winner, including 2017 and 2019 Best Novel of the Year.

She also loves hearing from her readers. If you would like to contact her, she can be reached through the following:

Website: www.traciabramson.com

Facebook page: facebook.com/tracihabramson

Facebook group: Traci's Friends

Bookbub: bookbub.com/authors/traci-hunter-abramson

Twitter (X): @traciabramson

Instagram: instagram.com/traciabramson